Hit Zero

Perrie Patterson

This is a work of fiction. The characters and the story were created in the author's imagination, but the inspiration came from the Navarro College Cheer documentary.

ISBN: 9798668330416   B&N Vendor #: Pub345076

First Edition Printing 2020

www.perriepatterson.com

Cover photo: Taken at sunrise on Orange Beach, Alabama. I enjoy taking the photos for all my covers.

To My Daughter, Laine

From the time I saw you perform in your very first cheer competition, I was impressed. You were amazing, and your team won a championship then went on to the Summit that year. It was a wild ride. From that point on and all through high school and Friday night lights, I loved watching you do your thing. Although All-Star didn't hold your attention and you went on to pursue many other activities, the days of competition cheer were some of the most thrilling for me to experience as a mom. As you prepare for your freshman year at college and close the door on your time as a high school sideline cheerleader, I send you all my love, and all my support. Remember that 2.3 minutes can mean the world, cherish every moment.

To Navarro Cheer

Your documentary story is an inspiration. I hope I've done justice to your sport and to the spirit of hard-working cheerleaders with this story I've created. May it also be an inspiration to others, regardless of whether they are competition cheerleaders or simply readers of the book. Thank you for what you do, your commitment to your team, and your love for the sport of competitive cheerleading.

Author's Note

All characters in this story are fictionalized as is the college. The names of cities and towns are real.

Leaving Home

1

Sitting up, struggling to find my clothes, I rummage through the covers looking for my shorts.

Jordan softly runs his fingertips down my back. "You okay?" he asks.

Even though the room is pitch-black, I can tell he's concerned. I don't know what I feel. I don't feel anything at the moment except the need to leave. I'm not sure what I was thinking coming here tonight, sneaking into his room the night before I leave for Texas. Maybe I thought seeing him one last time and giving him my virginity would be a good farewell gift for my boyfriend, especially since we've been dating more than a year. In the moment it just seemed like the right thing to do, I guess. But now . . .

"Yeah, I'm fine," I say. "But I should go. I don't want to get caught, and I know it's probably after midnight." I slip on my T-shirt and slide my feet into my flip-flops.

Jordan picks his jeans up off the floor and puts them on.

"I love you, Landry," he says, pulling my face close to his. "I'm glad you snuck into my room. And I'm really glad . . ." He grins. "Um, you know." He kisses me softly.

I blush. I know he can't see the color of my cheeks without turning the light on. I look into his eyes. They are shining and bright even in the darkness. I'm glad he's happy, and I'm glad I'm leaving him feeling this way.

He raises his window and helps me crawl through. Once I have my feet over the side, I hop onto the thick boxwood shrubs just below the window then leap to the ground. Jordan jumps down after me.

The night is quiet, with only the sound of crickets chirping. The air is warm and humid. It's thick like frothy liquid on our skin as we move rapidly around the side of the house to the driveway. Jordan's car is parked at the edge of the drive, near the road. With haste we get in and he starts the ignition but keeps the headlights off until we're down the street.

"What time do you guys leave in the morning?" he asks, putting his mod to his lips and taking a draw.

I glance at him through the cloud of smoke. He offers me a drag, but I wave away the offer. "I think I should quit vaping since my 'new life' starts tomorrow and all," I say, smiling at him. "We're leaving at seven a.m. It's almost a seven-hour drive. It's gonna suck."

"New life. That sounds serious. You know I'm happy for you, Landry. I'm going to miss you every day you're gone, but I'm glad you get this opportunity." He places a hand on my knee.

I look out the window, listening to the music lofting through the speakers as "Dissolve" by Absofacto plays quietly. I reach for his hand and loop my fingers through his. I take a deep breath as I listen to the lyrics about dissolving slowly in a pool of love, play through my mind.

"I'm going to miss you, too, Jordan."

Once we're on my street, Jordan cuts the headlights, creeps into my driveway, and kills the engine. He pulls me in, kissing me passionately, and for a moment, I'm lost in him. When we pull apart, he says, "I don't want to say goodbye. I know we'll be almost four hundred miles away from each other, but I just can't officially break off with you. I've been dreading this moment all summer. It's here now, and it doesn't even seem real."

"Jordan, you know I love you. I don't feel like breaking up with you either, and I don't think I could say it even if I tried." Our hands are still clasped together. He pulls them to his lips, kissing my fingers. "But we both know we're going to have to move on," I say. "I want you to get into art school after you graduate next spring. You know I'll always care about you." As I glimpse at my hand wrapped in his, my voice becomes quiet and shy like a whisper. "You were my first love and have a piece of my heart. But, if you meet someone else, I want you to feel like it's okay to move on." I lean into him and hold him for what seems like a long time. When I release my arms and pull away, he wipes a tear from my cheek.

"I'm going to miss looking into your amber green eyes. I think you'll soon have guys falling all over themselves for you." He says it softly, moving his hand from my cheek. He reaches for his left ear and unhooks a dangly cross earring, which he hands to me. I take out one of my small silver hoop earrings and place it in his palm. He puts it in. It looks good, and it suits his e-boy style. We whisper good night as I slide out of the car.

I scurry around to the back of the house, where I've left the door unlocked. In slow-motion, I open it, trying to be as quiet as I can. The cat blocks me as I take a step inside. She meows, letting me know she wants out. As I step over Rocky, she slips through the doorway, crouching in the grass, waiting and watching. She'll be out until morning, so I close the door, take off my flip-flops, and tiptoe toward my room, stopping first to use the bathroom.

There's ---blood in my underwear. Reaching under the sink, I unwrap a pad and fix it into place. I feel sore and uncomfortable, so I pop the medicine cabinet open above the sink

6

and pull out three ibuprofen and swallow them with a handful of water. Turning off the sink, I notice my reflection in the mirror. I don't look any different. Tonight was a hasty decision, maybe a bad one on my part. Chalk it up to another bad choice along with the others I've made this year. Flipping off the light, I slink into my bedroom then pull my phone from my back pocket and plug it in. Pulling the covers back, I crawl in, closing my eyes, longing for sleep. Tomorrow's a fresh start, a new beginning, and I'm leaving the old me behind.

Fresh Start

2

"Landry, hon. Landry, wake up." Mom is shaking my shoulder. Squinting at her, I mumble something that sounds like, "Huh?"

"It's almost six a.m. I've made you breakfast, and Grandma and Aunt Jackie are in the kitchen waiting for you," she says, walking toward the door.

"Okay, Mom," I say, trying to come to life.

In the kitchen, my grandma and my aunt smile and gush at me. It feels nice to receive some positive attention. I know they're happy for me. Mom has made pancakes and bacon. I pour myself a glass of orange juice before sitting at the table with them. Mom is a bundle of nerves and energy, moving at a fast pace, talking about laundry and suitcases and other things like stopping for gas. I'm half-listening. I cut a slice of my pancake and pop it into my mouth.

"Do you think you have everything packed?" Mom asks. "You packed clothes and shoes for all types of weather, right?"

I nod, still chewing my breakfast, hoping Mom's nervous energy doesn't send me into a panic.

"Yes, Mom. I think I did. It's all in two suitcases and a large duffel."

"Uncle Joe and I wanted to give you something. We got you these." Aunt Jackie pulls a bag from under the table and hands it to me. Inside are two sets of Nike Pros with matching sports bras.

"Wow. Thank you." Standing, I give her a hug. "You guys didn't need to get me anything. It's nice enough you're letting Mom drive your SUV all the way to Texas and back. " Mom's old Honda is probably unsafe, and they were unsure of us driving it all the way there then her driving it back home. I feel my throat tighten a bit. I'm filled with emotion, knowing how much my family has helped me pull off going to college a year early.

The first time we drove to Natchez College from my hometown of Lacombe, Louisiana back in February, Mom and I rode with Aunt Jackie and spent the night at the Motel 8 in Nacogdoches, Texas. The next morning, I had to meet with Coach McKaye and do a mini tryout for the team. Normally, their tryouts are in April, but I had a special situation. I got kicked off my all-star team in January after they found out I'd gotten arrested for shoplifting makeup from the local drug store right before Christmas. I was put on house arrest and got suspended from school too. So my junior year had gone way downhill to say the least. I felt worse for my teammates, because they had to find a replacement who could tumble almost as well as me, which was hard. I can do a handspring, whip, whip, full, full, and land it with never a tumble bust.

After the arrest, my cheer coach called me into his office to tell me he had to remove me from the team. Obviously, I understood, but I cried my eyes out anyway, knowing what a screwup I'd become. Jordan and I had started hanging with some people who were---how would you say it? ---'not the best influence' on us. The summer before junior year, we started partying with them a lot, including drinking and smoking pot on weekends. It all seemed cool and stuff, but I snuck around, trying to keep it all on the down-low so Mom wouldn't find out. Then

9

they dared me to steal something when we were in the CVS, and I did. Boom. Life as I knew it ended.

For weeks after that I felt full of regret. I stopped talking to those girls who had dared me to shoplift. Since it happened right before Christmas break, I didn't have to see them at school, and I was glad of that. Of course, being on house arrest and suspended from school until February helped to put distance between us. Mom was relieved I was stuck at home. She even started tracking my phone. Going back to school didn't appeal to me at all. I mean, hey, after being off for over a month, when I thought of going back, I was, like---*No thank you.* I spent a lot of time with Jordan during the holidays, but I didn't want to show my face at school, knowing people would talk and judge. The emotional stress of high school is tough enough without that. By the end of January, I'd sunk into a depressed funk.

Even though my cheer coach took me off the team, he was a great source of support. He suggested I get my GED, and he helped line up a tryout for me at a college known for its competitive cheer program. Having spent so many years at the cheer gym, I had shown my coach how much I loved it. It would be hard for me to give up the only sport I've ever known, something I'm really good at. I've been offered a second chance--- a way out---and I'm glad to take it.

It's been just me and my mom and my grandma for the past seven years. The last time I saw my dad, I was ten. He told me he was moving to Seattle to help with a start-up company. At the time, he and Mom were separated. I was too young to understand a lot of what was really going on. I just knew I missed my dad. I missed him until I finally decided to push the hurt as far down inside me as I could. At one point after he left, he sent a card with a $500 check in it, and that was it, we never heard from him again. Well, we never heard from him directly. My uncle told us he had re-married after the divorce was final. Mom and I were already living with Grandma.

Since my tumbling skills were so advanced, I was able to stay at my cheer gym because I was needed to complete a high-level team. But the girls my age figured out I was on "scholarship" at the gym, and they started snubbing me. Mom could no longer afford the expense, and she was already working two jobs. By the time I started high school, I had taken up with the wrong crowd.

"Landry, help me carry the shopping bags from Target to the car, please," Mom calls. "There are three large bags with sheets, pillows, and bedding sitting in the laundry room."

"Got it, Mom." Grabbing two of the three bags, I load them into the back of Aunt Jackie's SUV.

Aunt Jackie comes out with the other large bag, and slides it in. "Can I help with anything else?"

"I've got two suitcases, a duffel bag, and a backpack still in my room," I say.

We walk back into the house and down the hall. I hear Mom in the kitchen putting the breakfast dishes in the sink. Once the car is loaded, we hug Aunt Jackie and Grandma goodbye, get into the SUV, and head toward I-12. *Ahh, my new life starts now*, I think, smiling to myself as I watch Lacombe fade into the distance outside the window.

Texas

3

After stopping for gas, we get back on the interstate. It's too early to text with anyone, so I put my earbuds in, select Billie Eilish, and chill, trying to get a little sleep in during the long drive. Around noon we pop into a Chick-fil-A for lunch and a potty break. When we hit the road again, Mom asks about the details of moving into my dorm.

"I'm supposed to go to my dorm and check in first. I'll meet my roommate, then she and I will go to the cheer meeting with Coach and the rest of the team later. I think that starts at six."

Thinking about my first meeting with Coach McKaye in February gives me chills. She's awesome, don't get me wrong. She's also a machine, a beast when it comes to coaching competition cheer, and her teams have won more trophies and national titles than a lot of football schools. She doesn't play around, and she means what she says. She runs a tight ship, and I just hope I can manage not to screw up this opportunity. In securing a tryout for me, my all-star coach had called her and told her what I'd done and how I'd been kicked out of school for the "incident."

Coach McKaye told me point blank she expects a lot from her team, especially the ones getting a full scholarship. She told me I'd first need to work to get my GED. Once that had been accomplished, I was to mail her the paperwork and my transcript. I'm glad I'd already taken the ACT earlier in December and gotten a decent score. After I mailed everything, she said she'd get me the scholarship I needed to join the Natchez College Chiefs cheerleaders.

I know I can't screw up anymore. It was a relief for my mom and my grandma when they found out I had been given the chance to start over with another team *and* at a college to boot.

By now in mid-July, had I not gotten arrested, I'd be hanging with my friends at the lake, tumbling every day at the cheer gym, and planning senior-year shenanigans with Jordan and my friends. Jordan wants to go to art school in Savannah, Georgia, when he graduates. He's an amazing artist and he's trying to get an internship working with mural artists in New Orleans, or maybe one in Atlanta next spring.

After a few more hours of driving, we're getting close to Nacogdoches. Our Waze app is saying it's only about twenty more minutes.

Those minutes pass quickly and, I'm full of nervous energy as we arrive on campus. When we were here back in February, the campus didn't look alive. Today, the thick green grass, flower beds full of blooming Azalea bushes, and regal oak trees grab my attention as I take in the impressively manicured grounds. Mom drives slowly as we search for the athletic dorms. I'm in Smith Hall. All athletes, whether they're involved in volleyball, softball, basketball, soccer, lacrosse, football or cheerleading, have to live in athletic housing their first two years on campus. All the girls' teams are housed together, as are the boys' teams, and the athletic dorms seem to be on the west side of campus. I suppose all the other student housing is on the east side. Only athletes have to be on campus in July, arriving early to start practice and team bonding. Since school doesn't start until late August, it's nice that I'll be able to get my bearings and feel comfortable before classes get started.

Mom and I load up with bags and suitcases, and head into the lower level of my dorm to check in at the desk. A friendly girl greets us as we enter.

"Hey, ya'll, I can send some guys out to help you load your stuff onto a cart to make unloading easier for you," she says, smiling. "What's your name?"

"I'm Landry Ann Woods."

"Nice to meet you, Landry. I'm Shawna," she says as she runs her finger down the list in front of her, all the way to the W's.

I pluck my driver's license from my wallet and hold it up so she can see.

"Found you. Cool, ----you're a cheerleader," she bubbles. "Your roommate is here. She checked in about an hour ago. Her name is Kandice Kingsly. Y'all's room is number forty-four." She stands and points. "If you turn right and go down that hall, you'll find it down on the right." She hands me a key card then picks up the phone to page someone to help us with our bags.

Soon, two cute boys show up with a cart. One of them goes back to the car with Mom, pushing the cart. The other takes one of my bags from me.

"I'll follow you," he says.

"I'm in forty-four. This way." I nod in the direction of the hallway. Stopping at the door, I knock, thinking my roommate will answer. She doesn't, so I use the key card to enter.

"I'm Paul, by the way," the boy says, setting my bags down.

"Hey. I'm Landry. Thank you so much for your help."

"No problem. Welcome to Natchez College. I'm a sports-med major, so I'm sure I'll see you again. I work with most of the teams on campus for my training rotation." He smiles at me.

"Oh, wow. I'm taking sports med and sports marketing this fall. I'm trying to figure out which one I want to major in."

"Then I'll definitely see you."

Mom and the other boy arrive with the rolling cart full of my stuff. They squeeze by us into the room. This boy leans in to shake my hand and says his name is Dave.

After they leave, Mom gives me a look and grins. "Texas boys are really polite."

Laughing, I say, "Yeah, and cute too. I may not have time for boys, though, with the tough schedule Coach McKaye is supposed to keep us on."

Mom stops unpacking and turns to me. "Landry, I'm so happy for you. You made a big mistake, but you pulled through, worked hard these past few months, got your GED, and earned a spot on one of the best college cheer teams in the country." She squeezes me tight, then pulls away, dabbing tears from her eyes.

14

"I'm going to do my best, Mom. I promise." I place a hand over my heart and look Mom in the eye. Reaching up, I wipe a tear from her cheek. "I want you to be proud of me again."

"I am proud of you, honey. I have confidence in you. I hope you'll like it here. I want you to make some good friends on your new team. Speaking of which, I wonder where your roommate went. She's definitely been here and started unpacking." She looks at the other bed and motions toward the opened containers and half-empty suitcases.

"I'm sure she's close by. Maybe she went to a friend's room to chat." I start opening suitcases and hanging clothes while Mom makes my bed. After closing the closet door, I notice a note taped to the wall. "Hey, Mom, I think this note is for me."

Hey, roomie, I started unpacking, then one of the other cheerleaders said we needed to go to the gym to get our ID-card pictures made. They wrap up at 5:00. I left around 2:45, so if you get here soon enough, make sure to head over.

"We should probably go over there now," I say. "I'm almost done unpacking anyway. All I need to do is put my toiletries in the shower, put my makeup away, and hang up some photos. I don't mind finishing that up later."

It's a ten-minute walk to the gym and the heat is ridiculous. I thought Louisiana heat was bad. Walking in, we see two lines set up---, one at the check-in table and the other at the photography station. Mom and I get in the check-in line.

A girl greets us with a super cheery-- "Hey, y'all. What's your name?" When I tell her, she says the same thing the girl at the dorm said, "You're a cheerleader----cool."

When she says that, two girls standing in the photography station line next to us look my way. The one with wavy, long blonde hair says, "You're Landry Woods? I'm Kandice Kingsly, your roommate. This is Gracie Brown." She tugs on the girl's shoulder. Gracie is pretty and tan with black hair pulled into a high ponytail. She smiles, then turns toward the photographer's assistant who's motioning for the next in line.

"Thanks for leaving me a note. We came here as soon as I read it."

"You guys got here at a good time. When we arrived, the line was out the door." Kandice steps over and gives me a quick hug then gets back in line with Gracie, whose name sounds very familiar to me. They're being handed their Chief cards by the time we get to the front of the photo line. Kandice and Gracie wave goodbye with their Chief cards in hand as they head out.

When Mom and I get back to my dorm room, we're drenched in sweat. The cool air in the hallway feels good on our skin. Walking into the room, we see Kandice sitting on her newly made bed. She's put her clothes and suitcases away neatly inside her closet, the door of which is cracked slightly open.

"Hey, I just made popcorn. You want some?" she asks, jumping up with the bowl in hand. I scoop up a hand full.

Mom looks around the room nervously like she's about to get emotional. Then she walks over to my desk, where she sets her purse and starts digging through it.

"I stuck your computer charger cord in here somewhere." She pulls it from her purse and sets it on the desk. "And here are some envelopes with stamps." She places those next to the cord. "I hate to run out on you so soon, but I need to get on the road so I can get home by midnight. I've got to work in the morning." She turns to Kandice, who's sitting on her bed with her legs criss-crossed. "It was nice to meet you, Kandice. I hope you both have a great freshman year."

"Thank you, Ms. Woods. You guys can call me KK, everyone does."

I walk Mom to the car and hug her again. We're both teary by the time she gets into the SUV. I stand in the parking lot, waving as she drives away. Mom works as a receptionist for a dentist's office Monday through Thursday and has to be there by eight in the morning. Friday through Sunday, she works as a waitress at Sal and Judy's restaurant, a longtime favorite in our hometown.

After we never heard from Dad again, she took the second job, and we moved in with Grandma. I know she's anxious to get back because she left her sister, my Aunt Jackie, to look after Grandma, who had a stroke a few months ago. Grandma's walking with a cane now, and she's lost her ability to speak except for a few words at a time. I may not be able to see them again until almost Christmas, but

16

I know we'll keep in touch through calls and texts. I've already spent most of the drive here texting back and forth with Jordan.

Mom's car disappears into the distance, and a feeling of fear and excitement engulfs me like a ten-story drop on a high-speed roller coaster. Texas, college, new team, and new friends.

I've got this. I tell myself while turning back toward the dorm entrance.

As I walk into the dorm room, KK is changing into cheer-practice clothes, which is a surprise to me since I was thinking we would just be in a meeting.

"Hey, I guess I should change too," I say, opening my closet.

"Yeah, I know it's supposed to be a meeting. But it's at the cheer gym, so we may tumble," she says, pulling her long blonde hair into a high pony. My messy mop of long, stringy brown hair is stuck to my head with sweat. I whip a brush through it and pull it back into a low pony, then I throw on a change of clothes and grab my cheer shoes, ready to head out with my new friend and roomie.

The Team

4

KK, Gracie, Gracie's roommate, Christa and I walk to the cheer gym together for the meeting. We try to leave in time to be at least fifteen minutes early to make a good first impression on our upper-class teammates and, of course on Coach McKaye. Strolling toward the mat, we see the rest of the team tumbling and cutting up with each other like they are already best friends. *I hope to God, I can fit in here.*

"Hey, y'all!" One of the guys is waving us over. He is full of energy. Moving toward us, he stops in front of us. Leaning in, he gives us each air kisses and says his name is Donte. Then he pronounces it for us Don-tay, drawing out the syllables. His hair is in sponge twists with a low fade.

"Hey, Jaz, come meet the new girls," he says, excited. Jaz is taller and really built. His arm muscles are huge. He's at least six-foot-three and commands attention. His hair is shaved very close to his head, and a looped-line design has been shaved into the side. "Are y'all all flyers? 'Cause if you are, your game better be tight." He wags a finger in front of us----very sassy. I get the feeling he's for real and expects us not to mess around.

I give him a shy smile. Then Coach McKaye arrives with two of the assistant coaches and asks us to have a seat on the mat.

"Welcome to Natchez cheer," she begins. "You have all been selected to be on one of the toughest, most competitive, competition college teams in the country. For some of you, it's your first year with us, and you already know I expect a lot." She steps closer, then looks down. As she glances up at us again, her look turns soft, and I see a ghost of a smile. "You'll be part of our legacy from now on. NCFFU. Those five letters that you will see emblazed on our shirts and logos mean, Natchez, cheer, family, faith, and unity. NCFFU represents our team and what we mean to each other. We have faith in each other. We are a family, and we stand united."

Her hands move to rest on her hips. "You should always be on time for practice." She motions to the two male assistant coaches standing on either side of her. I expect you to communicate with me or the assistant coaches, if you are injured, sick, or have an emergency. Y'all are my kids when you are here. I'm going to treat you like my own, but I expect you to respect me, respect this team, and respect this school. As a Chiefs cheerleader, you have a *big* reputation to up-hold. You're expected to act with character in public and around town, and that goes for your social media accounts as well."

She pulls her cell phone from her back pocket. "The reason I asked you for your Snapchat, Twitter, Tik Tok, and Instagram accounts is because I get an alert on my phone when one of you posts something." She holds her phone up in the air toward us. "I know a lot of you are "cheerlebrities" and have a *huge* social media following, some of you with as many as three hundredK." She tucks her phone back into her pocket. "What you send out into the world on your social media reflects our team, me, this program, and this campus. I have an open-door policy, and as those who have been on the team already know, I'll do anything for my kids. But you have to try, and you have to follow the rules."

She pauses a beat then smiles at us. "We'll start working in stunt groups tomorrow and work on tumbling. Even though it's eight months from now, we'll begin looking tomorrow at who we want to have on the mat for nationals in Daytona. Not all of you will make mat. We can only take twenty, and this year we have thirty on the team. Those who don't make mat will be alternates, and you will need to be ready to fill in at any given moment due to an injury or whatever the situation. Also, those on scholarship-----, almost half of you-----are required to cheer for football and all basketball games. All of us as a team are required to perform for local elementary schools and town parades when asked----in addition to our preparation for the national competition. We also host three cheer clinics per year. So there will be other routines to learn throughout the year, not just the competition routine. Of course, the competition routine will be your hardest and most important one."

She clasps her hands together. "Now, we do like to have fun together as a team." She lays a hand to her chest. "I, as well as Zack and Matt, want you all to bond like family. We have a team bonding party at my house tomorrow night after practice. It's a pool party and cookout in my backyard, so wear a suit and bring your appetite. We'll take any questions you may have now, then we'll do some conditioning before you're dismissed."

A few hands go up, and Coach Matt calls on a girl named Lisa.

"Do we have practice every day of the week?" she asks.

"We have practice Monday through Friday, usually from four p.m. to seven p.m. but sometimes on Friday's we might be done by six." Coach Matt continues. "On Saturday we practice from one to three except for game days, and on Sundays we practice from three to five." Coach Matt looks for anyone else with their hand up. He calls on one of the new guys named Josh.

"I've heard there are all-day practices too."

This time Coach McKaye answers.

"Yes, once we have chosen who will be on mat, we will start with all-day practices on Saturdays and add more of them as needed. By the time we arrive in Daytona, you will have gone full-out with the routine over forty times. You'll do it until you know it, then you'll do it until it's impossible to get wrong."

A few deep breaths are heard among my new teammates. Donte stands and adds, "You guys can do this! We are family! Faith in our family makes unity!"

Suddenly, the older cheerleaders stand and chant NCFFU! Donte reaches for my hand and pulls me up, and everyone gathers in a circle, chanting NCFFU. Jaz runs into the middle of our circle, lifts his hands, and yells, "Welcome to the ring of fire." The rest of the team converges on him in a huge group hug with a few screaming, "The ring of fire!" We all begin jumping up and down in unison, and that's when I know I'm gonna love it here.

Team Party

5

"The first practice was pretty cool. There's a lot of talent on this team," KK says, opening her closet to pick an outfit to wear to the pool party later today. "What did you think about Donte and Jaz?"

"Donte is funny, and he seems like he's always in a good mood. He's a great guy. Jaz, on the other hand, is a bit intense. The other guys all seem pretty chill. What do you think about the other girls? I realized last night that Gracie Brown is pretty famous. I remembered her being in a lot of cheer magazines and ads for the Varsity company. Is she the one who has so many followers on social media? I only have, like twelve hundred." I let out a short laugh.

"Don't stress about that. By the time our team has won another national title, your social media is gonna blow up too. I only have three thousand followers. Some of the other girls have like ten-K and twelve-K, but, yeah, Gracie is def the cheerlebrity here."

"I got a really good feeling about the team last night," I say. "I was concerned I might not fit in, with my background and all. I know the coaches are the only ones who know about it, but I was scared I wouldn't belong. I don't have many friends back home anymore. After what happened, I didn't go back to school. I stayed clear of the girls who were a bad influence on me and stuck close to my boyfriend, Jordan. And it's just me and my mom living with my grandma. My dad's been out of the picture for years." I pause, wondering how much about my past I should share with my new friend.

"Jordan and I haven't officially broken up, yet," I add. "We've been talking and texting back and forth since I got here. But we are so far away." I slip a tank top over my sports bra and bend down to gather my sandals and swimsuit. "We told each other that if either one of us meets someone that we're interested in, we would tell the other."

KK walks over to me and puts an arm around my shoulders. "It's okay. I know how you feel being far from home. I feel the same, but I think this team is gonna be like family." We move over and sit together on the edge of her bed. "I live with my grandparents too," she says. "My mom left when I was two. I have a brother who is three years older than me, and he took off to find his way after he graduated from high school. Right after that, my dad remarried, and he started a new family. That's when my grandparents took me in and I got back into competitive cheerleading."

She gets up and gets a photo from her desk. "My gym is small-time compared to some of the big-name gyms a lot of our teammates come from." She holds the photo out for me to take. "When I had my first interview with Coach McKaye, she told me that she recruits from all over the country. A lot of the most talented kids, she said, come from broken homes with stories that would break your heart. She said she gives them a chance and gives them hope, telling them that as long as they play by the rules, and give it a shot, everything will be okay. She had me believing from the start. No one has to know your story if you don't want them to, but I think if you want to make friends feel like family and develop the bond Coach was talking about, it may be best to open up and share and let others be there for you. As a flyer, I feel sometimes like I have to have blind faith. You'll have to hope teammates catch you when you fall."

I nod and smile at KK. She's genuine and makes me feel better, bringing my spirits up from the low place I often find myself sinking into. We gather our bags and walk into the hall to meet up with our teammates Gracie and Christa who live four doors down from us. Both of them have cars on campus, and KK and I ride to Coach McKaye's house after practice in Gracie's car. When we arrive, there are already a lot of cars in the drive, so we park along the street and walk through the gate.

Slipping into the backyard, we see festive party lights, and red and black balloons in the Natchez College colors. Teammates are splashing in the pool, and a top 40-hit is blasting from the outdoor speakers.

Donte sees us walk up and says, "Hey, y'all, come on in here!" He sets a bowl of chips on a table set up for food and pulls us into a group hug. A man working behind a grill calls out, "Mandi, bring me a large tray to set these burgers on." A small group is at the edge of the pool making a Tik Tok video.

Jaz and a few more guys come through the gate, doing back handsprings and landing with a pose, with their hips out and their hands in the air. Cheering breaks out, and Donte in his loud, high-pitched voice screams, "Whoo, hoo!" That's how you make an entrance. Work it, boys!"

Gracie and Christa drag me and KK over to the hot tub to join more members of the team who are hanging out there. Another group of guys I think two are named Mark and Brodi---- have girls on their shoulders doing stunts and flips in the pool. Everyone is having a lot of fun, and I settle in with the other girls, laughing and being silly too.

After we've been there for a while, the man behind the grill calls out, "Mandi, the ribs are done. We're ready to eat." He must be Coach McKaye's husband.

Coach moves from under the large covered porch and gathers us in a circle. The guy next to me reaches for my hand, and Gracie on the other side of me reaches for the other. Coach asks us to bow our heads. Everyone seems cool with the prayer, which is pretty short, mostly to bless the food and our time together as a team.

I haven't been to church in a really long time. We stopped going once Mom took on two jobs and started working every Sunday. Church just wasn't a thing for us anymore. But it seems that Coach McKaye and her husband -----I think I heard her call him Brad, -----must be church goers.

After the prayer ends, one of the boys' yells, "Let's eat."

Coach corrects him and says, "Ladies first."

He steps aside with the rest of the boys to let us girls go first.

Coach holds a stack of beach towels above her head. "Ya'll can grab a towel to sit on and find a spot in the grass or along the edge of the pool. After we're done eating, it will be time for the big-little reveal."

Once we're sitting with plates of food and drinks in hand, I ask Gracie and Christa if they know what big-little is.

Christa explains. "I came to one of their clinics last year, and I learned a lot from a friend of mine who used to cheer for Natchez. She said that the upper-class cheerleaders will each be given a "little" to take under their wing for the year." She nods in my direction. "I think the seniors will get sophomore cheerleaders, and the juniors will get the freshman cheerleaders. I think the coaches have selected who our new "bigs" will be."

When everyone seems about done eating, Coach Zack gets out a stack of envelopes. He holds them above his head. Cheering and applause break out, and he begins, "It's time for this year's big-little reveal. Each big will get an envelope with clues as to who their little is. It's the littles' job to pay close attention to the clues. If they guess wrong and you know it's really you, then you stand. After all big-littles have been revealed, you guys find a spot somewhere in the yard or inside the house to hang out for a few minutes and get acquainted. We'll give everyone twenty minutes, then we'll gather in a group and each little will share something new they've learned about their big. Ready?" He begins passing out envelopes to each of the upper-class cheerleaders. When he's done, he asks, "Who wants to begin?"

Mark stands, opens his envelope, and reads the first clue about his little. "She can fly, she can base, she can tumble, and she can pose for pics, and be back home by six. Okay, my guess is Gracie Brown." She pops up and goes over to sit with Mark.

A girl named Sherry stands next and reads her first clue. "Was on the cross-country team in high school. Lives on a farm in northern Oklahoma." She pauses. "I'm still not sure, so I'm gonna read the next clue. Started back tumbling with her cheer gym her sophomore year. I'm going to take a guess. Landry?" I shake my head.

KK pops up and waves to her.

24

Next, Donte jumps up, opens his envelope, and easily figures out his little is a boy named Josh.

Brodi goes next. "She was on Smoed and Stingrays Peach. She's a flyer." He looks toward us. His eyes land on me then move to Christa. He points at her and she pops up to go sit with her big.

Jaz gets up next and opens his envelope. "She's from a small town in south Louisiana on the bayou. She can tumble like a boy." He stops, puts a hand on his hip, and says, "Girl, I know who this is now. Landry Woods, you are my little. Come here, girl!"

I'm a bit shocked that I got Jaz, but I know it's all about team bonding, and the coaches hopefully know who my best fit will be. I stand and move over to sit with Jaz as the rest of the bigs open their envelopes to reveal their littles.

Once all thirty of us are paired up with our 'bigs,' Jaz says, "Let's find a spot to sit."

We move away from the crowded pool deck to a large oak tree in the corner of the yard on the far left. I spread out a towel and we sit.

"Girl, I'ma be straight with you," he says. "I am serious about this team. Cheerleading for me is life. I used to play football, but I didn't really want to play. I was just told I was really good. But that wasn't me, ya know? I can be who I am and feel like myself as a cheerleader. It got me through a lot of struggles growing up. I don't want to weigh you down with the bad stuff that happened in my life. But just know this, it was some bad shit. I don't know what you've gone through or if you've led a princess life, but either way, we're a team, and we're family. I got you. You dig me?"

I nod, fixed in place, taking in his words.

"Girl, you look scared to death. Don't be. You don't need to tell me anything you don't want to but tell me something. My real name is James, by the way."

I smile at him shyly and clear my throat. "Okay. It's just me and my mom living with my grandma. I got in trouble my junior year and got kicked off my all-star team, and my coach called Coach McKaye to see if she'd give me a tryout. I was on scholarship at my gym because of my tumbling skills and was always on the level five teams with older kids. Most of the girls my age snubbed me. I had one real friend at the gym who was always nice to me. She's a year older, and her name is Nicole. I'll be honest. I was scared I wouldn't fit in here." I stop and bite my lip, not sure of what to say next.

Jaz leans in and hugs me. "Girl, I think you will fit in just fine."

Practice Makes Perfect
6

So, what's it really like in Texas? Jordan's text comes in as I'm walking to practice. We've texted back and forth a little since I've been here, but mostly about what he's been doing. Because I just go to practice and hang out at the dorms with the other cheerleaders, I haven't felt like I've had anything of interest to add to our conversations.

It's hotter here than in Louisiana, I think. It's a small town like Lacombe. There's not a lot to do. But I'm getting to know my teammates and I think I'm gonna like it.

I miss you, Landry.

I miss you, too. But I gotta go. Practice is about to start. I add a smile emoji.

Strolling into the cheer gym, I see my team stretching on the mat. I move over to join them.

Coach Zack walks over and says, "Tomorrow we'll have an all-day practice with the choreographer to get ready for a performance during halftime at the first game. Be here by nine and bring lots of water and snacks. Coach will have lunch brought in at noon. If everything goes well, you may get to leave early, but gear up for a long day. After you stretch out, run two laps then get into your stunt groups."

Later that day, I'm glad to be resting on my bed when there's a knock on the door. "Come in," I say, sitting up.

"Hey, Landry, we're going to make a run to the grocery store. You guys wanna come too?" Christa and Gracie are standing in our doorway with wallets in hand. My mom gave me some money before she left, but I know she expects me to eat on campus since that's covered in my scholarship. I have to watch what I spend.

Before I can answer, KK comes back from the bathroom, squeezing in between the girls as she slips back into our room.

"You want to go to the store with Gracie and Christa?" I ask her.

"Sure. I need to get a few snacks and stock up on Pop-Tarts. Tomorrow's practice is going to be a long one." We grab our bags and happily join the other girls, bounding out of the dorm, laughing, and giggling.

In the parking lot, a group of guys is standing by a car parked next to Christa's. They look over at us, smiling, and give us the cool-guy nod. One of them has a beautiful smile, showing off adorable dimples, gorgeous creamy light-brown skin and shoulder-length dreadlocks which are tinted blond at the end. He looks in my direction and says, "Hey." It's a very confidant, cool-guy, kind of *hey.*

I smile at him and respond with "Hi," before getting into the back seat of Christa's car.

Once Christa starts the engine and backs out of the spot, she looks back at me and says, "OMG, Landry. Cole Collins just said hey to you."

"Who is that?" I ask.

Christa bursts out laughing.

That's when Gracie turns around from the front passenger seat and says, "Just the Natchez College star quarterback, that's all."

KK and I look at each other with raised eyebrows.

Christa glances at us from the review mirror as she drives. "And did you notice the drip? He had on some bomb-ass tri-color Nike Air Max tennis shoes."

"Cool," I say, very nonchalantly. *I mean, I guess having the star quarterback say hey to me is cool?*

*****

Getting up at eight the next morning for a shower is rough. All of our practices until today have been in the afternoon, allowing us time to sleep as late as we want. But not today. We have to be at the cheer gym by nine and work with the choreographer all day. I shuffle over to KK's bed to make sure she's awake before I wander down the hall to the showers.

After meeting up with more of our team, we walk into the gym together. Donte holds the door open for us as we walk through. He's all smiles, bursting with enthusiasm. "Let's get this, y'all," he cheers. KK and I high five him.

With a few run-throughs under our belt we sit along the edge of the mat and watch the stunt groups. Unfortunately, KK's stunt group is a little shaky. She's not getting her heel stretch all the way up before she brings her leg down to regain her balance.

Dale, the choreographer, tells us to move into our beginning positions. "Landry, set up between Gracie's and KK's stunt groups. Begin with a handspring to whip then land a full, pose with a hand on your hip, do a chin pop, then move to the front left corner. Let's do a full-out and see where we get to. Ready? Five, six, seven, eight."

After we go full-out three times with this new routine, Coach McKaye decides to end practice. "Tomorrow is Sunday, so we don't have practice until three. There's also an open invitation to anyone who wants to join me for church on Sunday mornings. If you need a ride, you can text me. You're dismissed."

I fall back on the mat, not sure I have enough energy to stand. Jaz comes over to offer me a hand and easily helps me up.

"Show-off," I say, joking.

He flexes his large biceps then turns his back to me and twerks.

Laughing, I shuffle toward the locker room. KK and I gather our bags and walk back to the dorms with the rest of the girls. Christa is chatting obsessively about one of the football players we saw yesterday in the parking lot.

"Although he's not Cole Collins," she says, giving me a look. I'm not sure what she means or why she's giving me that look. I don't really know Cole Collins except that he said hi to me yesterday.

I shrug. "Not sure what you mean," I say, trying to sound uninterested.

"You should take any opportunity you can ----if you happen to run into him again. He's a total catch."

29

"It sounds like you want to date him."

"Girl code. He spoke to you. I was there. I saw how he was looking at you. I'm not going to mess with girl code. It's bad juju."

I laugh. "I definitely don't want any bad juju."

First Day of School
7

I've been at Natchez a little over a month, and I'm still alive. Classes start tomorrow. Since I've been here, I've memorized the campus layout but still want to figure out where my classes are and how long I'll need to get from one class to the next, grab lunch, get to practice, and get to and from my dorm. Plus, I want to figure out how late I can sleep every morning before having to crawl out of bed. Feeling pretty confident with my route to my first two classes, I plop down on the steps of the clock tower to answer a few texts from Mom.

Good luck with classes tomorrow. I love you.

Thx, Mom. I'll text u ltr and let u know how it goes.

We're so proud of you.

Love you too. Standing, I hit send, and refer back to my schedule as I look for the next building.

I really hope Coach doesn't keep us over today with classes starting tomorrow. I'm going to have to get used to a whole new schedule, with classes in the morning to early afternoon then practice into the evening every day. Staying busy definitely helps keep my mind off missing home.

After practice, KK and I pick up a pizza from the cafeteria to take back to our room. She sets the pizza on her desk.

I pick up a slice and take a few bites before setting it on top of a notebook on my desk. "I'm going to take a quick shower," I say in KK's direction. Gathering my towel, I wander down the hall.

"You excited for classes tomorrow?" I ask, a little later, drying my damp hair with a towel.

KK is sitting on her bed, busy typing on her phone. She finishes her text and tosses her phone onto her bed.

"Yes. We should compare schedules and see if we have any classes together or in the same building at the same time. We could try to get lunch together, but if that doesn't work. I'll see you back here before we go to practice."

I pull my schedule from my bag and read it aloud.

"I think we might have the same English class. I also have a marketing class, but mine is at a later time on Fridays."

She walks over with her schedule so we can compare. "Awesome. We have English together first thing tomorrow," she says, folding her schedule.

Popping the door of my closet open, I comb through my clothes. After looking through everything I decide on a white cropped top with bell sleeves that ties in the front, blue and white paper bag-style shorts, and my Converse high-tops. I move to my desk and eat the rest of my pizza while packing my backpack full of notebooks and pens. Looking around the room, I feel confident I'm ready for my first day of college classes. I set the alarm on my phone before drifting off to sleep.

*****

The first day of class wasn't too bad. Jogging into the room, I drop my bag to the floor, and yank open my dresser drawer. I pull out some Nike Pros and throw on a tank before meeting the rest of the girls to walk to practice together.

"Did you get Thompson for sports marketing too?" I ask KK as we wait in the hallway for Gracie and Christa.

"I do have him. I like that class. I know you're also taking sports medicine. How was that class?"

"I like both. I know eventually I'll have to choose a major."

Gracie and Christa pop into the hall and the four of us make our way out of the dorm and into the late-afternoon Texas heat toward the football stadium.

"I'm glad we have a change of scenery today for practice," Gracie comments.

"It's still hot as blazes out here, even though it's four in the afternoon." Christa spritzes some water on her face from her water bottle.

We meet the rest of the team at center field to stretch out before we begin. I'm glad we get to show off this routine during the first football halftime. From the loudspeakers, Coach Matt's voice booms, telling us to get into position. He's up in the stadium box on a microphone, barking orders that eco throughout the stadium. Squinting and holding up a hand to shield my eyes, I can see his shadow inside the press box. After an hour of practice, we've hit the routine full-out three times in a row and with the approval of Coach McKaye, we're dismissed.

Stepping out of our team huddle at center field, I walk toward the fence at the edge of the field where I left my bag and my water bottle. I pick up the bottle, taking a long drink. As I go to set it back into my bag, I see the football players walking onto the field for practice. My eyes dart to Cole Collins right away, taking in his creamy tan skin, and handsome looks. Today he has his dreadlocks pulled back with a thick rubber band. I throw my bag over my shoulder as KK walks up next to me. The two of us are walking toward the gate when he notices me. Well, I guess I might have been staring at him a little too long, causing him to look. But when he does, he gives me a grin. I glance down, embarrassed. KK's chatting about practice and uniforms or something. I'm not listening to her since I'm too busy staring at Cole. She doesn't realize I'm distracted and keeps talking all the way back to our dorm.

When we arrive back in our room, I'm still lost in my daydreams, but I've got to get some homework finished before calling it a night. I need to refocus and get my mind off Cole Collins. *The star quarterback is not into me.* I laugh out loud, shaking my head.

"What's so funny?" KK asks.

"Nothing, girl. I just thought of something silly and a little bit ridiculous. I've got to finish this assignment before I can go to sleep tonight."

*****

Ah. New uniforms. I take the plastic bag from Coach, slide it off the hanger, and stare at two beautiful, crisp, shimmery, perfect new uniforms. One is black and white with a rhinestone embellished collar. It's a two-piece uniform with a short, straight black skirt. The other is mostly fire-engine red with black and white piping along the edges and *Chiefs* spelled out in black sequins across the chest. I open the box of Rebel Athletic cheer shoes and take a deep sniff. Christa laughs. "Smell good?"

"I've always loved the new-cheer-shoe-smell." I take my stuff with me to the locker room to change.

Coach wants to decide which bow and what uniform we will wear tomorrow for the game. The uniform and bow she chooses will be our football and basketball sideline performance uni, and the other bow and uni will be worn for competition.

"Be in place for photos after you try everything on. We're meeting in front of the building across from the clock tower. If anyone needs a new shoe size or uniform size, let me know now." Coach McKaye's voice blasts from outside the locker rooms. "After photos, we'll come back here and start with two laps then hit the mat for conditioning," she shouts.

"It's Friday, Coach," Brodie interjects. "Can we have a short practice after photos are done? Maybe celebrate the first week of school and our first game performance tomorrow?" Brodi asks, walking out of the boy's locker room, flashing Coach a radiant smile.

"Show me how good your performance during halftime will be. Give it all your energy! And I'll consider letting you go early," she anounces, then claps her hands to get the rest of us to hurry.

The next day, I'm thrilled to have the first week of school over with, and I'm looking forward to cheering at tonight's football game and our halftime performance. Meeting on the field for a quick practice, we run through all the cheers, then I do a few warm-up tumble passes along the sideline. My stunt partner is Jaz for game days. On the sideline, we don't do a lot of stunts since some of the girls on the sideline team are not flyers. We've learned easy stuff like pop chairs, side birds, and shoulder stands. Gracie, KK, Christa, and a few other girls who are flyers do some more difficult stunts like liberties, full ups, and basket tosses with their stunt partners.

Our halftime routine hits perfectly, and the Chiefs win their first game of the season. Standing next to the chain-link fence along the edge of the field, I slide my cheer backpack on.

"It's time to celebrate," Jaz says with a smile. His white teeth glow under the stadium lights.

"You going to a party?" I ask.

"The tradition around here is that the players, cheerleaders, the band, and some student fans head to the local pizza place after home games. Our pizzas are always half-price. Come on." He waves his arm above his head, walking toward the parking lot.

I glance at the girls.

"We're game," Gracie says.

"I don't want to mess with tradition. I'm going." Christa starts walking then looks back.

"We're coming too," KK says with a grin.

I pile into the back of Brodi's SUV with Jaz, Gracie, and Christa. KK rides over with some other girls and Donte in Mark's car. A short while later, Brodi pulls into a parking spot next to Mark. As we're walking in, we notice a group of band members coming in along with us. The band members are in shorts and T-shirts having changed out of their heavy uniforms. Our team, however stayed in uniform. Some football players meander in, fresh from their showers with wet hair and flip-flops. Our team pulls two tables together and sets up extra chairs along the ends. We order five large pizzas to share. The football players pile into booths wherever they can squeeze in, and soon the entire restaurant is full of Natchez College students.

During dinner, Jaz and Donte keep us in stitches with descriptions of a TV show they love to watch. It sounds like a crazy show. I'm laughing so hard I almost choke on my pizza. Grabbing my Coke, I take a slow sip while glancing up at Cole and some other football players walking by our table. They stop and give fist bumps to Jaz and the other guys. Cole notices me and smiles. Nervous, I turn my eyes away and pick up the slice of pizza on my plate. He walks over to me, still smiling and I look up at him. "Great performance tonight," he says. "You've got some mad tumbling skills."

"Thank you," I say, embarrassed.

"I'm Cole." He reaches his hand out for me to shake.

"Hi. I'm Landry."

"It's nice to meet you, Landry. I'll see you around," he says as he lets go of my hand.

When they leave, Jaz and Donte hoot and holler. "What, what, what. . . girrrrrrrl. He likes you. Sho nuff," Donte's says, with a sassy nod.

I roll my eyes. "What are you talking about?"

"Cole Collins, girl. He has eyes for you fo sho!" Jaz says with confidence.

Jaz and Donte stand up and start dancing. "C'mon' girl. Get it, girl, get it." Their antics aimed at me.

Everyone at the table is looking at me totally amused. I've turned about five shades of crimson and I roll my eyes like they are all crazy. But in my mind, I'm wondering if they are for real? Could Cole Collins really be interested in me?

Hot Mess

8

Every freshman athlete has to meet with a tutor twice a week. *Gross.* Tutoring starts the third week of school. I guess by then we'll know which classes we need the most help with. It's mid-September now, and I've been here for about two months. I miss Jordan, Mom, and my grandma, but I've made some great friends here so far, and my team really does feel like family. I'm meeting my tutor after my last class of the day, right before I go to cheer practice. I'm anxious to know who I got. I'm supposed to go to the third floor of the library. Entering the elevator, I push the button.

Stepping out onto the third floor, I see students studying at tables while others sit on couches with their laptops. There's a hallway with classrooms on the -right side of the room. I'm not sure where to go, so I'm just looking around when I see a familiar face striding toward me. It's Paul, the guy who helped me the day I moved in. I remember he said he was a sports med major. He's also an upper classman.

"Hey, Landry," he says, stopping in front of me. "Guess what? I'm your tutor this year. Come on. Let's go down the hall. There are some empty rooms down there where we can be away from the noise and get started." He points toward the hall and starts walking. Hopefully, he's good at math since that's my least favorite subject and where I need the most help.

We're working on my pre-calc homework when a loud alarm startles us.

"That's the tornado siren. Let's move to the hallway and close all the doors to classrooms that have windows. We'll need to stay

37

in the hall until it's safe." He gets up and closes the blinds on the window, then we close the door to the room.

As I'm stuffing my book back into my backpack, more people come out of the classrooms along the hall, closing the doors behind them. Some of the people who were on the couches are now sitting along the wall in the hallway.

Paul pulls up the weather radar on his phone and wonders out loud about the likelihood of the tornado heading toward campus. I'm crouched in a sitting position with my knees up and my back against the wall when I hear a familiar voice. I look up and see Cole Collins and two other football players sitting at the far end of the hallway. I quickly look away, hoping he didn't see me looking at him. I send a quick text to KK, letting her know I'm huddled in a hallway on the top floor of the library with my tutor and some other students waiting out the storm.

She quickly texts me back. *Good, ur safe. I'm in the lower hallway of the dorm sitting on the floor with everyone from our floor.*

This may make us late to practice, but if it's a tornado I guess we'll be excused. I add a laughing emoji.

Who is your tutor? I don't meet with mine until tomorrow.

This guy named Paul. He's really nice. I'm getting him to help me with math.

I set my phone down after sending the texts and notice Cole looking at me.

When our eyes meet, he says, "Hey, Landry."

I blush and smile back. "Hey."

I start to pick up my phone to read another text that just came in, but before I do, Cole gets up, walks over, and sits right next to me. I think I'm going to hyperventilate. His creamy tan skin is beautiful. He's wearing his shoulder-length dread locks down today. His dark brown eyes are soft and warm, and he's smiling at me,---- *Those dimples.* Hopefully, I'm not panting out loud, but I realize I'm staring at him with a goofy smile on my face. I'm sure I look like a hot mess with my hair piled on top of my head in a messy bun, and no makeup on. I'm wearing a Natchez cheer T-shirt and running shorts, probably looking like I just rolled out of bed.

"Fancy meeting you here," he says with a short laugh.

I laugh too. "Yeah. Um, meeting during a natural disaster is not my usual."

"I'm glad we can sit and talk for a few minutes. I'd love to get to know you and find out more about you. I'd love to get your number."

I am literally dead right now. I don't even know if I'm breathing, but I manage to say,

"Sure." I tell him my number and watch as he types it into his phone. Then he asks my last name and where I'm from. I reply and to keep the convo going, I ask about him.

"So, where are you from?"

"A small town in Texas not too far from here called Tyler. Ever heard of it?"

"No. I've only been in Texas since July. I haven't ventured too far from my small town in South Louisiana. I guess you played football there, too." *Duh, that's obvi. What am I even saying? Landry get a grip. It's not like you've never talked to a cute boy.*

He laughs and is still smiling----with those amazing dimples---- so I don't feel like a total goofball. Perhaps it's his to-die-for dimples, but I'm feeling pretty comfortable around him now.

"Yeah, I was the quarterback."

Just then an announcement comes on that the tornado is out of our area and it's safe to move about campus. Cole stands and offers his hand to help me up.

"Bye, Landry. See ya," he says, walking away.

Paul cocks his eyebrow in a playful question. "That was interesting." He checks his phone for the time and says he has another tutoring session that is supposed to start in ten minutes. He hands me a homework sheet.

"I need to go back to my dorm to get ready for practice anyway. I guess I'll see you next time. Bye, Paul," I say, throwing my bag over my shoulder to head out.

Walking into my room in an excited rush, I can't wait to tell KK who I sat next to during the tornado warning. She's lacing up her cheer shoes when I walk in.

"You'll never guess in a million years who I was with in the hallway just now," I blurt out.

She looks up at me like she's trying to come up with something really good to say. "Cole Collins." She stands and does a ta-da-style dance step adding jazz hands.

"Um, yeah. I can't believe you guessed it."

"OMG, for real. It was just the first thing I could think of. I wasn't totally serious. But that's cool, right?"

"Well, it is, actually, because he legit asked for my number." I fan my face like I'm having a hot flash.

"No freaking way." She twirls around with a hop, grabs my hands, and we both bounce up and down a few times, silly and giddy.

While at practice, I am totally on top of the routine, energetic, smiling, and happy. Today, I could even give Donte a run for his money with the positive energy I'm evoking into the world. I can only think of one reason why I'm so enthusiastic. And sitting with Cole Collins in a cramped hallway during a tornado warning is most definitely it. Christa was right. He might just be the sexiest man alive.

Just a Text?
9

A loud knock on our door wakes me from a dream. I glance at my phone for the time. It's only nine a.m. on a Saturday.

"Hey, you guys up?" someone shouts from the other side of the door.

"Hang on," KK, says, getting out of bed, and shuffling to the door, which she opens.

"You guys want to go to Waffle House?" Christa asks in a burst. She is dressed in shorts and a T-shirt. With her sandy brown hair pulled into a bun. "Bring your laundry. We can get that done before we go to practice today."

KK glances at me, and I nod. "Give us a few minutes," she says, before closing the door.

"OMG, morning people," I moan.

"I know," KK snorts. "But we gotta eat, and getting laundry done is a must too."

The girls I hang with most are KK, Gracie, and Christa. We've gotten pretty close these past few months, and I love that I have girlfriends I can trust.

My phone dings with a text while we're eating breakfast. It's from Jordan. I'll read it later. I flip my phone over on the table just as another message pops up. I don't recognize the number, so I read the text to see who it's from. It's from Cole. Realizing it's him, plagues me with butterfingers, and I drop my phone in my lap. Holding my breath, I read his text. *Hey, just wanted to see if ur going to Pop's after the game tonight?*

Yes, that's the plan. I type while trying to be calm, but I'm starting to sweat.

Would you like to sit with me and order some pizza? Holy moly, I'm not sure how to answer. I need to see what the girls say about this before I send a response. Looking up from my phone, trying to be casual, I mention, "I just got a text from Cole Collins." Christa drops her fork on her plate with a loud clank. KK claps her hands like a two-year-old about to eat a huge bowl of ice cream. Gracie is smiling at me and asks, "What does it say?"

"He wants to know if I can sit with him tonight at the pizzeria, and it sounds like he might be asking me out, but I'm not one hundred percent sure."

"Read it to us," Christa says, about to burst with enthusiasm.

"It says, "Would you like to sit with me and order some pizza?""

"That sounds like a date to me," KK announces. All three are looking at me like they are about to combust from holding their breath too long. Christa starts tapping out a beat on the table then KK and Gracie join in, matching the beat. Then they start up a rap song about my text.

KK begins with, "Landry's got a boy, and he's the star QB.

Gracie adds, "It sounds like she's got a hot date tonight, if you ask me." They finish their rap and we all burst into loud laughter, causing everyone in the Waffle House to look our way.

"You did answer his text, right?" KK asks.

"No. I wasn't sure how to respond. What do you guys think I should say?"

"That's a no-brainer," Christa blurts.

"What do you want to say?" Gracie asks.

"I think he's really cute, and he seems nice," I say with an unsure voice and a shrug to my shoulders. "I think I want to at least get to know him better. But I want to sound casual when I respond, like it's no biggie."

"Okay, so send him a text that says, "Sure, sounds good. See you there." KK says.

"Yeah, do that." Gracie urges.

Christa and KK nod in agreement. I type out the text and hit send. And within a few minutes, he responds.

"Just got a new text. It says, "Sounds good, can't wait." I say, sounding pleased with myself. And in a great mood for the rest of the day, even while doing laundry.

"Hey, Mom," I say, holding my phone to my ear with my shoulder while shoving my wet clothes into the dryer.

"How is everything going?"

"It's good. I met with my tutor." I turn the knob and push the button to start the dryer. "Do you remember Paul from move-in day? He was the guy who helped us unload. He's a sports medicine major. He's helping me with my calculus. We have a home game later tonight. I'm finishing up some laundry now before we have to get ready for practice before tonight's game. How's Grandma and everyone there?"

"Everyone is good. They all miss you. Are you and Jordan still talking?"

"We are, but our lives are so different now. He's doing senior year of high school stuff and I'm in college. We talked about letting each other know if someone new comes along. I think I like someone on campus. But I don't want to say anything to Jordan too soon. You know, too soon before there's even a relationship."

"Just be honest with each other. Trust me. I know from experience how important having an honest partner is."

The conversation starts to feel too deep, so I quickly change the subject.

"How's work going?"

"I'm staying pretty busy. I know you are too. I'm glad you found time to call."

After talking with Mom until the dryer buzzes, I tell her I need to go.

"I've gotta get my clothes out of the dryer and head back to the dorm. I'll call you later, Mom."

Tossing my phone onto the warm clothes just out of the dryer, I lift the basket and wander out of the laundry room thinking about my plans for after the game tonight.

Wanna Pizza Me?
10

Talk about being *way* more interested in football. I was very much invested in the game tonight. I watched as Cole made plays and scored. He ran the ball in for a touchdown and I was impressed with the way he could scramble to avoid tackles, --- not to mention how fast he can move.

The girls are talking in whispers, trying to give me encouragement for my so-called date with Cole. Gracie is handing me her lipstick, and KK is spritzing me with a Bath & Body Works fragrance since we're going straight from cheering to Pop's Pizza. We ride with Sherry in her car because we're trying to avoid letting the guys in on the sitch with me and Cole. I guess they'll notice I'm not sitting with the other cheerleaders tonight, but the girls and I want to avoid their questions or silly teasing for the moment.

Following everyone into the restaurant, I don't see any football players yet. The guys go about moving tables around and setting up chairs. KK announces that we're going to the bathroom and takes me by the hand, leading me in that direction. After using the bathroom and washing my hands, I stare at my reflection in the mirror, checking my hair and makeup. I pull the cheer bow from my hair and slip it onto my wrist then flip my long, brown hair over and swish it around to fluff it up.

KK squeezes my hand and says, "Just be yourself. Be you. I'm excited for you."

I nod and we shuffle out of the bathroom. The dining room is crowded now with band members, and football players, and the group of cheerleaders at our table sounds loud and boisterous. Then I see Cole. He's standing next to a table talking with another football player. KK urges me forward, and I make my way toward him.

He glances in my direction and smiles big, showing off those dimples. His eyes are shining, and he starts walking toward me. His dreadlocks are pulled into a ponytail. He's wearing Nike athletic shorts, a Natchez football T-shirt, and Adidas slides. He reaches for my hand and says, "Hi, Landry. Let's sit over here."

I think a couple of the players were holding a booth for us, because when we get there, they give us a grin and move to a different booth with the rest of their teammates. Cole slides in, and I sit across from him.

"What kind of pizza do you like?" he asks, grinning, showering me with a dazzling smile and total cuteness.

"I like thin crust with pepperoni. I also like basil and tomatoes, and sometimes pineapple and barbecue chicken." I smile back at him.

"Pineapple and barbecue chicken slaps. Awesome. It all sounds good to me right now. I'm so hungry."

"Great game tonight. I was impressed with your running game."

"Thank you," he says as a waiter appears at our table. After we order, we continue getting to know each other while waiting on our pizza.

"How long have you been a cheerleader?"

"I started tumbling at the cheer gym and taking lessons when I was five. The first team I was on was a mini level two. By the time I was seven, I was on a junior level three. I moved up to a higher-level team as my tumbling skills advanced. I started out as a flyer, but when I got older, I was needed as a base and a back spot. That's what I am now. I've been told I tumble like a boy," I giggle. "The highest-level cheerleading is level eight stunting. I was on several teams that went to Worlds, which is a competition for level five and up. You have to earn a spot to go to Worlds. I've never been on a team that's won at Worlds, but we did come in second one year."

"Did you always know you wanted to cheer at the college level?"

I stumble around with my words, not sure how to answer. "Um, no, I actually wasn't thinking about cheering in college, and I wasn't even thinking about college at all before I was introduced to Coach Mckaye. I'm only seventeen and was supposed to be a senior in high school right now." I glance down and pick up my drink and take a sip. I don't want to divulge too much.

Our pizza arrives, and he lifts a slice, placing it carefully onto my plate, ----very polite. To take the focus off me, I ask about his life back in Tyler.

"I have three older brothers," he begins. "They all played football. Not all of them were quarterbacks, but they all got scholarships, same as me. My oldest brother, Chris, still plays in the NFL. He plays for the Falcons. The next oldest, Colton, didn't make it that far in the NFL. He played safety for a few years with the Panthers then he moved back to Tyler with his wife and opened a car dealership. And my brother Corbin, who is four years older than me, graduated last May after playing for Texas Tech. Now he runs the high school and middle school Young Life programs in greater Houston, and he's a volunteer coach for a Pop Warner football team."

"I've heard of Young Life. I know it's a high school program. Isn't it like, a Bible study or something?"

"It's an out-reach for middle and high school students with some great young leaders. It's a fun program that is very social. It's non-denominational and involves a worship band, food, fellowship, crazy games, and definitely a good time. It's not church, but it's designed to help students know they have someone to lean on, and someone to come to with their problems. And because it's so social, it gives them a great resource for finding a great group of friends. My brothers and I were involved with it big-time. My dad is a pastor, and he and my mom also work with Young Life. My brother felt a calling, and he's reaching out to teens in places no church would be able to reach. Just being a friend, lending an ear, and showing up means a lot. We have the same program here at Natchez. They call it Campus Club."

I'm impressed by this but not sure what to say, so I just nod and smile. Then Cole changes the subject back to me. "So, you're seventeen and in college. That's cool that you graduated early. I'm eighteen, and I'm honored that I was picked for QB1 this season. When do you turn eighteen?"

"In about a month, late November. When is your birthday?"

"At the end of February. The last day of February, in fact, the twenty-eighth."

"How often do you guys practice? I've heard Coach McKaye is a perfectionist, but that's why your team has so many national titles." He laughs.

"We practice every day, usually late afternoon. Sometimes we have all-day practices on Saturdays. When do you guys practice? It's so hot. Hopefully it will start to cool off in a few days. I can't believe it's going to be October already. Pumpkin spice lattes and all that." I laugh. Cole nods and grins at my joke.

"We practice at six a.m. on the outdoor field twice a week. But most of our practices are in the indoor facility late afternoons. We practice every day except Saturdays, which are game days of course. Sometimes we practice on Sundays, but it's rare."

Our check arrives and I try to hand him some money, but he reaches for my hand and holds it gently. "My treat. It's not often my head turns for a pretty girl. You're beautiful, and I think you are very talented. I'm glad to know you, Landry Woods, and I hope you'll let me see you again."

I'm shocked by his words. My cheeks are flushed, and I feel drops of sweat pop out on my skin, which feels tingly with him holding my hand. I say, "Thank you," quietly.

He pays the check, and we walk together to the parking lot to find my friends waiting in the car for me. He walks with me over to them, leans in, and kisses me lightly on the cheek before turning away and walking toward his truck. As I slide into the car, the girls are giggling with anticipation, waiting for me to spill the tea.

Homecoming
11

The mid-October weather has cooled off the state of Texas, which is no longer a pot of boiling heat. I'm loving the change of seasons. Aside from classes and cheer practice, I'm looking forward to Homecoming, which is just around the corner. Cole and I have been meeting up for lunch when we can, and sometimes walking to class together. Nothing too serious yet. But sometimes he takes hold of my hand while we're walking, and sparks fly. The chemistry is there. Thoughts of Jordan flood my brain, I wonder if I should tell him about Cole, but I tell myself it's nothing major at this point. But the other day Cole invited me to the Homecoming dance as his date. Now this I feel like I should mention to Jordan. But I don't know what to say about it, and he hasn't texted me that he's met someone new. I think I'll just wait and see if anything serious develops between me and Cole. I mean, I really like him, he's so cute, very nice, and fun to be around. I'm not in love with him. I think I'd know if I was. Because I've been in love before, right? Ugh. I don't want to think about this anymore. I push thoughts of boys to the far corner of my brain as I walk into the gym for practice.

During cheer practice this afternoon, Coach wants us to concentrate on the pyramid. I think she wants us to stretch our skill to see what the bases and the flyers are capable of for nationals. So far, we have some cool elements down pat for the pyramid we've been doing for shows on the field and the one we did at a local elementary school last week.

Today's practice is focused on adding a front tuck mount with a front flip to cradle to load then a rewind into liberties. The first try doesn't go well for KK's stunt group. She kicks Jaz in the nose, and he is cursing and bleeding when they stop. While the rest of us hit the mat for push-ups, Jaz leaves to get help from the trainer. If we miss a stunt or a base or back spot fails to catch a flyer causing them to get injured or hit the ground, we have to immediately do fifty push-ups. We're never allowed to let anyone hit the mat, especially if a stunt goes bad and the flyer loses her balance.

Jaz comes back to the mat with a tampon sticking out of his nose and a bad attitude. I walk over to try to cheer him up. "It's all good, Jaz. It was the first try with a new stunt and a flyer who's never tried it before. You guys will get it down soon. Don't get frustrated."

He gives me a condescending look, but says, "Thanks, Law." He found out my middle initial is A for Ann, and that my initials spell out law, so he calls me that sometimes.

I smile and give his shoulder a squeeze.

When the bleeding stops, his stunt group goes back to the mat to try again. The rest of us watch from the side. We're all cheering them on, but Donte is the loudest with his high-pitched voice and enthusiastic approach to team spirit. "Come on," he yells. "You got this. Push! Squeeze. That's it. Go! Go.! Yes, girl!"

They perform a lot better this time. I can tell KK is feeling more confident in herself, and Jaz is more chill, too.

"That looked a lot better. I'm going to let you guys go a few minutes early." Coach McKaye walks out onto the mat. "Don't forget we're meeting in the Piggly Wiggly parking lot Saturday morning to decorate the trailer for the parade. Those who are on Homecoming court will get your sashes after practice tomorrow. You'll wear those over your cheer uniform during the parade."

*****

On Homecoming morning, we're up early, working on our makeup, and Gracie and Christa are in our room too. They called Logan, one of our senior teammates, to come to our room to work on our hair. He can do the best poof. I'm terrible at the poof. He's working on Christa's hair now, and I'm next.

49

"Hand me that can of plumping powder, would you please, KK?" he asks, holding a long strand of Christa's hair in the air with the teasing comb in his other hand.

When Logan finishes with my hair, he takes a photo of the four of us girls, then we take a selfie with him. I post it to my Instagram. I haven't posted anything in months. I think the last time I posted was in August before classes started. The girls and I had gone to the pool at Sherry's apartment to hang out. I'd posted one of my newly painted pink toes with the pool in the background, adding something about the dog days of summer for the caption.

The five of us, shiny red pom-poms in hand, pile into Christa's car and head to the center of town, where we'll park and walk to our float. The early morning October air feels cool and breezy. Most of the team is already on the float, putting flannel blankets over the hay for us to sit on. Coach McKaye pulls up next to our float with her husband, Brad. They get out and start unloading pumpkins and some scarecrow decorations from the back of their truck. The guys jump in to help them carry the pumpkins, and we create an adorable pumpkin scene at the back of the float. Some of us will be riding on the float, and some of the guys will walk behind it, carrying the Natchez College Chiefs flags that they run up and down the field with during football games.

When the parade starts, I wave to Cole, who is with the football players on the float in front of us. Jaz notices me waving and comments, "Mm-hmm, I know he's cute, girl. Like delicious chocolate mousse on a designer cupcake that makes you drool."

I crack up, laughing at him.

After the parade, our team walks to the town green in front of the gazebo. The mayor makes a speech, then the president of Natchez College speaks. When our team is introduced, we perform a routine with our latest stunts. The crowds cheer us on. When the music ends, we're escorted to some tents next to the gazebo, where we sign autographs and take photos with members of the community who have come out to see us. The football players have similar tents for autographs and photos set up next to us. Long lines are starting to form in front of all the tents. They only give us about an hour to sign autographs, so thankfully we won't be out here all day. By the time we're wrapping up, my cheeks hurt from smiling. Cole walks over to our tent and asks if he can give me a ride back to the dorm.

I happily hop into his black truck, tossing my pom-poms on the floorboard in front of me. As I start to pull my seat belt across my chest, he leans in, placing his hand on my chin, slowly bringing his lips to mine in a soft, sweet kiss. "You look amazing today. I love your hair in long curls. I've always thought cheerleaders have the best hair."

Blushing and a bit taken aback by the kiss, I say, "Thank you. I had one of the guys on our team do the poof. You know what they say -----the bigger the hair, the closer to God." We both laugh.

"Everything's bigger in Texas," he says, grinning at me while starting the truck.

"I can pick you up at your dorm tonight after the game. I know you'll need some time to go back and change. I was thinking after we went to the dance, maybe we could have dinner? Since the game starts at three thirty, it will most likely end by six thirty ----- with us winning of course." He glances at me with a cute grin. "Will picking you up an hour later work for you?"

"Perfect."

He pulls the truck into the dorm parking lot, shifts into park, and turns to me.

"I'm looking forward to seeing you later."

I smile then lean down and pick up my pom-poms. He brushes his hand across my knee as I slide out of his truck.

"See you later," I say, blushing.

Date Already

12

The local country club is the gorgeous location for the Homecoming dance tonight. Twinkling lights greet us as we enter the ballroom. Hand in hand, we follow the lights and the sound of the music over to a table and sit for bit, whispering in each other's ears and trying to talk over the noise.

Reaching for my hand, Cole leans in close. "Would you like to dance with me?"

We scoot out to the dance floor just as the music changes to a slower song. I wrap my arms around his neck, and he puts his hands on my hips as we sway together. Suddenly, I realize this is something I missed out on in high school. Emotions well in my heart as I realize that if I were still at my high school, I might not have gone to Homecoming or prom. I'm not sure if Jordan would have been into going to prom. He didn't go in the spring because I didn't go back second semester. We hung out together that night. He took me to Clancy's in New Orleans for dinner. It was just the two of us, and it took my mind off prom and fancy dresses, and all the fuss. His thoughtfulness made me happy. He had skipped prom, to be alone with me, and try to make me feel special. But tonight, I feel a sense of joy to be experiencing Homecoming at my school with my friends and my teammates, -------not to mention the school's football star is my date!

"Just so you know, I'm not big on dances or getting dressed up," Cole says as we're dancing. "I wanted to be with you tonight. We don't get much time to spend together due to our schedules, and I wanted tonight to be a special time for us to enjoy and get to know each other more."

Looking into his eyes, I say."To be honest, I never went to my school's Homecoming dance or to the prom. It's nice to be able to have this experience tonight. But if you feel uncomfortable, we can go."

"Really? You never went to either? That's hard to believe. I would have guessed you were the Homecoming Queen. I'm not uncomfortable, just not one for loud parties or crowds. I spend most of my time with my buddies at the gym lifting weights or in my room playing Fortnite or the latest Call of Duty game." His eyes move up and down my body, checking out every inch of this tight dress I'm in. "You look amazing tonight," he says. "I would want to be here just to see you wearing this," he adds, twirling me around.

Gracie loaned me one of her formal dresses. It's a fitted, satin gown in lavender with a plunging neckline. Christa loaned me a pair of her strappy high heels. I didn't want to worry Mom for money to buy shoes and a dress. Gracie brought three formal dresses with her, and so did Christa. Those two have closets anyone would love to go shopping in.

"I've been known to play a little Fortnite myself," I say. "I've spent most of my time in a gym, too, although a cheer gym." I smile, biting my lower lip while staring into his eyes.

"I did make special arrangements tonight. Since this dance is at the country club, I asked if I could get a private dinner for two. The staff made arrangements for us in the dining room. It's not really a private room, but they promised to seat us in the most secluded section."

"That sounds nice."

"Whenever you're ready, we can walk upstairs and over to the main dining room."

"Okay. I'm ready now if you are."

"Right this way," he says, gently kissing my hand and leading me down the hall to the stairs that take us to the club's main restaurant. Cole is always the gentleman. I like that about him, not just that he's polite but the way he seems to put my feelings first. He's thoughtful in a mature way. He must have a great mom.

When we get to the hostess, she smiles like she knows who we are and leads us to our table, which is by far the coziest spot in the restaurant. Off to the side in a back corner is a table for two lit with candles, and there's a fresh bouquet of mixed flowers sitting on the table too.

Cole picks up the flowers. "For you," he says, handing them to me. I dip my nose into the bouquet. Its fragrance is sweet. The stems have been cut short and tied with a red satin ribbon, almost like a bouquet a bridesmaid would carry. I know a lot of girls these days use bouquets like this for Homecoming and prom pictures instead of corsages.

He pulls out my chair.

"Thank you," I say. "The flowers are amazing." I set them on the edge of the table as I sit down. A waiter comes by and fills our glasses with water and offers us a menu.

"Cole, this is so special. Thank you for putting this dinner together for me."

"I'm glad you like it. It's not very often I get dressed up and have the opportunity to take a beautiful girl out on a date."

I flush with embarrassment. And those dimples are getting to me. A warm feeling spreads through my body. We definitely vibe.

"Cole, tell me something else about you. You seem full of surprises tonight. I already know the basics. But I've noticed . . ." I pause, tilt my head, and smile. "You're extremely polite and you don't seem into yourself like some superstar athletes are."

He laughs, totally amused.

"I don't mean to embarrass you. But honestly, I think you are confident without the cocky," I say in a teasing tone.

He pauses a beat as he thinks about how he will respond. "I play the ukulele."

"What?" I spew a little bit of water from my mouth. "Wow," I say, setting my water glass down.

"And I play the guitar a little too, and I can sing."

"You do? I don't even know what to say. I'm . . . I'm so impressed," I stammer. In my mind, I'm really thinking, *Hot, superstar athlete, confident, kind, and a rock star to boot. Yes, please!* "Could you play and sing for me sometime?"

"Absolutely."

54

When our food arrives, we move on to topics like proteins, healthy foods, and the best protein shakes for maximizing workouts. He thinks KK and I should invest in some protein powder and a blender. Before we leave the clubhouse, we wander back over to the dance floor and dance to one more song, taking a few selfies while we move to the music. We're being playful and goofy, cutting up and acting silly, enjoying just being together.

Later, he takes my hand, entangling his fingers with mine as we slowly walk to the parking lot to get into his truck. Stopping before he opens the door for me, he bends down to kiss me. Leaning in, I surrender to the kiss, which is soft at first then becomes more passionate as his tongue moves softly with mine. Slowly, one of his hands slips down to my rear while the other moves up to the back of my neck as he pulls me closer. When we break apart, I feel dizzy with passion. He lightly kisses my lips again before he opens the door for me to climb into the truck.

Back on campus, he walks with me into my dorm and gives me a hug and a kiss on the cheek. The goodbye is sweet and polite. I can see he wants to be respectful and not initiate a full-on make-out session in front of anyone who might walk by. We whisper our good nights as we pull apart, and I stride dreamily back to my room.

When I walk in beaming with a euphoric smile, KK, Gracie, and Christa squeal, abandoning for a moment their efforts to change into comfy clothes. KK kicks off her shoes and runs over, pulling me into the middle of the room.

"Tell us all the details. We are dying here," she says.

"It was totally amazing." I sink down on my bed. "He had the club set up a table for two. We danced then had dinner. He's so cool and sweet and down to earth. We went back to the dance after dinner and danced to another song. When we were walking to the parking lot, he stopped to kiss me, ------and I *mean* kiss me." I tilt my head back and close my eyes, remembering his lips on mine. The girls squeeze in next to me on my bed.

"So, he's a good kisser too?" Christa asks.

"Mm---hmm." I nod but keep the other details to myself.

We spend the next hour talking about how fun the dance was. Christa mentions she danced with several different guys. Gracie and KK say they mostly hung with the rest of our team. When we notice it's after midnight, Gracie and Christa walk back to their room. I snuggle up in my bed, still relishing the memories of my night. As I start to drift off, a sudden thought bolts me back into consciousness. *Should I tell Jordan about Cole?*

I pick my phone up off the nightstand and send him a quick text.

Hey, J. How's it going? Anything new?

A few minutes later I get a text back.

Not much, but I was chosen to do a special mural at the school. It will be on a wall in the gym. Only two top art students were chosen, and I was one. That's going to take up a lot of my time. I applied to SCAD. Fingers crossed. Anything new with u?

Of course, I can't tell from his text if he's dating or interested in anyone, and I have no idea if he would tell me if he was. I don't want to throw this on him yet. I'm going to wait a little longer before I say anything. I should probably not tell him in a text anyway. It would be best to give him a call-----just not tonight.

Fall Fever
13

Halloween is tomorrow so KK and I have been planning what we want to wear for our Halloween practice and the party afterwards. Most of the team are planning to twin or create group costumes. We're trying to decide between being M-&-M's or Thing One and Thing Two while passing time on the bus riding to an away game. There's a lot going on around us. Some of the guys are using the aisle as a runway. Jaz and Donte are standing in the middle of the aisle talking about their Halloween costume choices, Donna Summer and Nicki Minaj. When we stopped to eat, Jaz bought a pink wig at the Dollar Store next door to the sub shop where we had lunch. He and some of the other guys are giving us a full runway experience with dance moves and all. Behind us there's a bubble gum bubble blowing contest going on. You couldn't say there's any lack of entertainment on this long bus ride.

"I think I want us to be Thing One and Thing Two. It's, like, a red T-shirt, and we would need black and white paint. Is their hair blue?" I ask, trying to get KK's attention. She's watching the runway show, laughing at Jaz with his wig.

"What? Is what blue?" she asks.

"Thing One and Thing Two, their hair. Is it blue?

"Yeah, I think that's right. We would need blue spray for our hair. Look up a photo to make sure," KK suggests.

I pick up my phone to look up images for our costumes and notice I have a bazillion Instagram notifications. The last post I made was a week ago right before we left for the Homecoming parade. I pull up my post and see there are tons of comments on the photo. I know a few are from my teammates, "We love you, girl," comments, one, but now these flooding in are mean, rude, hateful, and down-right scary and they're all from some weird-named account I've never heard of.

KK looks at me. "Did you find a pic?"

I'm so engrossed in the comments on my post that I pay no attention to her.

"Landry, did you find a picture of Thing One and Thing Two?"

I start to cry and shake my head.

"Oh, no, Landry. What's wrong?"

I hold my phone up. "Someone has been posting nasty, hateful comments on my Instagram for the past hour. There are over a one hundred on there now."

"Give me your phone."

I hand it over and put my head down to cry. The commotion has brought the dance music and the runway show to a pause as the focus turns to me and KK.

"What's wrong, Landry?" Jaz asks, walking over to our seat. He touches me on the shoulder to get me to look at him.

With tears rolling down my cheeks, I say, "Someone started trolling me hard on Instagram. It's bad."

"Yeah, look." KK hands my phone to Jaz.

He takes my phone from her and scrolls through the comments.

"It looks like whoever this is created a fake, anonymous account and they've blocked you from it. I'm sure it's not someone from the team. Do you have any idea who it might be?" he asks.

I shake my head. "That's only the second thing I've posted since I got to Natchez back in July."

"Do you have any enemies back home you think might do something like this?" KK suggests.

"I wasn't even in school the second half of my junior year. I got my GED and came here. I stopped talking to a lot of people except for two friends. There's my friend Nicole from the cheer gym, but she's a cheerleader at LSU this year, she's a freshman. It wouldn't be her. And there's my old boyfriend, Jordan, but it wouldn't be him either. I used to hang out with a bad group. They dared me to shoplift. I took the dare and ended up in a lot of trouble." I take a deep breath, feeling somewhat relieved that KK knows a little more than I'd told her previously. "When I ran out after them, they were already in their cars, pulling out. I was left to take the blame and I haven't talked to them since."

"Well, whoever is doing this is jealous. Check your Twitter and see if they're doing anything on that account." Jazz says, like he knows what's up.

I pull up my Twitter and notice a few posts "I hope you die." "You're an ugly bitch." Not as many as on my Instagram.

"Before you delete these comments, screen shot them, just in case charges need to be filed," Jazz continues. "Put a block on this anonymous account and report it on Twitter and Instagram. And make sure you block anyone you don't talk to anymore on Instagram and SnapChat. It's gonna be okay. Don't let some troll get to you. If it keeps happening, tell Coach. She'll help."

"Thanks, Jaz."

He leans in, giving me a hug. Gracie hands me a tissue.

"Try not to let it get to you," Gracie says. "I've had it happen to me many times, and you just have to block it out. There are some mean people in the world for whatever reason. I know it's hard, but you can't take it personally. Make sure you turn off the comment setting."

"Thanks, Gracie, I will." I try to smile as I wipe my tears away. We're pulling into the parking lot of the college that our team is playing against tonight, and it's time to put on a happy face. The show must go on.

*****

The game is tight, and in the fourth quarter we are down by three points. We have the ball, and if we can score now, we'll win. Time is running out, and I'm holding my breath as I watch Cole step back in the pocket to launch a rocket into the endzone. He gets sacked. I bite my lip, hoping he's okay. He gets back up and sets up for a pass. It's two and twenty-six. He looks right, hoping to throw the safety off, because it looks like there's a receiver on the left ready for a long pass. Cole throws fifty-one yards; it's caught, and the receiver runs it into the end zone. We win! I'm so happy.

The guys grab the flags and run up and down the sideline. The rest of the team gets in their shoulder stands. I'm on Jaz's shoulders with my poms in hand waving, yelling, and cheering as our players converge in celebration on the middle of the field. Cole gives me a wave and a smile, putting those dimples on display. I wave my poms over my head, and let out a loud hoot in triumph. Today was rough, but it's ending on a high note. The stress from earlier has been pushed from my mind.

I meet up with Cole at the buses before we load up to head back to campus. I rush over to give him a hug and congratulate him. He leans in and kisses me sparking a feeling like a swarm of butterflies rushing into my stomach.

"I'll see you tomorrow," he says, softy before pulling away to hop onto the bus.

Smiling, I say, "See ya," and walk over to our team's bus, hopping on.

Logan asks our driver if we can stop at a Walmart to pick up some snacks for the ride home. He agrees, giving us the perfect opportunity to buy supplies for our Halloween costumes for tomorrow night's festivities.

*****

Coach Matt is having us work on running tumbling today before working on stunts. My mind is on the Halloween party tonight. Some of our teammates came to practice wearing pieces of their costumes. KK and I wore our Thing One and Thing Two T-shirts to practice. Everyone is excited about going out tonight, ------especially me ------until Coach Matt's voice jolts me to attention.

"Landry, I want you to work on an x-out. Throw a handspring, whip, full, then x-out whip."

I try it and it's okay, but he wants me to do it again. After I do three more tumble passes, Coach Mckaye gathers the stunt groups, giving me a chance to take a break and cheer on my teammates from the side of the mat.

"I want to see your flat back pancake toss to liberty then tik tok, to superman then full extension," she says. "Make sure you have smooth transitions. Then work on handspring to into inverted handstands. Do those well, and we'll wrap early so ya'll can get ready to have a great, Halloween," she says, pausing to look at us.

60

"Safe, but fun, Halloween. Okay, load in. Let's go. One, three, five, seven."

Finally done with practice, we rush into the locker rooms to freshen up and change into our costumes. I'm glad Halloween is on a Sunday. That gave us time to paint our shirts this morning, so they'd have time to dry before today's late afternoon practice.

KK pulls out two cans of blue hair paint, her hairbrush and a bottle of hair spray. She takes her brush and teases her high ponytail until it looks like a giant bird's nest. I slip on my black leggings. KK sprays her teased hair with hairspray then picks up a can of blue spray.

"Shake the hair paint really good, then spray my hair," she says, handing me a can.

Then she sprays my hair blue after I tease it as best I can. We gather our bags and walk out of the locker room with blue teased hair and our Thing One and Thing Two T-shirts look even better with our complete ensemble.

Gracie, Christa, Sherry, Mark, Logan, and Josh are dressed as M-&-M's. Donte is Donna Summer. Jaz is Nicki Minaj. Other teammates have decided to pair up as salt-n-pepper shakers, Star Wars characters, while others are wearing animal themed pajamas. When everyone is ready, Coach tells us to smoosh in for a group photo. After photos, KK and I wave bye to our teammates since most of them will be heading over to Sherry's apartment for a party.

After walking out into the cool fall air, we stroll across campus. The sounds of crunching leaves under our feet, the rustle of the trees in the wind, and the smell of a wood-burning fire fill the night air. I'm meeting up with Cole at the Campus Club party tonight, and I'm glad KK agreed to come along. Pulling my phone from my bag, I text him, letting him know we're headed that way.

On the way.

Can't wait, babe.

Song on My Heart
14

KK and I follow the crowd up the stairs. A girl in an elaborate Queen Victoria costume blocks our view of the entrance. Music is playing as we walk into the building. We're greeted by a guy dressed as a scarecrow and his friend in a cowboy costume complete with chaps. They hand us headphones for the silent disco later tonight. As I place the headphones around my neck, a mummy pops out and ushers us into what appears to be a haunted hallway.

KK and I squeeze through the fake cobwebs at the entrance that leads to a large room full of costumed students. The dark room is lit by strobe lights flashing discotheque rainbow sparkles across the ceiling and the walls. What I first thought was a soundtrack playing a song by a top ten American Idol runner-up is in fact live music. Up on the stage in front of us singing "Out Loud" by Alejandro Aranda is Cole. His voice is similar to the American Idol star's and his guitar skills are bang on.

I grab KK by the arm, determined to get to the front of the stage, and we slip our way to the front. We manage to get to the second row, center stage. Cole is really into the song and sings with his eyes closed through most of it, so he hasn't' noticed us yet.

When he finishes, the crowd breaks into screams and applause. I call his name. He looks down, smiling at me. There are two more microphone stands set up on either side of him, and two girls join him on stage. The next song begins, and I'm not familiar with it. It seems to be a worship song, and this new selection resonates in my heart with hauntingly truthful lyrics.

Whispering the words, I half-hum, half-sing softy about a reckless love. "It chases me down, fights till I'm found, leaves the ninety-nine. I couldn't earn it and I don't deserve it."

On stage the singers' voices blend perfectly. Around me, hands are in the air and praises are going up. Caught up in the emotion and touched by the lyrics, I raise a hand, close my eyes, and listen with my heart. When the song ends, Cole and the girls step away from the microphones just as a guy pops up at center stage to make an announcement.

"Welcome to Campus Club Halloween!" he says in a loud, enthusiastic voice, inspiring cheers and hoots from the massive crowd. "We're so glad you're here tonight. We hope you and your friends have a blast. We certainly don't want you to go hungry, so we've got pizza and refreshments set up along the back wall. The restrooms are located in the foyer, where you first came in. And we'd love to see you back next month for our Thanksgiving feast and flag-football fun. There are flyers about that event you can take as you leave tonight. Before we crank up the tunes on the silent disco so ya'll can hit the dance floor, let's bow our heads for prayer."

By this time Cole has made his way off the stage and is standing with me and KK. He reaches for my hand as he bows his head. I lower mine as he gives my hand a squeeze. When the prayer ends, we put on our headphones and dance to the music blaring in our ears. Cole is a great dancer. KK has paired with a guy dancing next to us and we are all having the time of our lives. A few songs later, I pull Cole's head close to mine.

"I'm ready for a dance break." I lift up Cole's headphones and whisper into his right ear. He nods, pulling his headphones off but leaving them draped at his neck. Hand in hand, we wander over to the food table. He hands me a bottle of water. Taking the lid off, I take a few sips then glance at Cole.

Teasingly, I say, "You really can sing. You were not even kidding."

He reacts shyly to my comment. If his skin wasn't so dark, he might be blushing. He grins at me, and those dimples catch my eye, -----so cute. "Yeah, it's a fun hobby that takes my mind off things."

"Well, I'm thinking American Idol status." I chug the rest of my water and toss the bottle into the trash can. Then I take Cole's hand in mine and wiggle and sway with him back into the crowd.

Things start to wind down around eleven thirty. KK is still talking with the guy she met. I wave to her to let her know I'm about ready to head back to the dorm. She waves back then leans in whispering to her new friend and pointing in my direction. As Cole and I are walking outside into the cool fall air, I see Paul, my tutor.

"Hey, Paul," I say, getting his attention. He turns and looks our way, and a smile breaks across his lips as he walks toward us. I'm not sure what he's dressed as. He's wearing a Hawaiian shirt and cut off shorts with white crew socks and brown hiking boots. "Who are you dressed as?" I ask.

"Hopper from *Stranger Things*," he answers.

"Oh, yeah, right. I get it now." He looks from me to Cole.

"Thing One and Thing Three?" he asks.

Cole and I laugh. Cole is wearing the red Thing Three T-shirt I made him with black jeans, although he didn't spray his hair blue. That probably would not have worked with his dreadlocks. Just then, KK and her new friend walk up, and Paul nods in her direction. "I get it now. Here comes Thing Two. Cool costumes."

"Thanks. I'll see you on Tuesday," I say as he turns to leave.

KK introduces us to the guy she's with. His name is Jared, and Cole already knows him. He's apparently on the football team too. The four of us walk together to the dorms.

"Thank you for inviting me tonight to this Campus Club thing. It was really fun," I say, cuddling up to Cole.

"I'm glad you liked it. Maybe you can come again to the next event too."

"Yeah, I would like that." We stop at the entrance of my dorm to say our good nights. Cole gives me a sweet kiss on the cheek. We whisper, "Good night," and I turn to go inside. KK hangs back a little longer, talking with her new friend, Jared.

I hop in the shower to wash the blue from my hair, then walk back into the room in my bathrobe and a towel wrapped around my hair. I plop down on my bed to look at my phone.

There's a text message on the screen. *You bitch. Think u can run off and start a new perfect little life. Think again. Ur still a thief and a loser!*

The serene, happy state I was in vanishes as fear and shock take over. I open the text and realize it's from Carla, one of the girls from the group I used to hang with. She was definitely the bossy, leader, and queen bee of the group. She's the one who pushed me to steal the stuff in the store the day we got out of school for Christmas. Suddenly, it dawns on me, she could have been the one who was trolling me on Instagram, posting those awful comments.

A Snapchat from Jordan pops up. He wishes me a happy Halloween, and it looks like he's at a party with a lot of people. His face is painted in an awesome skeletal design-----impressive.

Hey, looks like you are having a great time. I went out with some people to a party tonight too.

Yeah, I went out with some art friends, had a blast. Hope all is going well with you.

Kinda. But I got a text from Carla just now. It was mean and hateful. A few days ago someone posted a ton of hateful comments on my latest Instagram post and some on my Twitter. They looked like they were from an anonymous account, and I've blocked them. Before I did, I screen shot everything. What do you think? Could it be her?

I don't know. She did ask about you a while back. I told her you got a scholarship to a college in Texas and were on their competition team. But that's all I said. She just smirked and didn't say anything. Don't let it get you down. If anything, she's jealous of you. I think she's always been.

I set my phone down. It does bother me, even though I know it shouldn't. What she thinks of me shouldn't matter. But for months after the incident I was depressed and down on myself. Since I've been here, I've been happy. Like actually feeling good about myself again. Now, I don't know. An old ugliness is creeping into my brain. I slip off the robe and put on my PJ's just as KK walks in.

"Um, hey there. You dating a football player now, too?" I sit back on my bed, trying to look cheery.

"There might be a date in the future, yes."

I lean back on my pillows, getting comfy. "Time to spill the tea, girl."

We talk about boys until the wee hours. When we can barely keep our eyes open, we say good night. I fall into a deep sleep then wake with a start when my phone alarm goes off the next morning for class.

Moping around the room while getting ready for my first class, I'm still reeling from the text message. It's put me in a funk, but I try not to let it show. When I leave for class, I give KK a cheerful wave as I walk out the door.

Later, after practice ends, Coach asks me to hang back.

"Landry, will you meet me in my office?"

I nod then go to the locker room to grab my backpack. When I walk into Coach's office, she asks me to shut the door and have a seat.

"I just wanted to talk with you for a few minutes and see how everything is going. Your grades are good, and I've gotten a good report from your tutor. You should be very pleased with yourself, and you'll end this semester well." She stops and leans forward at her desk, focusing on me. Her eyes look soft and filled with concern. "You are very talented, Landry. And you get along well with everyone on the team. But I noticed you weren't your usual, confident self during practice today. Is something bothering, you? I'm here to help any way I can. You know that, right?" She pauses, waiting for my response.

I bite my lower lip and look down into my lap. "Someone's been trolling me on Instagram then I got a nasty text message from a girl from my old school. She's always been a bit of a bully." I look up now seeing the concern on Coach's face. "It brought up some old memories and reminded me of things from my past I wish I could forget. Everyone's told me to ignore her and she'll go away. They think she's doing it because she's jealous of me. At first, I wasn't sure who it was since the comments on Instagram were from an anonymous account. But later I got the text. I've blocked the account and I've blocked anyone who I don't speak to anymore. I did screen shot the comments, and I even made a screen shot of the text message before I blocked the number."

She leans back in her chair. "Your friends are right to tell you to ignore it. If this girl is jealous of you and you don't give her the attention she wants from what she's doing, she'll move on to someone else. Why don't you send me the screen shots you took, and I'll speak with a friend at the police station about this. In the meantime, I want you to focus on the positive. You have a lot going for you; don't get down on yourself." She stands, walks over to me, leans in, and gives me a reassuring hug. I stand and smile at her. She reaches for my hand and holds it for a brief second. "Come to me anytime you need to talk."

I leave the cheer gym feeling a lot better. I reach into my bag for my phone to find a sweet text from Cole. Yeah, I should definitely focus on the good things I have going on right now.

Football, Fire, and Fellowship

15

My flag football skills seem to be limited to looking cute on the sidelines. KK ended up on the winning team. My team lost by a touchdown, but I gave it my best. A lot of these girls who have come out to play flag football tonight are soccer and lacrosse players, and they can *run*. Unwrapping the yellow flags from my waist, I drop the belt into the pile with the others and plop down on the grass to get a drink and recover. KK and her team are still in celebration mode, taking selfies with the make-shift rubber-turkey trophy.

Some of the football players helped coach our game tonight, and Cole worked with my team. It's about time for the boys' game to start, but first he strides over and sits next to me in the grass.

Giving him a defeated look, I say, "Sorry, Cole. I wish I could've held onto the ball a little longer on that last play before they grabbed my flag."

"I think you did great for your first time playing the game. You don't always win; it's a fact. I've had to deal with losing games every now and then. Sometimes it's more about the team and just being on the field able to play." That infectious smile and positive attitude radiates good vibes all over me. He reminds me of Donte a little that way.

When the winning girls' team exits the field, Cole stands. He starts jogging onto the field then turns around and jogs backward, throwing me an air kiss. Mmm, he looks good with his dreadlocks pulled into a low ponytail at the back of his neck. His creamy almond skin, his super-athletic body, and those dimples when he smiles give me all the feels.

"Hey, Landry," KK says, pulling me out of my dream state. "Are you staying for the bonfire thing after the boys' game ends?"

"I think so. Why?"

"I'm tired from practice and this game tonight. I ran my ass off out there. I want to go back and take a shower and chill while getting some homework done."

"Sure. I understand. I'm beat, too, but I want to watch Cole and the guys. I'm gonna hang."

"Okay. If you don't mind, I'm going to head back to our dorm with some of the other girls."
She picks up her bag and unzips it, handing me a can of corn she brought for the food donation tonight.

"Here. Add this to the food drive for me, please." Throwing her backpack over her shoulder, she turns to leave.

My attention returns to the field, where the guys' game is about to start.

Paul is one of the refs. Before he blows the whistle to start the game, I hear him say, "First team to get to fourteen wins. We've still got a bonfire to light, and we don't want any unnecessary injuries to the football players who came out in support of the flag-football fun tonight."

Cole's team gets to fourteen first. Like the girls' team they get a make-shift rubber turkey trophy. When Cole's team finishes posing for pictures with their trophy, we walk to where a local barbecue restaurant has set up a catered meal next to the bonfire. We follow everyone as they get into the line forming for food. With plates filled and drinks in hand, we circle up near the fire.

The guy in charge of Campus Club hops into the middle of the circle to get our attention.

"Thank you for remembering to donate a canned-food item. Those will be delivered next week to local families in need. If you can help with delivery, make sure to sign up with Kirk." He spins around until he locates Kirk, who waves a hand. The Campus Club speaker leads us in prayer before we sit down to eat.

Thanksgiving is just a week away. But tonight's meal is not the traditional turkey feast. Instead, it's barbecue brisket, beans, and potatoes with banana pudding for dessert. Cole explains that brisket is big in Texas. It's delicious. When we are done eating, Cole takes my plate and his to the trash can and throws them in. I watch as he walks over to the duffel bag he brought, opens it, and pulls out his ukulele. I clasp a hand over my mouth, surprised but happy to hear him play.

He sits back down and starts to strum, getting the attention of the crowd sitting around the fire. There's a hushed silence as everyone focuses on him, and he begins to sing. A beautiful and tender song about blessings, very fitting for our Thanksgiving gathering tonight. There are several others who know the words too, and they join in. As the beautiful tune fills the air a joyful, peaceful feeling washes over me.

Cole's voice rises as he belts out the chorus, "Bless the Lord, oh my soul," he sings. When he finishes the song, he sets his ukulele down, and we all stand in a circle, holding hands. A few upper-class students begin naming things they are thankful for. Others join in, and comments move around the circle until it's my turn. I blush, worried about what I should say. I don't want to say something dumb or sound like I'm copying someone else. I quickly say, "I'm thankful for the friends I've made since I've been here, and I'm grateful for second chances."

Cole glances at me with a sweet smile as he squeezes my hand. He's next and says, "I'm thankful for my family. I'm thankful for new friends I've made recently who have made my year special, and I'm thankful for my Lord and Savior."

I glance at him with a shy smile and give his hand another squeeze. A warmth fills my insides, and I feel more drawn to him than ever.

The night becomes chilly as Cole and I head back to the dorms, and we walk close together, his arm around my waist, and my arm around his. Being this close to him makes me feel warm and cozy.

"You sang another beautiful song tonight," I say. "A lot of people knew it."

"It's called '10,000 Reasons' by Matt Redman. It's a pretty well-known worship song."

"I haven't been to church since I don't even know. I guess maybe I was twelve and it was Easter. We just stopped going. My mom was working a lot, and I was getting older, and my grandma wasn't up to driving anymore."

"I go on Sunday mornings to the church here in town. In fact, a lot people from tonight's group go, and I've seen a few of the cheerleaders there. Coach McKaye and her family attend."

"Oh, yeah, she told us if we wanted to go to let her know. I really didn't pay much attention when she mentioned it, but now, I might be interested."

"Cool. You can come with me sometime."

When we arrive at the entrance of the dorm, Cole kisses me softly, reaching his fingers into my hair. We say good night, and I watch as he walks to the dorm across from me. After getting ready for bed, I decide to ask KK about church.

"Hey, what do you think about going to check out the church Coach McKaye attends?"

KK looks like she's half-asleep, so I don't know if she understands the question. She mumbles something that sounds like "mm-hmm." Well, it's something to think about anyway. I close my eyes, feeling truly thankful for the friends I've made, and the team I'm on ----and I'm definitely thankful I met Cole Collins.

Thanksgiving

16

With Thanksgiving just a few days away, it sucks our team doesn't get much time off. We practice up until Thanksgiving then take the Friday after and the weekend off. The football team has the same schedule we do. Our team has made it into the playoffs for our small Division 1 college. So, they might make it into a bowl game. I don't have enough time to go home to Louisiana and come back. It's too far to only have a few days at home. A lot of my other teammates are in the same boat. Some have come from as far as Canada and Hawaii to be on this team.

Gracie and Christa and a few others will be able to fly home on Wednesday night and fly back here on Sunday. And some can drive home since they are from other cities in Texas. But many of us just don't have the money to fly and live too far to drive. And some, I think, would rather be here with their cheer team than home with their families anyway. Cole's hometown is about two hours away, and he leaves Wednesday afternoon to be with his family. Students left on campus have been invited to their coaches' homes for Thanksgiving Day, and that goes for me and those of my teammates who'll be sticking around.

Since we don't have classes on Wednesday, Coach has us do a two-hour practice that morning. After practice is over, I get a text from Cole. *Hey, can I meet up with you before I head out to go home?*

Yes, I'm just wrapping practice now.

Let's meet by the clocktower.

Ok, see u n a few.

Cole is sitting on the steps of the clock tower. He stands when he sees me walk up. "Hey, you." He wraps his arms around my waist, pulling me in for a sweet kiss. I put my arms around his neck, pulling him in closer as our kiss becomes more intimate. As we pull apart slowly, and he looks down at me, he's all smiles and dimples.

"You know, I'm really wishing you were coming home with me today," he says with a smile, showing off his dimples. "And to be honest, I almost asked you if you would. I chickened out, of course." He grins, shyly.

"Really, you wanted me to come home with you for the rest of the week and spend Thanksgiving with you and your family?"

"Yeah. I did. I do, actually. My brothers and their families will be there. My brother who lives in town, Colton, will be there with his wife and baby. My brother who lives in Houston will drive up with his girlfriend. And my oldest brother Chris, who plays for the Falcons, won't be able to make it with his schedule." He pauses and looks down at his shoes then looks at me. Hesitating, he finally says, "After thinking it over, I started to feel unsure about asking you. I thought it might be a little soon for you to meet my whole family and all. I don't want to scare you away. I want to take things slow. It's a big deal to bring a girl home to meet the family, you know?"

"Right." I nod. "It can make the relationship seem more serious. I really think it's cool that you considered asking me though."

He takes my hand and leads me to the steps of the clocktower, where we sit. "So, just hypothetically speaking, what do you think you would have said if I had asked you to come home with me?" He gazes into my eyes sweetly. His look ----searching, serious, and full of longing -----gives me butterflies.

"I kinda feel like I would have said yes."

He slides a hand around my neck, pulling me in for a kiss. It's sweet, soft, and passionate. When he stops kissing me and we pull apart, he says, "I'm really trying to take things slow with you. But I want you to know I'm having some strong feelings."

I'm not sure how to respond, because even though I'm extremely attracted to him and I really do like him, I haven't thought about deep feelings. But now that he's said that, I know

I'm on the same path. I'm starting to feel more than school-girl giddy, puppy love. I'm starting to have real feelings for him. But I want to guard my heart. I'm not ready to reveal my feelings just yet. I gave my heart and myself to Jordan whom I'm supposed to tell when I feel something for someone else. I just don't feel ready to start getting serious. I'm afraid of letting go and letting someone else in, too fast. At least Cole is trying to take things slow. He's being real with me about his feelings, and he's being very respectful. I appreciate him for that. So instead of a verbal response, I loop my fingers through his and lay my head on his shoulder.

"When do you need to head home?" I ask.

"My parents expect me home tonight. I'm supposed to text them right before I head out. It'll be a two-hour drive. I just have to pull myself away from you," he says, leaning in, to nip at my neck. I giggle and start squirming.

Finally, we stand. I pick up my backpack, throw it over my shoulder, and walk hand in hand with Cole across campus to his truck. We say goodbye with one more slow kiss that leads to another. I pull away first, whispering, "Goodbye" in his ear. "Call me as soon as you get there."

"I will, babe." He slides into the driver's seat.

I walk into my dorm room, toss my bag next to the closet door, and flop down on my bed. I lie there, staring at the ceiling for what seems like forever, my mind focused on my feelings for Cole. I'm also trying to decide if I should go ahead and call Jordan and tell him what's going on.

My thoughts are interrupted when KK bursts into the room.

"Hey, Donte, Jaz, Logan, Sherry and a few others are going to see a movie in a little while. They invited us to go with them. Are you up for it?" she asks, walking over to the side of my bed.

"Yeah, for sure. Let me change really quick."

*****

Coach McKaye told us yesterday after practice to come to her house around noon for the Thanksgiving meal. After the movie last night, we decided to pop into the Piggly Wiggly and pick out a pie to take with us along with a bag of chips and dip. We didn't want to show up empty-handed even though I know Coach will be prepared for all of us. Her kids will be home from college, but since she is graciously having twelve of the team over, we don't want to look ungrateful or add stress to a day meant for family and down-time.

We carpool over, arriving as Coach is sliding casseroles into the oven. Everything smells wonderful. We set the food we brought on the kitchen island. Her son and daughter come into the kitchen, and we're introduced. The TV in the living room is showing the Thanksgiving parade. It snags our attention, and we stop to take a look at the performance on the screen. Coach's husband, Brad, motions for us to come and sit in the living room to watch the parade.

"It's going to be at least another hour before we sit down to eat," he says. "Y'all come on in and make yourselves at home. When the parade is over, I know there will be a game on to watch too." He stands and waves us toward the couch.

When the turkey is done, Brad jumps up from his recliner and helps Coach in the kitchen. Their daughter, Kim, goes in and helps set food along the counter and the center island. I hear Brad ask, "Mandi, are we using paper plates today?"

Once everything is set, Coach calls us to gather in a circle, and we pray. As I listen to the prayer, a sense of longing fills my heart for my mom, Grandma, Aunt Jackie and Uncle Joe, and their twin boys------knowing they're all together now. After lining up for food, KK and I walk carefully to the dining room with our filled-to-the-brim plates. There, we find extra seats at a card table set up along a wall next to their dining table. KK and I sit there with Sherry and Brodi, feeling a little like we're at the children's table.

When everyone heads back into the kitchen for dessert, some family members show up at the house with balls, ready for a game of touch football in the front yard. After dessert we head outside where Kim her brother, Nick and their cousins pick teams. Donte, Jaz, and Logan opt out of the game, choosing to tumble and cheer for us instead.

After an hour of running and being tackled, I'm done. The game wraps up, and we traipse into the house, where the guys help themselves to second plates. When they finish eating, KK and I give them the signal it's time to go. We hug Coach and Brad, thanking them for the wonderful meal, and for opening their home to us, making us feel like part of their family.

When we get back into the car to head to the dorm, I notice a text from Mom and one from Cole. I quickly text Cole back and decide to wait and call Mom once we are back in the room.

"Hey, Mom," I say when she answers. "I miss you guys a lot. We had a really good time at Coach's house today. What did you guys do?"

"Grandma and I went to Aunt Jackie's for lunch. We cooked a pumpkin pie while we were there that turned out really good. We had some turkey and dressing. We watched a little of the parade and some football. Grandma fell asleep during the game." She laughs. "After I helped Aunt Jackie clean the kitchen, she and the boys and I put a puzzle together. It was a good day. We were missing you though. I'm hoping it will work out for you to come for Christmas. We might be able to drive out and get you, or maybe I could get you a bus ticket."

"I should be able to come home for Christmas. We'll have a few extra days off. We have Christmas Eve off and three days after Christmas. I would be able to leave the afternoon of the twenty-third."

"It'll be good to have you home even if it's just six days. I love you, baby."

"I love you, too mama."

After I hang up with Mom, my phone rings again. It's Cole. A smile graces my lips as I slide my phone open to answer his call.

For Real. . .

17

"Is it too late to call?" he asks.

"No. I just got off the phone with my mom. I've only been back at the dorm for about twenty minutes. I'm alone. KK is hanging with some of the team in Brodi's room. I think they started up some card game or something, but I'm a little tired. We played touch football with Coach McKaye's family in their yard. I'm just chillin' now. I was telling Mom I'll get more days off during Christmas and will be able to go home for a week. It'll be good to see her. What's going on with you?"

"Thinking about you mostly."

"No, really. I want to hear all about your day. I want to know what I missed out on by not coming home with you this weekend now that I know that was an option." I giggle.

"Oh, do you now? I can indulge you in that. In fact, I'm gonna get comfortable and settle in for a nice, long conversation since I have your undivided attention. At least until your roommate comes back." We both laugh. I snuggle under the covers and get comfy, glad to be talking to a cute boy, just him and me. I'm feeling giddy and-----who knows-----maybe a tiny bit like I'm falling for him too.

"So, we had sweet potatoes, which I love, by the way. Corn soup, chicken and rice, turkey, and a traditional dish of mango, pineapple, peppers, lime, salt, and onion. My father is from Trinidad. He and my mother met when she was a senior in college. She spent a summer on the island doing some mission work at the same church where my dad was working. My mom is white, so I'm bi-racial. I guess we haven't talked about that yet." He lets out a short laugh, as if he is uncertain how I might react.

"I don't know if you've ever dated a black guy before." He pauses a beat then says, "We're definitely dating. I want you to be my girlfriend if you're okay with that." His voice sounds adrift. It fades a little in the distance as if he's unsure of my response. I knew he was light skinned, but I had no idea his mom was white. And honestly, I haven't thought about his race. I was attracted to him the moment I saw him that day in the parking lot.

"No, I haven't dated many boys at all actually. I've had one real boyfriend so far. We became good friends the summer between our sophomore and junior years. Then we started dating, and we didn't actually break up officially when I left to come here back in July. We said our goodbyes and told each other we could date other people -------and that we would let the other know if real feelings developed for someone that we met. We text every now and then. I have thought about calling him and telling him I have feelings for someone, but I haven't done that yet. I'm not sure I'm ready, or maybe I'm just scared to do that. In a way, I'm afraid of letting go."

I take a breath, and there's a long pause on the other end of the phone. I hope I haven't offended Cole or hurt him by telling him about Jordan.

"Hey, you still there?" I ask cautiously.

"Yeah, I'm still here. I'm not going anywhere. I want you to know I really like you and I'm going to take things slow. I don't want to blow it with you."

"You're not going to blow it with me. I have strong feelings for you, Cole. I'm just a bit guarded with my heart."

"That's good. Let's try to be open with each other. My parents have always said it's important to be honest and open. Sometimes things can be hard to say, but my mom and dad have taught me to be respectful. And my mom taught me to be even more respectful toward women."

"So, if you break up with me, I can expect it to be such a nice experience that I may not even realize we broke up?" I laugh at my own comment, which makes him laugh, too.

"Well, I guess you can say something like that. I for sure don't want to hurt you in any way." His voice sounds sweet.

"Do you want to tell me about any serious girlfriends you've had?"

"I've dated other white girls, and a few of them were cheerleaders." His voice changes in inflection, possibly to make the point that he has a thing for cheerleaders.

"Cheerleaders, huh?" I say, teasing.

"I had a serious relationship my freshman and sophomore years. She and her family moved away, and we broke up the summer before my junior year. We talked a lot on the phone for a while, but soon we both got busy with new friends and life, you know. One day we just stopped talking. I dated other girls------, sometimes for a few months at a time. I had a girl cheat on me with another guy, and from then on, I've tried to be picky about who I chose to date. And you might even say I'm a mama's boy, because she and I talk a lot about stuff."

"Well, I might be a mama's girl, since my dad's no longer in the picture. I may have daddy issues. Which quite possibly may be true, but I haven't self-diagnosed or anything."

KK walks in as I finish saying that.

"Hey, Cole, KK just walked in," I say. "I'm glad we talked tonight. It was a really nice chat. I feel like I can tell you anything, and that's a good feeling."

After hanging up, I wonder if I really could tell him anything. He doesn't know about my dad, and I don't want to talk about him. He's no longer in my life and probably never will be.

Practice Makes Perfect
18

I feel as if Coach is working us hard at practice, maybe since we were off so many days in a row. We were supposed to run every day. KK and I did run on Friday and Saturday, but yesterday we were lazy. Everyone is complaining about having to run extra laps during practice today, and I joke with Jaz about all the food he ate on Thanksgiving.

"Girl, you know my metabolism is on point. Look at these abs, girl." He lifts his shirt, showing a perfect six-pack.

I roll my eyes and take a spot on the mat to stretch out for conditioning.

"After you stretch out, get into your stunt groups on the mat. We're going to rotate flyers in and out of these stunts just to see if I need to move anyone around." Coach McKaye claps her hands, pulls a chair up to the edge of the mat, and opens her iPad to film us. "Let's start with the beginning sequence with the four stunt groups throwing backflip baskets. At the same time, I want my four best tumblers to each start out between a stunt group. Landry, I want you to start between Gracie and Christa's group. You'll do a handspring, whip to full. Tumblers, after you land, you'll grab the signs. Back spots, once the basket tosses end, pick up the signs to hand the flyers, because once they're caught from the toss, they'll load into shoulder stands holding the cheer signs. Okay, let's try that and see if everyone lands at the right time. Tumblers, once you land and pick up the signs, you'll start the NC cheer and chant. Ready? Five, six, seven, eight."

After we do this segment four times in a row, we switch a couple of flyers and two of the tumblers out and do it again. After taking a ten-minute break, the tumblers work with Zack and Matt while the flyers work on load to inversion into splits. Bases and back spots switch out, and when Sherry is partnered with someone new, her inversion goes sideways, and she crashes. She hits the back of her head, and Paul rushes over to take a look. I can hear them talking about a concussion, and coach wraps practice after the rest of us hit the mat for pushups because of the mistake.

"I have some good stuff on film to go over," Coach says, while Paul and the other coaches tend to Sherry. "Tomorrow we will be working on different stunts, and I will keep moving people around as we work on different skills. Lisa, I'll need you to fill in for Sherry the rest of the week. She may have a concussion, and she'll need to be checked again tomorrow. The rest of the week I'll be looking to see what we're capable of and where we need the most work. Next week the other coaches and I will be looking specifically at who we think we want on mat. So, everyone bring your A-game this week and next. The week after next, you guys will be studying and taking your final exams, so practices will be very light. I appreciate your flexibility while we are working on these details. Once we're back from Christmas break, we will announce who's on mat, and you'll work with a choreographer for the routine you'll perform at nationals. But remember, if there is an injury or if something isn't working, you can be pulled out and replaced at any time." She looks toward Sherry who is being helped into the training room. "Be ready to step in if your team needs you, and don't be flustered if you don't make mat. There's always next year. We want to support each other at all times. You guys are dismissed. I'll see you tomorrow."

Back in the room, KK and I discuss who we think may make mat.

"I think you have it over Lisa," I tell her. "I think you have smoother transitions, and your heel stretch has gotten so much better."

"Thanks. I don't want to get my hopes up just yet. I'm positive Gracie will make it, and I think Christa, too."

"I agree with that. I hope Sherry's okay. I'll text her and see how she is and if she needs us to bring her anything." I pull out my phone and send the text. "I'm glad the game this Saturday is in the afternoon. I like early afternoon games. It gives us more time to ourselves on Saturday night. Coach forgot to mention that we won't have practice on Saturday due to that. Surely, she won't make us practice Saturday night." I give KK a look.

"Yeah, you're right. This will be the third time we've had an afternoon game at home since the first game of the season and the Homecoming game, I think we'll get the night off. That means we'll get to Pop's Pizzeria a lot earlier on Saturday and still have a whole evening ahead of us to do stuff.

"Maybe you and Jared and me and Cole should plan a double date for Saturday," I say with raised eyebrows and a whatcha think look. "Sherry texted back. She says Coach gave her a note to be dismissed from classes the rest of the week, and she has to set an alarm to wake her up in the middle of the night. She said her roommate is home, and Brodi is going to stay with her tonight."

"God, that sucks. I know she's bummed. But, yeah, mention the double date to Cole and see what he says."

"Okay. I'll see him tomorrow when I meet with my tutor. I bet he'll like the idea."

*****

"Hey, Cole," I say when I see him in the library. He's heading in to meet up with his tutor but stops and turns around when he hears me call his name

"Hey, pretty girl. What's up?" He leans in and kisses me on the cheek.

"I was thinking since the game this Saturday is in the afternoon, we'll have all of Saturday night to hang out. KK and I thought that you and Jared may want to double date." I tilt my head, looking at him with pursed lips and dreamy eyes, thinking his answer will be what I was hoping for.

"My family will be at the game on Saturday. It's a big playoff game, and if we win, we get to play in a championship game. They haven't been to any of my games since the last time we had an afternoon game at the beginning of the season. It's because my

82

dad's a pastor and he's got to be at church early on Sundays; it's a two-hour drive from here. They always came to my high school games, of course, but those were on Friday nights, so it was a lot easier for them to make it to all the games. They are looking forward to driving down on Saturday morning, and I was planning to introduce them to you at the game, then afterward maybe we could all go to Pop's together." He sounds like he's asking me a question. He lifts an eyebrow, waiting for an answer.

"I would love to meet your family. We can always go out with KK and Jared another time."

"I was hoping you would say that." His smile is radiant and his dimples divine.

Paul waves at me then taps his watch, giving me a subtle hint.

"I'll see you later, Cole. We both need to get to our tutoring sessions. Paul is looking antsy," I say, giving him a smile as I shuffle over to where Paul is waiting on me.

Shhhhhh! It's a Surprise
19

On Friday morning I wake up to a text from Mom. *Happy 18th Birthday! I love you. I sent you something in the mail. Make sure to check your box today.*

I don't think anyone else remembers it's my birthday. I don't want to say anything about it because that would seem uncool. But I probably wouldn't remember anyone else's birthday unless I had it written down or it was melded into my brain for some reason like Jordan's birthday, January twenty-fifth. I'll probably always have that memorized---- and my mother's on April sixth. Anyway, whatever Mom sent will be a nice surprise, and I'll go to my mailbox after my marketing class.

Wrapped in a robe, as I walk back in from the shower, KK yells, "Happy Birthday" as loudly as she can. I scream and drop my shampoo bottle on my toe.

"Oh my gosh, Landry, I am so sorry I meant to surprise you, not kill you. But I did get you this." She pulls out a happy-birthday balloon from behind her back. I wonder where she was hiding that?

Smiling, I say, "Thank you," and lean in to give her a hug. "I'll tie it to my bed frame."

"So, I can't wait to hear about the plans you and Cole have for tonight. A big birthday dinner or surprise maybe?"

"I really don't know if Cole even remembers it's my birthday. I mean, we did talk about when our birthdays were about a month ago, the first time we went out. His is easy to remember because it's the last day of February unless it's a leap year. Can you imagine being born during a leap year on February twenty-ninth? You would only have a birthday, like, every four years."

"I bet he remembers. Cut him a little slack," she says, laughing.

"I'm not going to worry about it. I can have a totally incognito birthday and be just fine. You remembered and so did my mom, so all is good in the world today."

I finish getting dressed and reach into the mini fridge to get a juice box before heading to class. "Bye, KK. I'll see you later," I say, scooting out the door.

After class, I happily walk to the commons to open my mailbox and see what I got. Along the way, I get a 'happy-birthday' text from Jordan, quickly I hit the heart button, showing I like his text. Opening the tiny door to my mailbox, I find two envelopes waiting for me. Reaching in, I pull them out and lock the mailbox back, then I walk to the campus store next-door to buy a smoothie before heading back to my dorm.

Tossing my bag down, I plop onto my bed and open my first card. It's from Aunt Jackie, my Uncle Joe, and their boys. She also sent me a Starbucks gift card. Sweet. Next, I open the card from Mom. Inside is sixty dollars in cash and a bus ticket for home for December twenty-third.

I stick everything back into the envelope and lay them on my desk. Picking up my phone, I quickly text a thank you to my aunt and then one to Mom. After texting back and forth with Mom and Aunt Jackie for a while, I pack a bag for practice, grab my coat, and walk across campus to the cheer gym. It's weird that KK isn't here. We normally walk to the gym together or with Gracie and Christa and some of the other girls, but no one seems to be around.

Opening the door to go inside the gym, I see that it's dark. *Hmmm. Did I get the time wrong today?* Suddenly, the lights come on, and my teammates and three coaches scream, "Happy birthday, Landry!" My second scare today. With my mouth hanging open and a look of shock across my face, I gingerly take a step toward the group. "Y'all really got me."

Everyone laughs. They have party hats on their heads and horns in their mouths. Jaz walks up and blows a handful of confetti into my face. KK, Gracie, Donte, and Christa run up and hug me.

"Surprise!" They scream, very pleased with themselves.

"Yes. I am very surprised. Thank you, guys."

Coach comes over, puts her arms out for a hug, and squeezes me. I'm feeling the love today for sure.

"We'll have cookie cake during our break," she says. "Okay, ya'll, let's get ready for practice."

"Can we still wear these hats?" Jaz asks. "Because I think they look good."

We crack up. Even Coach McKaye laughs at that one before getting serious again.

"Let's get back to business, guys," she says. "I will let you out a little early today in honor of Landry's birthday, but I need to see effort. Let's go!" She claps her hands to get us to shift into practice mode.

After an hour and a half, Coach calls break. She has set out bottled water, a cookie cake, birthday napkins, a card, and a gift box. Zack lights the number-one and the number-eight shaped candles on the cookie cake, and everyone joins in to sing the traditional birthday song at a rambunctiously loud level. Zack hands me a slice of cookie cake. Donte puts his party hat back on and puts one on my head.

Jaz picks up the gift and says, "We all chipped in and got you this." He hands it to me.

I open the card, which everyone has signed. Then I tear open the gift wrap and take the lid off the box. Inside is a Natchez College hoodie. I stand up and slip it over my head. Coach McKaye comes over with a selfie stick and tells everyone to put their hats back on and scrunch in for a selfie. She sends me the pic, and I post it to my Snapchat.

"I'm not going to make you practice for another hour. You guys are dismissed. Have fun," Coach says, helping herself to some of the cookie cake.

In the locker room as we pack up our stuff, there's talk of ordering Chinese and hanging in Gracie and Christa's room watching Netflix on Gracie's computer. KK and I agree that sounds fun.

Christa asks, "Have ya'll seen that old John Hughes' film *Sixteen Candles*?"

I shake my head.

Gracie says, "Yes."

KK says, "I've heard of it."

"I'm cool with watching it if you guys are," I add. I sit on the bench to lace up my fake Doc Martens. The girls seem in a hurry to leave. They're already walking to the door.

"We'll meet you outside," KK calls over her shoulder.

I wave bye to Coach and the rest of the crew, who are still hanging out, nibbling on cookie cake. Then I step out of the gym into the cool night air. When I look up, Cole is leaning against his truck, which he has pulled up to the curb, and is holding flowers and a teddy bear that has on a tiny Natchez College T-shirt.

"Cole. Oh, my gosh," I say, running towards him.

He hands me the flowers and the bear. "Happy eighteenth," he says, smiling at me with the sweetest look on his adorable face. He leans in to give me a gentle kiss.

"I have another surprise for you if you want to come with me," he says, taking my hand. We walk around to the other side of the truck, where he opens the door for me to climb inside. He drives to the library, where he turns off the ignition and glances at me.

"Ready?"

"Um, yeah," I say, unsure of what we are doing on a Friday night at the library *on my birthday*, but I'll roll with it. I set the flowers on the seat but carry the cute teddy bear inside with me. It's almost deserted inside the library, with only three other people, it appears, and one of them works here. Cole takes my hand and we get on the elevator. He pushes the button for the third floor. *Oh, no, is a tutoring session about to happen?*

When the doors close, Cole reaches for my waist with one hand, pulling me toward him. With his other hand he gently touches my cheek and kisses me. My lips part with his, and I slide my arms through his, gripping the back of his jacket.

The elevator doors pop open. Darn. I would have liked to have gotten stuck on that elevator for a few hours alone with Cole.

Stepping onto the third floor, I notice that it's dark. I'm tensing up, thinking someone is about to pop out from the hallway, from behind the couches or from under a table to scream, "Happy birthday." But as we move farther into the room, I find we truly are alone. And surely no one has a tutoring session at six-thirty on a Friday night!

Cole leads me to a table, pulls out a chair for me then slides his chair near mine. He unzips his coat and pulls out a small pink box with "Sugar Shack" printed across the top. He opens the lid and gently removes a chocolate cupcake piled high with pink, fluffy frosting and sprinkles. He sets it in front of me then reaches into the box again, pulling out a birthday candle, which he sticks into the icing. Then he takes his coat off, tosses it aside, and reaches into the pocket of his jeans to retrieve a lighter. He lights the candle, and the glow shimmers and reflects off the table, creating a romantic ambience in the dark room.

"Make a wish," he says, reaching over to hold my hand.

As we stare into each other's eyes, I pause, gathering myself; my heart is beating fast. I make a wish and gently blow out the candle. My wish is simple. I just want to keep it going, this thing I have with Cole that I'm not sure how to describe just yet. What I do know is I don't want it to end anytime soon.

"You can take a bite if you want," he says, pulling the candle out.

"Mmm, yes. I do want." I carefully peel the wrapper back and take a bite, getting icing on my nose.

"Com'ere." Cole leans over the table and kisses my nose, making me giggle.

"Here." I pick up the cupcake and hold it toward Cole. When he leans in to take a bite, I push it into his nose. Now he has pink icing on his nose. I lean in close and lick the icing off. He grips my wrist and pulls me in for a kiss. I open my mouth, and my tongue softly moves with his. Setting the cupcake on the table, I scoot closer. Cole pulls me onto his lap as we continue making out. When he breaks off the kiss, he stands, pulling me up with him.

"I have another surprise for you." He pulls his phone from his front pocket.

"Wow. This birthday is full of surprises. I think it may be the best one ever. I thought it was weird when we pulled up in front of the library, but this was a great idea. No one is here. We're totally alone in the dark. I couldn't have thought of anything this romantic if I'd tried."

"Well, one of the reasons I picked someplace here on campus is because the football team has to stay on campus the night before games. We have a curfew."

"Oh, right. That makes sense, but still I have to give you props for this date." I pull him in, putting my hands behind his neck and tilting his head down to meet mine, kissing him slowly.

"I love kissing you," I say.

"Mm--hmm. Me, too. But I do have another surprise." He slides his phone open and pulls up a Spotify playlist and taps the first song. He pulls me close and we slow dance, swaying to the beat and holding each other tight.

"I don't recognize this song, but I like it."

"It's "Butterflies" by Michael Jackson. I put together a playlist of the seven most romantic, chill songs I could find."

He kisses my neck gently, definitely giving me butterflies. When the next song starts, I don't know it either. He tells me that it's "You Don't Know My Name" by Alicia Keys. He sings a little to me.

We're having the best time twirling around, having a private dance party in the dark. After a while, we sit on the couch wrapped up in each other, softly talking, holding hands, kissing, and cuddling. At nine an announcement comes over the speakers, letting us know the library is closing. We sneak out of the library, hop into his truck, and drive back to the dorms. After parking, he leans over and pulls me in for another passionate kiss. My hands slip under his shirt. He lets out a soft moan, before he pulls away, giving me a quick kiss on the nose.

My room is dark and quiet when I walk in. KK's still with the other girls, watching a movie, I guess. I bet they knew Cole was planning a special surprise tonight. Flipping open Spotify on my phone, I continue listening to the romantic playlist Cole made for me. While changing clothes, I dance around the room to "1000 X's and O's" by Prince. By the time KK walks in, I'm singing out loud to "Love on the Brain" by Rhianna.

"Wow, someone is in a great mood, and I want the tea!"

I hit pause on the music. Grinning from ear to ear, I tell her all about the most romantic date I've ever had. When I tell her about the candle and the cupcake, she says, "That sounds like the final scene in *Sixteen Candles*."

"Tonight was definitely the stuff they write songs and movies about."

Playoffs
20

The last Saturday in November is sunny with a high of only forty-seven. The playoff game this afternoon is our final home game. I spend extra time curling my waist-length brown hair into ringlets and add a touch of glitter eyeshadow to my lids. I'm nervous and excited to be meeting Cole's parents at the game today. I slip my cheer jacket on over my uniform and lace up my cheer shoes. I grab my red pom-pom's, and KK and I meet up with the girls in the parking lot, where we pile into Christa's car to head to the stadium.

When we arrive, the football team is on the field warming up. Cole is throwing practice passes to the running backs as they go over last-minute plays. Crowds are starting to trickle into the stands. My team stretches out along the edge of the field as we warm up.

"Aren't you excited to meet Cole's family today?" KK asks, while pulling her arm over her head and leaning into a split. I sit next to her and slide into a split to stretch out, too.

"Yes. But I'm more nervous than I thought I'd be."

"Nervous about what?" Jaz asks.

"I'm meeting Cole's family today. They're coming for the game."

"You have nothing to worry about," he says. "It's all good. Just be yourself. And don't act like you're nervous. First, impress them with our performance today then impress them by being charming and friendly." He offers me a hand to help me up.

The football team finishes their warm-up, and some of them start toward the locker room. Cole stays back, motioning for me to come to him. As I meet him on the field, he's all smiles and dimples, carrying his helmet with one hand.

"Hey, Landry. I want to make sure my family knows which one you are while they're watching the cheerleaders during the game." He reaches for my hand with his free one. "Turn around." He leans into my shoulder as he points to his family sitting in the crowd just to the left of where the cheerleaders stand. They are down in the front row.

"That's my brother Colton, his son, Tyler, who's almost two, and his wife, Tracy. Sitting next to Tracy is my dad, and my mom is next to him."

He waves to them. They notice and wave back. I give a shy wave.

"I've gotta go. I'll meet up with you guys after the game." He winks at me before he sprints toward the locker room.

"Have a great game," I yell, then I turn and give another shy wave to his family as I walk back to my place with my team. There I do a tumble pass to warm up before we get the crowds going with cheers and stunts.

In the second quarter, we're up by two touchdowns and it's looking good for our team. I know Cole wants to win this playoff game so we can play for the championship in a televised game. I know that's what Cole is counting on, bringing home the championship and finishing the season undefeated. Also, at stake is nationwide recognition of Cole as a freshman quarterback, possibly allowing him to enter the transfer portal and end up as the quarterback at a much bigger college.

With three minutes to go until halftime, Cole sets up for another pass with the hope of making it a three-touchdown lead. As he goes to throw the ball, he seems to be searching for an open receiver, but he doesn't have time to get the ball off before he's sacked. He's hit hard. He goes down and stays down. My breathing stops. I'm frozen, waiting for Cole to get up. He looks like he's in pain.

Paul jogs out onto the field with his med-training gear, water, and towels. He leans down to talk to Cole, then he removes his helmet and helps him sit up. Paul turns around and motions for the coaches to come over. They're all huddled over him, and I can't see. Tears pool in my eyes, I have no idea why Cole hasn't gotten up. Jaz steps up next to me and puts an arm around my shoulders. KK takes my hand in hers. Then we all kneel as we watch and wait.

I haven't prayed in a while, but my thoughts quickly turn into a silent prayer as I repeat over and over, *God, please let Cole be okay. Please, God. Help him get up. Help him to be okay. Please.*

Soon a golf cart appears on the field, and Paul and the coaches help Cole onto the back. Cole waves to the crowd, and I can see him smile a little as they take him away. Relief washes over me. He's going to be okay. He may not be back after halftime, but maybe I'll find out something if Paul comes back to the field. A few minutes later, I notice Cole's parents get up and leave the stands with one of the coaches. I hate not knowing what's happening.

At the start of the third quarter, our back-up quarterback enters the game. We end up losing by three points, so we won't be bringing home the championship this year. As soon as the game is over, I find Paul folding up the training table on the field and packing his gear away.

"Paul," I say, and he turns around. "How's Cole? What happened?" I ask, feeling panicked.

"It's his ankle. He'll be okay. But they took him to the hospital for X-rays. His family is there with him now."

"Thanks, Paul." I run back to my teammates, who are gathering their bags to walk toward the parking lot. I grab my backpack and meet up with Christa and the girls at her car. "Guys, Paul told me they took Cole to the hospital for X-rays. He hurt his ankle. Can you drop me off there?"

"Yeah, get in. We'll go with you," Christa says, and we take off in the direction of the local hospital.

We arrive within a few minutes, park, and head into the emergency room. I stop at the desk. The receptionist looks up at us, takes in our uniforms, and says, "Cole Collins may still be in triage while they're waiting on his X-ray results. His family is with him, so you may not be able to see him just yet. You'll need to wait until he's been admitted and we have his room number. Tell me your name hon, and I'll let them know you're here."

"Please let him know that Landry Woods is here to see him."

"Sure, hon. Have a seat. I'll send a nurse out to you once we have his status update." Her soft smile is reassuring.

The girls and I take seats in the almost empty waiting room. There's only a mom with a baby and a toddler waiting at the moment. After we're seated, KK takes my hand, and Christa pats my back.

"He'll be fine. You'll be able to see for yourself soon," KK says in a soothing voice.

After we've waited a while, I dig through my backpack looking around for my phone. It's getting late. The game ended at six, and now it's almost seven-thirty.

"We've been here long enough for someone to have come out to tell us something. I know they know we're still here," I say, looking over at Gracie and Christa, who are thumbing through magazines, looking bored to death.

"I'm going back over to the desk and ask again if we can see him." I stand and walk to the reception desk. "Ma'am, can you please let me see Cole? I'm his girlfriend," I say, pleading with her.

"Let me check with a nurse and see what his status is. He knows you are here, sweetie. I promise." She gives me a smile as she picks up the phone to page a nurse. I listen as she talks and nods in response to whatever information she's being given. She puts the phone down and glances up at me. "They have just moved him into a room. He's in room 213. You and your friends may go and see him now."

I practically skip back to the girls. "They've moved Cole into a room. We can go and see him," I say, picking my bag up off the floor.

We get on the elevator and go up to the second floor. Then we walk down the hall, cautiously looking for room 213. When we find it, the door is cracked open, and I hear voices. I tap softly on the door while peeking through the crack.

Someone pulls the door open and says, "Come in."

The girls and I step inside.

Cole's face lights up when he sees me. "Landry. I'm glad you're here." He waves me over. His ankle is wrapped and elevated. His mother is sitting in a chair next to his bed, and his dad is sitting next to the window. His brother is leaning against the counter next to the sink.

Just after we arrive, his sister-in-law pops through the door with a chatty toddler in her arms.

"Hi," she says, and I turn toward her.

"Tracy, this is my girlfriend, Landry. Mom, Dad, everyone." Cole motions around the room with his hands. "I wasn't expecting you to meet her in a hospital room." He chuckles. His mom and dad get up and walk over to me.

His mom takes my hand and holds it in both of hers. "It's very nice to meet you, Landry. We've heard a lot about you. Cole speaks very highly of you."

His dad reaches out to shake my hand.

"Thank you," I say. "It's nice to meet you too." I turn to my friends, who are still huddled together near the door. "These are my friends KK, Christa, and Gracie," I say, pointing to each of them. They smile and wave.

KK says, "We can give you guys a few minutes. Landry, we'll meet you back downstairs in the waiting room. Nice to meet everyone. Cole, I hope you are better soon." She waves and leaves with the girls.

Tracy puts her son down and he toddles over to his grandmother, who scoops him up. Cole pats the side of his bed inviting me to sit.

"I heard we lost by a few points," he says, looking defeated.

"I'm so sorry, Cole." I say, knowing he must be heartbroken.

"No need to be sorry. It's football. It's a game, and sometimes it happens." He smiles. He even looks cheery, which is strange after his injury left him in the hospital, unable to bring home a championship.

"We have next year," he continues, not skipping a beat. He's still smiling, -----happy even.

"How are you?" I ask.

He points to his ankle. "High ankle sprain. They took X-rays and are sending them to a hospital in Dallas. We won't know anything until Monday morning. But there's talk of transferring me to the hospital in Dallas on Monday, and a possible surgery."

"Oh, no," I say, alarmed.

"It's all good," he says. "The surgery would allow for proper and quicker healing of the muscle in the ankle. I'd be back practicing with the team by spring, as if nothing happened. The recovery time is quicker, and with the surgery, my ankle would get stronger. And since it's a few weeks away from Christmas break, I can spend more time at home recovering." He squeezes my hand with a sweet grin on his face that prompts me to grin back.

"So, Landry." Cole's dad clears his throat, pulling my attention from his son. "Tell us about yourself. Your performance at the game today or the part of it we saw, was impressive."

With the focus now on me, I give them a brief history of my small town in Louisiana and a little info about Mom and my grandma. "I'm really enjoying Texas and cheering at Natchez." I finish.

A nurse walks in with a tray of food for Cole and sets it in front of him. His brother walks over and takes Tyler from his grandmother.

"I think we should get some dinner and come back. This little guy isn't going to last much longer," he says, looking at his wife.

"I should probably go too." I move from Cole's bedside.

"Don't go just yet. When my parents get back from dinner, they can drop you off at the dorm. They're driving home later tonight so Dad can preach in the morning."

"We don't mind taking you back later when we leave, Landry. Stay and keep Cole company. We can bring back a burger for you if you'd like," Cole's dad suggests.

"No, thank you. That's okay. I'm fine right now." I watch as they walk out the door, closing it behind them, and leaving Cole and me alone.

"I'll text the girls and let them know they can leave. They were sweet to come with me, but I know they're ready to go," I say, with a laugh.

"Come back up here and sit next to me," Cole says while putting dressing on his salad.

After sending the text, I set my phone down and scrunch up next to him, letting my feet dangle off the side of the bed.

"Do you want some of my dinner?" he asks. "I have chicken soup, rolls, and cheesecake. You want a bite?" He playfully offers me a spoonful of soup.

"No, that's okay. I'm good," I say, with a hint of a smile.

"I know hospital food is not that great. I get it." He nods. He reaches out and takes my hand.

I lean my head into his shoulder and whisper, "I'm so glad you're okay."

Finals Week

21

Now that Cole's been transferred to Dallas for surgery this week, I find myself feeling stressed. For one, I'm worried about Cole. Two, finals are next week. Three, he's leaving to go home after finals. And four, I have to stay a little longer to cheer at the basketball game before leaving on break. He'll get extra time at home now that his team's season has ended sooner than they thought. I guess it's good he'll be at home to recuperate, but I'm going to miss not seeing him. On the other hand, I'll be glad to go home for a few days too. It'll be nice to see Mom and just be home to chill. In the meantime, I have practice. We're performing on New Year's Day after the town parade, and Coach is working us in stunt groups, carefully watching our tumble passes to see who will make mat. That announcement will be made once we return from Christmas break. I have my fingers crossed that both KK and I will make it. Making mat for nationals in Daytona would be like Christmas all over again.

On Tuesday afternoon on the way to practice, my mind is filled with thoughts of Cole. It's the day of his surgery, and I hope to hear from him soon. So far, no news. I switch my phone to silent and join my team on the mat for conditioning before our two-hour practice begins. At the end of practice, Coach reminds us that next week we have shorter practices each day since it's finals week. I'm half-listening to the schedule as she drones on.

"Remember we have four home basketball games coming up. For those who are flying home on the twenty-second, I know you won't be cheering at that game, but for anyone who is still in town, we'll still have practice." She glances around at us, making eye contact. "Please make plans to be back on the thirtieth for the basketball game that evening and the performance after the New Year's Day parade on the first. You may all be wondering what you'll be able to do in town on New Year's Eve." She laughs. "I'd like for you to come to a special event that my church is hosting. It will be a dessert and mocktails evening with a live band, a short message, and prayer time that leads into the new year. It will be a good time that I promise you'll enjoy. I encourage you to attend." She gives us a big smile before she dismisses practice.

I pull my phone from my bag and notice a voice mail. As I walk back to my dorm, I click play to listen to it. "Hey, babe. I've been out of surgery for about two hours, and I'm just hanging out in my room waiting on the doctor to come in to tell me how it went and give me my rehab instructions. I wanted to call and let you know I'm good. I miss you."

Arriving back in my room, I send him a text to ask when a good time to call him back would be. He has told me his mom is staying with him and that she'll drive him back to school later this week when he's released. It'll be good to talk to him tonight.

*****

After classes on Thursday, I wander into the campus store to look for a welcome-home gift for Cole. Finally settling on a knit cap with the Natchez College logo emblazed on the front, I pay and make my way back toward the dorm as a text pops up. *Almost back on campus. Can you come by my dorm to see me?*

Can't wait. C u ltr.

When I get there, Cole is in the living room of his dorm hanging out on the first floor with some of the other guys from the football team. They're watching a college basketball game on the TV in the large common room. Cole is in a wheelchair with his bandaged ankle propped up, and he's laughing with his friends.

I rush over, giving him a quick kiss on the forehead.

"I'm so glad you're back. I got you a little something." I hand him the knit beanie.

"I love it."

He pulls it on, takes my hand, and pulls me toward him, kissing me sweetly on the lips. When this happens, the other guys make excuses to leave, saying they want us to have our time together. Once we're alone, he pulls me onto his lap.

"I have to get some studying done since I haven't had time to think about finals yet. My tutor is meeting me here in a few minutes, and we have a major study session planned. But first I need a little of this." He leans in and gives me a slow, sweet passionate kiss.

"I'm so glad to see you," I whisper.

"Me, too." He nuzzles my neck. "It's good to be back. And it's really good to be back with you." He grins, showing his cute dimples.

"How long will you be in the wheelchair?" I ask.

"They want me to use it to get around easily. This way, I can get to classes without having crutches. I'll have to use the elevators for some of my classes," he says, rolling his eyes. "But once I'm back home after finals, I'll be using crutches to get around. Resting and hanging at home. I'll be back on campus when school starts back in January, hopefully with a walking boot. While I'm home the next three weeks, I'll have to make a trip to Dallas to see the doctor before I come back to campus. They'll do some scans to make sure everything is healing the way it should. And if everything goes well, I'll be back at spring workouts in March." He smiles.

"I know you'll be excited to get back with your teammates playing football again. I guess it's kinda good that this happened at the end of the season and near the holidays, giving you time to recoup," I say, trying to sound positive.

"I can agree with you on that. Things didn't go the way I planned. I'm not heading into the transfer portal, and I don't have SEC coaches reaching out to recruit me. But I'm looking on the bright side. Because I'll be back here for another year with you." He lightly rubs my arm while looking into my eyes with a hopeful grin.

I smile back. I don't say anything, but I'm really happy he will be here next year.

"There's always next year. Our team will be even better. I can feel it."

"Yes. Next year," I say, nodding.

His ukulele is sitting on the couch. He picks it up, and I slide off his lap and sit next to him. He strums out a tune then starts singing. He's cheerful, radiating positive energy, despite his situation. He's peaceful. He seems grateful, and I am too. He has found a way to be positive and hopeful in negative circumstances.

"Let's plan on studying together this weekend. You want to meet at the library tomorrow night after your practice ends?" he asks.

"Absolutely."

*****

A week later, after finishing my last final, I'm feeling happy and glad to be free from studying. Cheerfully, I head back to my dorm. Tossing my bag down, I plop onto my bed to text Cole.

Hey, how were finals? I'm done.

Me too. Let's get together, maybe order pizza, tonight?

Sounds great.

He could be leaving to go home right now, but I'm glad he's chosen to stick around until Sunday before he drives home for Christmas.

Walking into the lower common room of the boys' athletic dorm, I see Cole near the big TV.

"Hey, you," I say, striding toward him. "Where's the wheelchair?"

"It's in my truck. Since I don't have to go in and out of classrooms and use elevators now, I think I'll switch to crutches. Have a seat." He pats the spot next to him on the couch.

The delivery guy from Pop's Pizzeria arrives and tells Cole it's on the house, compliments of the owner.

"Get better, man. We're rooting for you next season," he says, handing Cole the box.

Cole lifts an eyebrow. "Free pizza. I'm down for that. Thanks, man." He shakes the delivery guy's hand and takes the box from him. He lifts the lid on the box. Steam rises, wafting our noses with the smell of delicious pepperoni.

"Thank you for sticking around for the basketball game tomorrow night," I say, taking a bite.

"Anything to be able to see you for a few more days."

"I wish I could head home on Sunday, but we have two more games to cheer at next week. I'll be glad to go home and relax for a few days and see Mom," I say, glancing at Cole.
He nods, chewing his pizza.

"My parents are driving down to help me. Dad's going to drive my truck home. I'll ride back with Mom in their car. Since it's my right ankle, they don't want me driving until I'm fully healed. Then they'll help me drive back down for the start of the new semester."

"At least the drive is only a few hours. I'll be on a Greyhound bus for a seven-hour trip. Mom is picking me up in Slidell, then we have a thirty-minute ride home. It will be exhausting. I'll finally get home around midnight. Her dental office is supposed to be closed the twenty-fifth through the first. It should work out that she can drive me back, so I won't have to ride the bus again."

"You're reminding me that you'll be here on New Year's Eve and I won't be." He pulls a sad face. "I'm calling you at midnight to whisper sweet nothings into your ear," he says, laughing.

Laughing too, I lean up against him. He puts his arm around me and pulls me close. Snuggled and cozy, we spend the rest of the evening talking about our favorite Christmas traditions and happy family memories. I avoid mentioning anything about my father.

On Sunday, I meet up with Cole as his parents are loading the final bags into his truck. With a little small talk and wishes for the merriest of Christmases and happy New Year, he's off and I'm headed to practice. A few more practices and two more basketball games to cheer at, then Christmas break for me, too! Yay!

The week goes by rapidly, even with the tough practices we're enduring. Coach has the stunt teams practicing a pancake toss to flyer switch tosses. As I'm watching the two stunt groups practice. I hope they both are on the same count, if one goes and the other doesn't, there's nowhere for the one who's in the air to land. Crazily, just as I'm thinking about that very thing, it happens. Luckily, one of our extra back spots steps up to catch Christa before she hits the ground. She lands on Mark's pinkie, and we think it may be broken. We hit the mat for pushups for the mistake, and Paul arrives to evaluate the injury. While he's looking at Mark's finger, I strike up a conversation.

"Hey, Paul. I'm surprised you haven't left to go home for the holidays yet,"

"I can't leave until after the basketball game Tuesday night. Since I'm a senior I'm doing my final team sports med clinicals this semester with the basketball team. Next semester, I get to work with both the lacrosse and the soccer teams. You'll be able to do rotations your senior year too, if you stick with sports medicine as your major."

"Cool," I say while watching him adjust Mark's finger into the right position then wrap the tape over the splint.

"I think you'll be okay," Paul says to Mark. "If it turns purple and is still hurting a lot, go to the hospital for an X-ray. Here is the request form. Have Coach McKaye sign it at the bottom." He closes his kit and heads out, leaving Mark with a bandaged finger and Coach McKaye looking a bit flustered over our lack of progress today.

"After Mark's injury, let's switch gears," she says. "Let's work on our basketball cheers and sideline partner stunts then I have a surprise for you." She claps her hands for us to line up for the first cheer.

As we're working on our basketball cheers, I notice out of the corner of my eye Coach Matt and Coach Zack carrying in a Christmas tree. They set it on the edge of the mat and plug in the light strand. Coach Zack goes into the office and comes back with a giant clear ball of what looks like Saran Wrap. Coach McKaye stops practice and motions for us to come sit on the mat next to the tree.

Once everyone is seated, she asks us to circle up. "We're going to play a Christmas game before everyone leaves for break." She leans down and picks up the giant ball of Saran Wrap.

"Inside this ball are gifts," she says. "Some of the gifts are cash. Some are gift cards to local restaurants, grocery stores, and other stores in town, and some of them are candy. The idea is when the song ends, whoever is left holding the ball has to strip away the wrap as fast as they can to try to reveal a prize. If they get to one before the music starts back up, they keep the gift. If the music starts before they unwrap anything, the group continues to pass the ball until the music stops again. Okay? Everyone ready?"

We all scream in excitement, ready to play. Coach starts the Christmas music, and we enthusiastically toss the giant ball of Saran Wrap to each other and watch as it goes around the circle, anticipating when the music might stop, and who will be the first to play.

When the music stops, Donte has the ball. Frantically, he begins unwrapping it, tossing pieces of clear wrap into the air to land where they may. The music starts back, and he screams, "No! I didn't get to it yet."

Jaz takes the ball from him and starts it around the circle again. This time the music stops abruptly with the ball in Christa's lap. She unwraps the first piece and unfolds a ten-dollar bill. She waves it in the air as the music begins again. This time, Coach Zack keeps the song going a little longer. The ball lands in Mark's lap next. The pinkie finger on his left hand is wrapped with a splint, and he struggles with the wrap, only getting a few strands undone before the music starts again. This time when it stops, I have the ball. As I work quickly, pieces of clear wrap fly everywhere until I get to a gift card for Target and hold it up. Everyone cheers, and the music begins again. Finally, after almost thirty rounds, everyone has something. Jaz ended up with twenty dollars. I ended up with a one-dollar bill and the gift card. KK has a gift card to Chili's and a ten-dollar bill. The practice wraps with us all in the holiday spirit. As I hug my teammates goodbye, thoughts of home, family, and Christmas float through my mind. I definitely need to see Jordan while I'm there.

Christmas

22

The next morning, KK and I talk Paul into driving us to Target so we can shop for gifts for our families. I shop for Mom and Grandma with the gift card I got yesterday. KK uses the cash she won at the party to buy something for her grandparents. We buy a roll of wrapping paper and tape to wrap the gifts back in our dorm. After wrapping gifts, we pack our suitcases and tidy the room up as we get ready to leave. KK's grandparents arrive, and they drop me off at the bus station an hour before my bus departs, then they make their drive home to Oklahoma.

I try to make the long bus ride bearable by texting with KK and Cole. Opening the book, I checked out from the library, I read until it gets dark. After dark I switch back to texting. There's an older lady sitting in the seat next to me who's getting off in Baton Rouge to visit her grandchildren. Hopefully her seat will remain empty for the final two hours of my journey and so I can put my feet across it and get more comfortable. I get a text from Mom an hour after the stop in Baton Rouge letting me know she's arrived at the Greyhound station and is waiting for my bus to pull in.

Just after midnight, we arrive in Slidell and pull into the station. I grab my duffel bag from the overhead compartment and eagerly hop off the bus to see Mom waiting. After running toward her, I collapse into her arms. With my energy drained, exhaustion takes over and I fall asleep on the drive to Lacombe. After we arrive at home, Mom wakes me, gets my bag from the trunk and we walk into the kitchen. As I walk through the door, I'm greeted by the familiar smells of homemade cinnamon cookies, the fresh pine from the Christmas tree in the family room, and floral scented soaps in the bathroom. I toss my bag onto the carpeted floor of my bedroom, pull back the covers of my bed, and fall into a deep, dreamless sleep.

In the morning, Mom pops her head into my room and calls my name. "What time is it?" I ask.

"It's noon. We're going to Aunt Jackie's to spend Christmas Eve with them. You need to get up and start getting ready."

"Okay," I groan. Pulling my phone from the nightstand, I see I have a text from Cole. I quickly text back that I just woke up but will call him tonight. My grandma was asleep when I got home last night, and I realize I need to go say hi before getting into the shower.

On the short drive to my aunt's, I fill Grandma and Mom in on the latest happenings on campus. "Our basketball team has won its last four games, and I'll have another game to cheer at on the thirtieth when I get back to campus." I rattle off more details as they listen, hanging on every word.

Before we pull into the drive, Mom mentions Cole and asks if I'm still seeing him. I blush at the mention of his name and shyly reply, "Yes."

Getting out of the car, Mom hands me a pie and a bag of gifts to take inside. She helps Grandma out of the car and hands the cane to her. All three of us walk at Grandma's slow pace to the front door. One of my twelve-year-old cousins marks our arrival by screaming, "They're here!" before he takes off running through the house.

The dog starts barking and runs to greet us. I can hear Aunt Jackie in the background telling the twins to settle down. It feels like walking into chaos, and I wonder how long we plan on staying. I set the pie on the counter in the kitchen, where Aunt Jackie has more pies sitting out. Evidence of meal prep can be seen on the island, and something's boiling on the stove. Whatever it is smells divine.

Both of my cousins burst into the kitchen, trying to snag cookies from a tray on the counter. They ask if they can take the bag of gifts from us to put under the tree. I gladly hand it over, thinking if I didn't, I might be attacked.

Uncle Joe wanders into the kitchen and hugs us while asking, "Jackie, when's the gumbo going to be done?" Mom asks about helping set the table, and Aunt Jackie gives us instructions on which tablecloth to get out and where to find the Christmas dishes. Uncle Joe leads Grandma into the living room to sit, and the boys come bounding down the stairs. I hear the backdoor slam, then the doorbell rings.

"Can you get the door, Joe?" Aunt Jackie yells from the kitchen. I'm starting to wish I were back in my dorm room, but it's Christmas and family time, and I'm sure I can endure a few hours of this, at least.

Uncle Joe's oldest brother, Marcel walks in with his son, John who dropped out of college at LSU last year and never went back -------too much partying probably. I think he works for his dad now.

"Mary got called into work early this morning, so she won't be coming to eat after all. I'll take a plate home to her for later." Marcel announces, tossing his jacket onto the back of the sofa. I'm starting to wonder how many more relatives we can squeeze into Aunt Jackie and Uncle Joe's home.

When it's time for dinner, we gather in a circle in the kitchen holding hands, and Uncle Joe leads us in prayer. After he says Amen, the boys lurch toward the plates, snagging one before Uncle Joe moves them to the end of the line. I help fix Grandma a plate then carry it for her into the dining room before I get back in line to fill my own plate. There are all sorts of delicious things to sample including jambalaya, gumbo, ham, corn bread, salad, oysters, and french bread. During the meal, everyone seems to be focused on me, and wants to know what college is like in Texas. I explain how much my team practices and how we'll find out who makes mat for the competition in Daytona after school starts back next semester.

"We'll start practicing all day on Saturdays from mid-January through the end of March and we'll have over forty full-outs before we leave for Daytona the first week of April."

One of the twins asks, "What's full-out?"

"That's when we do our entire routine from start to finish without stopping, and we include all our jumps and running tumbling. Sometimes we may only be working on a certain segment of the routine like the pyramid, and we may not do a full-out until we have all our stunts exactly the way Coach wants them."

"Sounds like they're keeping you busy," Marcel, comments.

"Yes, sir. We definitely stay busy."

"I heard you date the quarterback." One of the twins says, cracking up, which causes the other one to start giggling, too.

"What happened with Jordan?" Uncle Joe asks.

I feel my cheeks flush and look over at Mom for some help. She quickly changes the subject by asking Marcel's son John about his plans.

When everyone finishes dinner, we take our plates to the kitchen and begin helping Aunt Jackie with the clean-up. The twins go outside to play with John and the dog in the yard. Uncle Joe helps Grandma to a seat in the living room and turns the TV to a sports game.

Later, Marcel calls the boys back into the house, and everyone gathers near the Christmas tree. The twins sit on the floor and start picking up gifts, and shaking them until they're reprimanded. The dog jumps up on the couch next to me and starts licking my face. I push him onto the floor. *Ugh. This is why I have a cat.*

"He likes you," Uncle Joe says, laughing.

"When are we going to start? Please can we open the gifts now?" The twins beg, looking very restless. I'm feeling the same. I'd love to be curled up in my bed talking to Cole on the phone right now.

"You boys can pass out gifts. They're all labeled." Aunt Jackie instructs, and the twins get busy rushing to and from the tree, handing out gifts until the area under the tree is bare.
They carefully check under the tree to make sure no gifts were missed.

"Santa definitely has to come tonight. Our tree needs a refill." Sam, the taller twin says, and the room fills with laughter.

Laughing at the boys, Aunt Jackie gets them settled, and we begin opening gifts. Everyone has at least two. Mom and Aunt

Jackie must have gone shopping for everyone they knew would be coming over. Grandma opens her package. She's excited to get new yarn for her latest knitting project. Mom gets a nice raincoat and matching umbrella. I open a gift card to one of my favorite stores, and my second gift is a super-soft Vera Bradley blanket.

After everyone has opened all their gifts, the room is filled with wrapping paper. The boys are running around playing, with their new Nerf guns and remote-control helicopters. Marcel and John start to gather their things to leave. I follow Mom and Aunt Jackie into the kitchen to get some trash bags. They're huddled together whispering frantically to each other and quickly stop when I approach.

"What do you need, sweetie?" Aunt Jackie asks.

"I just came to get some trash bags to clean up the wrapping paper."

"Sure. Here they are under the sink." She opens the lower cabinet for me to take some from the box. When I'm out of earshot, they go right back to their hushed conversation. I fill two trash bags with wrapping paper and boxes, and as I'm walking toward the kitchen, the hushed conversation between Mom and Aunt Jackie seems to be coming to a head. Mom looks stressed. She raises her hands to her face, and I hear her say, "Tomorrow, I'll tell her, tomorrow."

Aunt Jackie nods, looking sympathetic. She runs her hand up and down Mom's arm reassuringly. When they see me returning with the trash bags, their demeanor quickly changes, and they act as if nothing is going on. Aunt Jackie takes the bags from me and tosses them into the garage. Mom wanders into the living room to help Grandma gather her things so we can head out to the car.

Finally, home. It's really late. Grandma's exhausted, and we say good night as she goes to her room. Mom comes to my room to let me know it's okay to sleep in in the morning even though it's Christmas. I smile. "Thanks, Mom. Merry Christmas. I love you."

"I love you too." She turns around quickly, walking toward her room. Is she holding back tears? I get the idea she is.

I text Cole to see if it's okay for me to call. When he texts back, *Please do,* I don't waste any time. The cat pushes my door open and wanders in, jumping onto my bed, purring, and trying to head butt me.

"Hey, babe," he answers. "How was your Christmas Eve?"

"Like a scene from the Griswold's."

He laughs, and we settle in for an hour of chatting, sweet talk, and a little flirting. We talk about how much we can't wait to see each other back at school. When I start to drift off, we say good night. I hang up feeling content, and calm, with fluttery feelings of falling in love.

The Nightmare
23

Christmas morning is here. I crawl out of bed and pad my way into the kitchen to find Mom and Grandma sitting at the table sipping coffee and eating fresh biscuits with jelly.

"These look amazing, Mom."

"I'm glad you're awake. Sleep well?" she asks.

"I did. I feel refreshed and ready to open Christmas presents. How about you guys?" I ask, looking from Grandma to Mom as I bite into a buttery biscuit.

Mom laughs. "Let me finish my coffee first."

After moving into the living room, I help Mom light a fire, even though in south Louisiana, it's not needed. It hardly ever goes below forty degrees in the winter, but I enjoy a fire and the ambience it creates, making our living room that much cozier.

"This tree is nice, Mom. I'm usually here to help you get it off the car and into the house and in the stand. I guess you asked Uncle Joe to come over and help this year?"

She just looks at me and changes the subject.

"Here's your stocking." She reaches for my stocking on the fireplace mantle and hands it to me. It's filled with shampoo, deodorant, nail polishes, earrings, and fun face masks.

"Cool. Thanks. I can always use this stuff. Let me get the gifts I got for you and Grandma." Moving over to the tree, I pick up two boxes and hand one to Grandma, who nods and smiles. Then I give the other one to Mom.

Grandma's eyes light up when she pulls out the cream-colored cardigan sweater, I got her. Mom gushes in approval of the blouse I picked out for her and comes over to give me a hug.

"Landry, I love the color. This is perfect. Thank you, sweetie." She goes over to the tree and retrieves more packages, handing some to me and giving another one to Grandma.

"Mom, this is a lot. It looks like you went a little overboard on me this year."

"We missed you. So maybe I bought more gifts than I should have."

After opening all the gifts, I have several new outfits, a hat, a Vera Bradly duffel, a beach towel that matches the pattern on the duffel, a pair of leather sandals, and a cute dress.

"I'm grateful. This is so nice of you. I love everything. I'll go try it all on to make sure it fits."

I start to collect everything when Mom stops me.

"Wait. There's one more." She goes to the tree, reaches up near the top, and plucks down an envelope. "I know you wanted to get your hair lightened with that . . . I don't remember what you called it . . . style."
I let out a chuckle. "You mean balayage? That's too expensive, Mom."

Tears run down her cheeks as she hands the envelope to me. Opening it, I find two hundred dollars in cash. "Mom, you must have saved up for months. How?" I shake my head in disbelief. "I don't know what to say."

She comes over to me, leans down, and puts her hands on either side of my face. She's crying now, and it's making me cry, too.

"It's been long in coming, sweetie. It's yours," she says, trying to smile through the tears.
I wrap my arms around her and pull her close.

"You're the best mom in the entire world."

Once all the gift wrap, boxes, and bows have been cleaned up, I gather all my gifts in my arms and make my way into my room, where I plop the stack down onto my bed.

"I'll be in my room trying everything on," I call over my shoulder before closing the door. After spending half an hour trying everything on and taking a few selfies, I change into running shorts and my Natchez College hoodie. I slip on my warm socks and my old but still very fuzzy fake UGGs. I stick my phone inside the center pocket of my hoodie, thinking while watching Christmas movies on the couch, I'll text a few of my friends, and maybe even Jordan. I should go see him today. Telling him about Cole in person would be a good idea, I think.

Before I can get to the living room, Mom stops me in the hallway. "Can I talk to you for a few minutes?" She still looks upset about something. I thought maybe me being home for Christmas and the emotions surrounding the expensive gifts might have been the cause of her tears, but now I know there's something wrong.

I take a step back inside my room as she steps closer to me. She reaches for my hand and holds it between hers, patting it softly as she tries to gather her words. I feel myself tense, waiting nervously for what I'm about to hear.

"Your father contacted me a few weeks ago. His wife passed away. She had breast cancer. She had been fighting it for several years, but it metastasized to her brain, and there was no hope. He found her dead one morning. She had overdosed on pain pills after she had gone to bed the night before. They had a little boy together. He's six, almost seven. His name is Todd." She pauses, wiping tears from her cheeks.

"That's very sad, Mom. But I don't think his life has anything to do with us anymore. He left us before your divorce was final. He married her as soon as he could. He left. He moved to Seattle with that woman. He ran away with her, and he left us behind. He chose her over us, Mom. We got one lousy card and one check from him after he left. That was almost eight years ago." I'm practically yelling now. I'm starting to feel angry. I don't care about my dad or his life. Why should my mom care?

"He's come home, Landry. He came back home to raise his son. The woman he married didn't have family. Her parents died years ago. He came back here to go back to work at his family's seafood market and to raise his son here where he was raised. He wants to see you. He doesn't want to be estranged from you. He wants to apologize and ask you to forgive him." She looks at me with a softness but also a sadness in her eyes.

113

"No. There's no way. No. I don't want to forgive him or even talk to him." I give Mom a serious look, squeezing her hand in mine. "Mom. Think about this. He cheated on you for years with more than one woman. He ran off with one, married her, had a son, started a whole new family in Seattle. He never tried to keep in touch. His story is sad, but maybe that's what happens to cheaters." I shake my head in disgust.

"Please, Landry. Please. He wants to explain. He wants to talk to you. Just hear what he has to say." I make my way past Mom into the hallway, still shaking my head.

"It's Christmas Day, Mom. Let's not ruin it. I was planning on watching Christmas movies the rest of the afternoon with you and Grandma and making hot chocolate." I look over my shoulder at Mom, who is still standing in the doorway of my room.

I'm walking toward the living room when I hear her say. . .

"He's here. He came to talk to you."

As I set foot into the living room, he's standing there, and our eyes meet. I scream, "No!" I run into the kitchen and out the back door. I run as fast as I can, making a right on my street and running a mile down Lake Road toward the waterfront. I'm crying and out of breath, but I push on, continuing to keep up my speed.

At the end of the road, where the rocks form a wall against the water from Lake Pontchartrain, I collapse. Out of breath, panting and crying, I climb the rocks and sit, looking out onto the gulf. This can't really be happening right now-----my dad back in my life and with a half-brother? This has to be a nightmare. I can't go back home with him still there waiting. I never want to see him again. I can't believe he came back. He couldn't possibly think I'd care about him or anything that's happened to him in the past seven years. And my mom thinks I should allow him to talk to me, and ask me to forgive him? She thinks I should let him back into my life? No. No. This is not really happening right now. Taking a deep breath, I look out over the water. The cool wind whips my hair around.

I pull my phone from my pocket and call the only friend here in town I can think of who would care. Jordan.

I start crying again when he answers. "Jordan," I say through tears and sniffles, "can you come get me, please?"

"Sure. What's wrong, Landry? Where are you?"

"I'll tell you about it when you get here. I'm at the lake front at the end of Lake Road. I ran all the way from my house."

A few minutes later, Jordan pulls up in his red Toyota, and I hop in. His eyes are sympathetic as they take me in. I'm sure I look like a crazy person. My eyes are bloodshot, my messy bun is loose with strands of hair dangling in my face, and I'm wearing shorts with fuzzy UGG boots.

"Hey, thank you for coming to get me. I had to get out of my house. I ran as fast as I could to the end of the road."

"Sure. But can you tell me what's going on?"

"Can we go somewhere first?"

"Yeah. We can go to my house. My parents, my grandparents, and my older brother are there, but they'll be in the kitchen working on dinner. We can go to my room and talk in private."

"Okay," I say, leaning my head back on the headrest, and clicking in my seat belt.

We pull into the drive and go in through the garage. Then we go down the hall into Jordan's room. We can hear commotion in the kitchen. There's laughter coming from that direction as well as a delicious aroma as the smell of comfort and Christmas fills my nostrils.

Jordan closes the door to his room. I sit on the edge of his bed, and he sits next to me. He lays a hand on my knee then looks at me.

"Tell me what's up."

"My dad is back. He showed up at my house this afternoon. My mom knew he was in town. She said he has moved back because the woman he ran off to Seattle with died. She had cancer, but from what my mom told me, it sounded like she committed suicide, and they have a little boy. I have a half-brother now. He's six. My mom thinks I should talk to him because he wants to apologize. Can you believe that? He wants to come back into our lives and start over with us?" I shake my head in anger as tears stream down my cheeks.

Jordan's hand moves slowly up and down my back. "I'm sorry about all of this, Landry. I know that is not something anyone wants to have happen, especially on Christmas Day. I don't want to tell you how you should feel because I know how hurt you were after he left."

"I know." I nod, looking at him through teary eyes. "It took years of pushing the pain down, before I could finally hide it, ----- before I finally felt free of it. I had come to terms with it just being me and Mom. We were doing okay. Then I got into trouble, but I got a second chance, a chance to start over. Everything was going great in Texas. I really feel comfortable with my teammates and the school. I even felt happy for the first time in a really long time, like actual happiness. Now a giant, festering wound has been ripped open in my heart and in my life. I want to stop the pain and sew that part of my life closed, forever." I glance at Jordan. Our eyes meet, and a warmth spreads through me. He wraps his arms around me and holds me, and I begin to cry harder.

There's a soft tap on the door, and we hear someone say, , "Jordan?" A girl pokes her head into his room. She's cute with dark hair and dark eyes, a thin frame, and a sparkling stud in her nose. When she sees us, she seems startled. "I'm sorry. I didn't know you had company," she says and goes to close the door.

"Wait. Michelle, this is Landry. She's had a bad day today with some family stuff, and I brought her here to talk. Do you want to hang out and wait for a few minutes?" he asks.

"Sure. Nice to meet you, Landry," she says then quickly closes the door.

"Um. So. I should explain," Jordan says.

"She's your girlfriend?" I ask.

"Yeah. We just started dating, and I was planning on telling you about it. We met during the project I was asked to do at school---- the mural on the gym wall. She and I were the two art students chosen for that. We spent a lot of time together on it, and we started hanging out a lot, and then we realized we had feelings for each other. Recently, we made it official and I asked her to be my girlfriend. I really was planning on letting you know." He watches me with a serious look on his face.

"I believe you. I understand. I've been seeing someone, too. I thought about calling you to tell you, then I thought about coming to see you while I was home and telling you in person. It's all out of the bag now. Honestly, it took me a while to figure out how I really felt about him. His name is Cole Collins. He's the quarterback at Natchez. He's from a small town in Texas. I'm starting to realize I have real feelings for him that are getting stronger the more I talk to him."

Jordan lets out a soft sigh as his lips curl into a smile. "At least there's something happy in your life right now. I know this is not the perfect way for either one of us to find out about the other's new relationship, but there may never be a perfect place, way, or perfect time. I mean, both of us wanted to say something, and both of us were struggling, right?"

"Yeah. I know. I should probably go. I don't want to keep you any longer from your plans." I stand, pause, and look at Jordan.

"It's fine," he says looking up at me. "Really. I'm glad I was there when you needed me. Do you want to call your mom first to let her know where you are?"

I pull my phone from the front pocket of my sweatshirt. I have three missed calls and two text messages. One of the texts is from Cole, and the other is from Mom. All the missed calls are from my mom. "I'll call her now," I say. "She's called three times and texted me." I slide my phone open and call Mom. She's panicked and freaking out when she answers. I explain where I am and that Jordan will drive me home, then I ask if my dad is still there. When she says no, I know it's okay to head back home.

After the Fact. . .
24

When Jordan and I walk out of his room, his brother sees us, starts laughing, and says, "Two in one day, Jordan? That's a record. The other one left, by the way. She said to tell you to call her."

Jordan rolls his eyes but doesn't say anything. He places his hand on my lower back as we walk toward the kitchen.

"Come say hi before you leave," he says.

"I hope I didn't mess things up with Michelle," I look at him, concerned.

"Nah. Everything will be okay. I hope it's alright if I tell her the reason you were upset and the reason you were here?"

"Of course. Anything to help smooth things over. The truth always helps, right?" I smile at him.

As we enter the kitchen, his mom is saying, "Tony, you need to pass the broom. I spilled some rice over by the stove."

His grandparents are at the kitchen table playing cards with his dad. They stop when they notice us walk in. "Landry, dawhlin,' where y'at? I didn't know you passed by. Come on in here."

"Thank you, Mr. Cassagne. I've been good. It's great to see everyone again."

"Margo, looks who's here." Jordan's dad gets his mom's attention away from what's she stirring on the stove. When she sees me, she throws her arms up in the air and walks over to hug me.

"I've wanted to pass by and see your mama so many times since you left for Texas. You made eighteen recently, too?" she asks, smiling at me.

"Yes, ma'am. About a month ago."

"Jordan makes eighteen next month. Did he tell you about the mural artist in New 'awlin's he's going to be working with? We're so pleased for him. We've been wait'n on pins and needles to hear from that school over in Savannah. He really wants to go there for his art degree," she says.

"I should hear from them soon, Mom, I need to take Landry home. I'll be back in a few minutes." Jordan reaches for his keys on the counter.

"Oh, just a minute. You can't leave without a little *lagniappe*. I just prepared these shrimps and made some remoulade." She scoops some sauce into a container and fills another container with shrimp. Then she hands me a loaf of french bread. "Take that to your mama, and tell her Merry Christmas and I'll pass by soon."

"Thank you, Mrs. Cassagne. I appreciate it," I say, taking the containers from her.

When we get into the car, I say, "I've missed your parents and their Cajun accents."
Jordan laughs. "You should hear them when they play Bourré and start talking in French." He starts the engine.

Pulling the car in front of my house, Jordan pauses, turns to me, and lifts my chin as he searches my face. "I'm glad you called me. I hope everything works out for you and your family. You will always have a piece of my heart, Landry." He looks sincere.

"I feel the same about you. Thanks, Jordan." I manage to get the words out just as tears flood my eyes. Quickly opening the door, I get out of Jordan's car and run up the steps to the front door.

Inside, Mom is on the phone with someone. "She's home," she says, setting the phone on the table in the kitchen. She runs toward me, enveloping me into her arms.

"I was worried sick."

"I'm sorry. I just had to get out of the house. I didn't want to see him. I can't believe he came here. Did you know he was coming?" I ask. She looks at me then turns her eyes away and keeps them down.

119

"He called me a few weeks ago and told me the whole story about what happened with his wife. He told me about his son and said he was back in town. That's when he asked to see you. I told him you had gone to college a year early and that you were in Texas until Christmas. I told him I'd tell you and that I'd let him know. He came by the house a few days after his call. He gave me some money to give to you for Christmas, and he helped me buy the tree and put it up. I met his son. He's a sweet boy who misses his mother." She looks at me and reaches out, grabbing hold of my arm. "He's sorry for leaving you and he wants to make it right. I thought it would be good for you to talk to him."

"Well, you thought wrong. Here." I hand her the containers. "These are from Jordan's mom. She said she wants to come by and see you sometime. She's been thinking about you." I turn away from Mom and walk into the hall. "I'm going to my room. I don't feel like eating anything."

When I get back to my room, I text back and forth with Cole, then he calls me, and we talk for an hour about his Christmas. The cat settles on my pillow, filling the air with soft purrs. I chat with Cole about the gifts I got for Christmas but don't mention anything else. I can't talk about my awful dad showing up. He doesn't even know about my troubled past. I'd feel like such a loser if I were to tell him. After I hang up with him, I drift off to sleep, hoping that the nightmare will have been just that and that I'll wake to the happy life, I've hoped for.

When I do wake up, it's early. Mom left a note for me on the table saying she's taken Grandma to her hair appointment. I pick up my phone to call her. "Hey, Mom. Can you ask if they can fit me in this week for a balayage?"

"Hang on. Let me see." I hear her talking with someone in the background before she returns to the phone. "They can do it tomorrow morning at nine."

"Thanks, Mom."

I hang up and fix myself some breakfast. I need to go to my old cheer gym and do some workouts today. I'll text Nicole to see if she's in town and if she'll go to the cheer gym with me. I want to hear all about her freshman year at LSU. After breakfast I shower and change into cheer clothes. I pull my old cheer shoes from the back of my closet and lace them up. Minutes later, a text pops up that Nicole is here. I walk outside and happily hop into her car.

"Hey, Landry. I'm glad you texted me. I've been thinking about you lately. How's it going at Natchez? I heard their coach is tough and the practices are hard," she says as she pulls away from the curb.

"It's a lot of practice. But I really like Coach McKaye. She's nice, almost like a second mom. She's a tough coach, but she's also down to earth, and I can tell she really cares about us. I like my teammates too. I feel like they get me. It's like family there. I want to hear all about LSU and the parties, the guys, and your cheer team," I say, smiling and feeling better now that my mind is no longer focused on yesterday.

Nicole and I walk into the cheer gym together. Everyone at the gym is excited to see their alums back.

Coach Reed comes up and hugs us. "How's it going, college girls?" he asks. Nicole and I fill him in on all the details. He asks me about the difficult partner and pyramid stunts that we've been learning at Natchez. He seems impressed and tells me how proud he is that everything is working out for me. After Nicole and I warm up and tumble for a while, Coach Reed wants to know if we can help with the holiday cheer camp that's happening at the gym this week.

"If you guys can be here at eleven tomorrow and the day after, we have three levels of camp classes lined up from eleven to three. Lunch and craft time is from one to two. I'll pay you guys thirty dollars per day. What do you say?"

We both agree that would be cool. I'd love the extra cash to take back for next semester, and it will keep me occupied until I head back to campus later this week. Coach Reed looks relieved he doesn't have to teach level ones for holiday cheer camp, and Nicole and I are thrilled with the opportunity to earn some extra cash. Before leaving the gym, I snag Coach Reed's attention and make my way over to where he is.

"Hey, Coach. I just wanted to say thank you again for getting me a tryout at Natchez. It really has been a good move for me. I love it there. I've made a lot of friends and I'm working hard. I want to give everything I've got for my new team. I'm grateful for the second chance I've been given."

He smiles, putting a hand on my shoulder. "I'm happy for you. I knew it would be the right move. Bring home that national title in April." He chuckles then turns to go back to the mat to continue coaching, he waves to me and Nicole as we head out the door.

When she drops me back at home, it's almost time for dinner. When I walk through the door, Mom gets up and hugs me like she hasn't seen me in months.

"Thank you for leaving the note to let me know where you were going. I almost had a panic attack when Grandma and I got back from her hair appointment and the grocery store and we didn't see you. Then I saw the note you wrote on the back of the one I left you this morning."

"Are you able to take me to my hair appointment in the morning?" I ask. "Also, Nicole and I are working holiday camp tomorrow and the day after from eleven to three. I'll make a little extra money, and it will be fun. Maybe something I can add to a resume for a summer job or something."

"That sounds good." She pauses and glances at the dishes in the sink. She walks over and turns on the water then turns around facing me. "Your dad called again to check on you. He still wants to see you."

"You know the answer is still no. I don't care what he wants. *Please* stop talking to me about him. It's my Christmas break and I want to enjoy the few days I have here at home. Can you understand, Mom?"

"Okay, hon. Will you set the table for dinner?"

The next few days are a lot more fun. Nicole and I are having a blast teaching the littles at holiday cheer camp. My new hair style looks really good too. The lighter style makes me feel prettier, it's a definite boost to my self-esteem. I've always thought my straight brown hair was boring.

When Nicole drops me off after camp, Mom wants my help with taking the decorations off the tree.

"We can pack away the decorations and take off the lights, then tomorrow we can take the tree to the curb. The trash service comes the day after," she says, setting a plastic container in front of the tree.

After packing the decorations, I haul the boxes into the attic. As I'm walking backward down the attic stairs, my phone rings. It's Cole. I slide my phone open and bound into my room, closing the door to be alone as we chat. Lying down on my bed, I curl up with a pillow to my chest and snuggle it as we talk.

"I have a new hairstyle. It's lighter now. I think you'll like it," I say, teasing.

"I'm thinking of getting rid of my dreads. What would you think if I came back with a shaved head?" He laughs.

"I think you'd still be just as cute and adorable as you are now."

"You're heading back to school tomorrow, aren't you?"

"Yes. We are leaving at the crack of dawn. My mom's sister, Aunt Jackie, and Mom will drive me back. I'll probably get there late afternoon. KK's supposed to come back the next day. We have a basketball game to cheer at later that night."

"I wish I could see you on New Year's Eve. But I'm going to Dallas to have scans done on the second. The Falcons didn't make the playoffs, so my brother is flying to Dallas from Atlanta that day. After my doctor's appointment, we'll pick him up. He'll get to be home with us for a few days. It will be good to spend some time with him."

"That sounds like fun. I want you to let me know how everything goes at your appointment. I hope you're healed up and ready to roll again soon."

"Affirmative. You'll text me on the long drive to Texas, right?"

"I will. You'll be sick of me by the end of the day tomorrow."

Laughing, he replies, "Not a chance."

Feels Good to Be Back. . .
25

Squealing with joy, I rush to the doorway as KK walks through, suitcase in hand. We embrace, then we do a hip bump, and a fist tap, and we high five each other. She grabs her bag from the floor beside her and tosses it onto her bed.

"Since my mom has taken off from working at the restaurant until the first, she and Aunt Jackie are staying until tomorrow. They'll watch me cheer at the basketball game tonight. I'm excited about introducing them to the team later," I say after our celebratory greeting.

"Gracie and Christa flew into Dallas earlier today," KK says. "They'll be back just in time to throw on their uniforms and head to the gym to cheer at the game. I'm glad your mom and your aunt could stay a few days. My grandparents will leave in the morning. I think they'll stay for most of the game tonight, but they don't like being away from home too long. It's an eight-hour drive back to Tonkawa, Oklahoma," she says, before turning around to unpack her bag.

"I'm glad most of the team is back. It'll be fun being together on New Year's Eve tomorrow night, too. I think everyone's agreed we'll go to the event at Coach McKaye's church."

KK, nods. "I'm looking forward to it. I'll show you the new outfit I'm planning to wear." She pulls it from her suitcase and holds it up to model it for me.

Later, walking into the gym, I hear my name and look up to see Mom and Aunt Jackie standing in the bleachers. They're waving their arms in the air, showering me with air kisses. I wave back and motion for KK to look up at them.

The game goes into double overtime, and we win by two points. Mom and Aunt Jackie rush down the stadium steps at the end of the game to hug me. I go about introducing them to Jaz, Donte, Gracie, Christa, and the rest of the team before the others scoot out to get pizza.

"That was some game," Mom says, looking relieved.

"We definitely got our money's worth," Aunt Jackie says, laughing.

"The team, pep band, and cheerleaders are heading to a place called Pop's Pizzeria. It's a tradition we do after home games. I'd like it if you guys came too," I say, picking up my backpack from the floor in front of me.

"That sounds like fun. I'd love to see a little more of the town," Mom says, following me toward the exit.

Yesterday after we arrived on campus, they dropped me off at my dorm, and helped me carry my bags inside before they went to check into their hotel. We grabbed some breakfast this morning then Mom and Aunt Jackie dropped me off at cheer practice before they drove around to see if there were any interesting antique shops to poke around in. I know they will enjoy this Natchez College tradition of going to the pizzeria after home games with my team and the other students.

As we settle into our seats at the end of the table, Mom and Aunt Jackie are totally entertained by Donte, Jaz, and the rest of the gang. They plan on leaving early in the morning, and I'm savoring these extra minutes with them as we munch on pizza, laughing and feeling light-hearted.

Early the next morning, my phone alarm goes off and I quickly silence it, hoping not to wake KK. Scurrying to the bathroom, I quickly get dressed, run a brush through my hair, and brush my teeth before I grab my coat and head out of the dorm. Walking quickly down the block and over one street, I meet up with Mom and Aunt Jackie at the coffee shop next to campus, and we go inside for goodbyes over coffee.

"When can we see you again?" Mom asks with tear-filled eyes. She picks up a napkin from under her coffee mug and dabs her eyes with it.

"We'll have a showcase in March for family members and alumni. I'm not sure we have an official date for that yet. As soon as Coach gives it to us, I'll let you know so you can make plans to take off work." I smile, trying to lighten the mood. I know it's hard on Mom to have me far from home. Aunt Jackie pats her arm.

"Maybe I'll come back for that too," Aunt Jackie says, giving Mom's arm a squeeze.

"It's almost eight thirty. Uncle Joe will be wondering where we are if we aren't back home by dinner time," Mom says, standing. "Have fun tonight with your friends, and please be safe. Nothing good ever happens after midnight. *Even* if it is New Year's Eve." She tries to smile then takes my hand and pulls me into a hug.

I watch as they pull out of the parking lot, before I turn and make my way back to campus.

*****

"What should I wear tonight?" I ask, opening my closet to comb through my clothes.

"I'm wearing jeans and a new sweater I got for Christmas with my new boots," KK says, looking up from the book she's reading.

"What do you think about these jeans with this top?" I ask, holding up a pair of black ripped jeans and a white top with a rainbow stripe down each sleeve. "I have a few more new things," I say, as I pull some other options from the closet and hold them to my chest waiting for KK's response.

"I like the rainbow-stripe sweatshirt with those dark jeans," she says, walking over and putting them together. "I have some red suede booties that will look divine with this."

After spending time getting ready, we're dressed to impress, with our hair curled, and makeup on point. We walk down to Gracie and Christa's room to see if they're ready to head to the party.

"Do you guys know how to get to Coach McKaye's church?" I ask.

"Yeah. We've been once before on a Sunday," Christa responds.

As we walk out of the dorm, Gracie says, "I'll drive."

126

When we arrive, we see that the building is large and modern. Orange and red lights illuminate one side, where large steel letters spell out "Community Campus Church." An all-glass garage-style door is open, and people are flooding through the entrance. Loud pop music greets us as we meander into a large open space. Spotlights flicker around the ceiling to the beat of the music. The scene around us is a flood of loud chatter and laughter. Suddenly we're greeted by a nice lady holding a tray of fun-looking drinks.

"Have a mocktail," she says, lowering the tray. "This one is blueberry with a spritz of tonic water. This one is lemonade with a dash of cherry." Each one is beautifully topped with a sprig of fresh fruit and a mint leaf.

"Thank you," I say, taking a lemonade from the tray. Gracie and Christa each take one as well, and KK takes the last one.

"If you want dessert, there's a huge selection on the tables over there." She points across the room, and we decide to go take a closer look.

The dessert tables are stacked with all sorts of cheesecakes, mini cupcakes, and other treats. There's also a donut wall featuring a wide variety of flavors. Each of us decides on a donut, making it easy to walk around while eating and talking. I point out a photo station where a line has gathered. On a platform, I can see a background has been created to look like the fountain scene from *Friends.*

They've built an actual working fountain on the platform and have added multi-colored umbrellas for everyone to pose with.

"Look, guys," I say, pointing to the photo stage.

"Oh my gosh. It looks just like the fountain from the opening credits in *Friends,*" Christa squeals.

"Let's get in line for pictures," KK says, making her way in that direction.

When we get closer to the line, we notice some of our teammates waiting and we squeeze in with them in line.

"This is the coolest church I've ever seen," I say, taking it all in.

"I agree," says, Sherry. "There's another photobooth that has the couch from "Central Perk" on *Friends.* You get to hold giant coffee mugs for that photo. We got photos there before we came over here. Donte and Jaz were with us for the first photo. I think they wandered off with Coach McKaye. We'll find them when we go into the auditorium later." Sherry motions for us to move up as the line in front of us grows shorter.

After we've stood in line for each of the *Friends*-themed photo stations, we decide to find the rest of our crew. "Send a text in GroupMe and find out where everyone is hanging out." I nudge KK's arm.

"Look, guys. They have *Friends* themed T-shirts for sale," Gracie says, pointing to a pop-up shop outside the auditorium entrance. Gracie picks up a shirt and examines it before flipping it over to look at the back. "There's a verse on the back," she says then reads it out loud. *"Bear with one another and forgive as the Lord forgave you. Put on love, which binds all virtues in perfect unity. Colossians 3:13-14."*

"They have seats saved for us on the fifth row on the right side," KK says.

Gracie tosses the shirt back onto the table, and we head into the auditorium to find the rest of our teammates.

Donte waves us over when he sees us walk in. He motions at the four seats he's standing next to.

As we make our way over to him, Coach McKaye comes over to greet us.

"Hi, girls. Glad you could make it," she says, leaning in for hugs.

"Your church is really cool," I say.

"I'm guessing the topic tonight is friendship," Christa mentions when we sit.

Laughing, Coach McKaye says, "I think it might have something to do with that."

A few moments later, the lights dim, smoke seeps from the stage, and laser lights flash as the band takes the stage. They break into the *Friends* theme song then move onto the theme song from *Toy Story*, "You've Got a Friend in Me." After that comes "Thank You for Being a Friend" before they begin worship and praise songs. The music has us all on our feet, dancing, swaying, and singing along.

During the worship music, I notice they've put words up on large screens so people can sing along. A lot of people have their hands up in praise, and a peaceful feeling washes over me. When the last song ends, the lead singer talks to us for a few minutes about God's love and peace before he asks us to bow our heads in prayer.

After we sit down, the band leaves the stage, the smoke settles, and a single spotlight focuses on a thirty-something-year-old guy as he walks onto the stage with a barstool in one hand and a Bible in the other. He sits down. He's wearing jeans and a long-sleeved button-down shirt with brown lace-up leather shoes. His shirtsleeves are rolled up near his elbows, and when he sits, I notice a cross tattoo on the inside of his left wrist. He begins talking, and it's like he's talking to us in the same way someone would who's just sitting in your living room having a casual conversation. He's easy to listen to. I like his mannerisms *and* I like what he's saying.

My mind drifts in and out of my own thoughts as he laughs and jokes about people making New Year's resolutions to go on a diet or to go back to the gym, only to find the resolutions are short-lived. He ties it into the way some relationships fizzle out, depending on how much effort you put into them. He moves on to talking about Jesus, his friendship with his disciples, and how they loved and trusted him. They trusted him so much they left their jobs and families to follow him as he traveled from city-to-city healing and teaching.

He moves off of the barstool and stands, moving closer to the edge of the stage. He talks about how Jesus tried to prepare his disciples for what was to come,-----the betrayal, the lies, the accusations,-----but they chose not to believe him, saying they would never leave him nor betray him. "But the cock crowed three times, and Peter knew what he'd done. Judas's body is found. He hung himself. And three days after the Crucifixion, Jesus appears to them in the locked room where they've hidden. Grace, love, forgiveness, and hope win in the end," he says, almost in a whisper.

At this point, I'm leaning in. I'm wholly focused, my mind refusing to wander. I'm stolen by his words, by the story. I'm captured by the way he begins to tie it to the present day as he continues.

"Have you been hurt, betrayed, or let down by someone who had no right to hurt you?" The old wounds I've tried to close begin to open. "How could God ask you to forgive what they've done to you?" the speaker asks. "How would it even be possible to forgive such a wrong?" He pauses, looking into the crowd. My breathing becomes shallow.

"We want justice served. We want wrongs made right. It's how we're wired. Being made in the image of God means we want good to win over evil. Where's my justice? We want something very bad to happen to those who hurt us. But when our anger becomes hate, it conjures bitterness and betrayal. We can't take justice into our own hands, even though we'd like to. But----but, look what they did?" He stutters his words to emphasize the fervency of the imagined plea. "Can't they see how they've hurt me?" He walks back to the stool and sits.

"A human father won't take kindly to anyone hurting his child. Think of God as the perfect father, better than a human. Then you realize that, as the perfect father, he won't take kindly to anyone hurting a child of his. His justice and his timing *are* very different from ours. Time doesn't pass in heaven, because it's always in the present. Thirty seconds could be the same as three years. Even though we may run on a tight schedule that doesn't mean God does. Hurt causes us to place blame, but that won't help us to heal. So, at the start of this new year, how do we begin to heal? How do we forgive those who've slandered us, wounded us, done something unspeakable to us? How do we restore broken friendships or broken relationships?"

A single tear rolls down my cheek, and I don't bother to wipe it away. I'm frozen in place with my attention glued to this man who is speaking into the depths of my soul. There's barely a sound in the enormous auditorium, which I know must be filled with close to a thousand people.

"What does the cross mean to you? What is grace? A gift that's freely given. To give forgiveness to someone who doesn't deserve to be forgiven,----to that, you'd say, *No way.* I can't do that, it's impossible. You're right. It's impossible for humans to feel they can forgive someone who's done something unspeakable. But the enabling force of God's free gift of grace and forgiveness is available to anyone. If he forgives you, then you are likewise expected to forgive. You may not forget, and you may not trust again. Trust is something that is earned while forgiveness is given. The easiest way to begin to heal is to pray and simply ask him to help you, to help you pray for those who've hurt you. Their hearts may need to be changed more than you will ever know or understand." He stands again and walks to the edge of the stage, and his final words are "Anything is possible with God."

The worship band joins him on stage, holding lit candles. The pastor takes one from the lead singer and holds it up.

"Join with me as we ring in the new year, and I pray that your hearts will be healed, your relationships renewed, and your joy made new. Our staff is coming around with candles to pass down each row. As you hold your individual light up, ask for what you know you need most this new year, and even if your diet only lasts a few weeks and working out at the gym only lasts a month, keep prayer and conversations going with God throughout the new year. He's waiting to hear from you."

The band begins playing softly. Voices join in singing quietly. The candles reach our aisle, and I stand, holding mine, and gazing into the golden flame. I don't know how to begin to pray, so I just say, "Thank you, God."

A countdown begins. "Happy New Year!" band members proclaim before they begin the familiar old tune. The audience sways, arm in arm. My teammates huddle close, reaching for each other's hands as we join in singing. When the song ends, we turn to each other with wishes and hugs to greet the new year.

KK reaches for me and pulls me close. She has tears on her cheeks. I know my mascara is running too.

"Tonight, was amazing," she whispers. "Do you want to come again on Sunday?" she asks.

Smiling, I nod. "I do."

Back in our dorm, I'm quiet. Both KK and I were moved by what we heard tonight. She doesn't know that my father came back to town and tried to see me. I wasn't planning on talking to anyone about that. I wanted to leave my past in the past, hoping it would all fade away, but maybe that's not really what I'm supposed to do. I don't have a clue what I'm supposed to do or how I should feel. What I do know is I want to go back to Coach McKaye's church, and I am glad KK does too.

Before I lie down, I plug my phone into the charger and notice I have a voicemail. I'd turned the volume off when we entered the auditorium tonight. I fold back my comforter and crawl under it, snuggling up to my pillow as I listen to Cole's sweet voice. I try to call him back, but it goes to voice mail. I glance at the time and realize it's almost two a.m. I leave a quiet message, trying not to wake KK since we have to be up early to get ready for the New Year's Day parade.

"Hey, Cole, I just got your voice mail. I'm sorry I missed talking to you. We went to Coach McKaye's church and I had the volume turned off on my phone. I'm in bed about to go to sleep now. You may already be asleep. Happy New Year. I can't wait to see you next week."

I drift off to sleep, feeling the year is starting off pretty good so far.

We Made Mat

26

Nervously, I walk to the mat and sit next to KK. She reaches for my hand and gives it a squeeze. Gracie appears relaxed. Christa looks as scared as KK and I do, keeping her head down, and staring at her feet. Coach Matt walks in with Coach McKaye, and Coach Zack follows them. Coach McKaye is holding a piece of paper in her hand, and I know it's the list of who made mat for the national championship competition in Daytona. We're all waiting with bated breath for the news.

When she reads my name, I let out a sigh of relief and say a quick prayer. *Thank you, God.* KK squeals when her name is read. When Donte's name is announced, he shouts, "Praise the Lord, oh, my soul."
Christa and Gracie clap silently when their names are called, and I give them a thumbs-up.

After all the names have been announced, Coach speaks directly to the ten people who didn't make it this time. Most of them are freshman, Lisa being one of them. I know KK was worried it might come down to a choice between her and Lisa for one of the flyer slots.

"For those whose names I did not call, you will still need to be on time for practice, and you will need to know the routine backward and forward, just as if you had made mat. You never know when we might need you to fill in at the last minute. Next Saturday will be a full all-day practice. Once we are into February, we will use most of our Saturdays for full-outs, and each Saturday in March we will do a full-out outside. You will do this routine until you can't get it wrong." She looks around, making sure we are all on the same page before she speaks again. Then she signals for KK to walk over. She whispers something to her. Then calls me, Logan, and Brodi over too.

"I need you guys to work with KK on her standing full during today's practice," Coach says before sending us off to get started.

Over the next few days of practice, we work on jumps, tumbling, and stunts. On Saturday we focus on the pyramid. As the day wears on, I'm struggling to focus, knowing that tomorrow afternoon Cole will be back on campus. We text back and forth a few times, then he calls me later in the evening. Full of anticipation, we chat about our plans to get together once he arrives.

"KK and I are going to church tomorrow with Gracie and Christa. We had a lot of fun together at the New Year's celebration, and I'm looking forward to going back."

"I usually go there with some guys from the team. We won't be back until later in the day tomorrow, but maybe we can get together for a quick dinner with my parents?"

"Sounds good."

"When I get to campus tomorrow, I'll text you. You can meet me over at the dorm then we can go eat before my parents head back home. I'm still not driving since I'm in a boot. We can all ride in my mom's car to dinner."

*****

Coach gives us the afternoon off today since we had an all-day practice yesterday. I know I'm glad to have the day off, but so are the other girls. KK and I meet up with Gracie and Christa to ride to church together.

During the service, I notice some girls sitting near us taking notes, and I wonder if I should get a journal. I used to write things in a diary when I was around eight or nine. I stopped using it when I got older, mostly because what I'd write became painful and unpleasant to think about. So, I quit writing in the diary. I forced myself to stop thinking about my dad and wondering whether he'd ever come back. Now that he is back, I wish he wasn't. Being in

Texas and far from home is good for me. I don't want to bring back painful memories. I hate thinking about my past.

Later in the afternoon, I pop the door of my closet open and pick out an outfit to wear to dinner with Cole and his parents. Then I spend extra time curling my hair. When he shoots me a text letting me know he's back, I unplug the curling iron and stare at my reflection, hoping I look good for Cole. KK notices I haven't moved.

"You look amazing, girl," she says with enthusiasm.

Turning from the mirror, I smile at my friend. "Thank you. I appreciate the compliment. I'm going to dinner with Cole and his parents. I'm not sure when I'll be back."

"Ooh, have fun, girl. Don't do anything I wouldn't do," she says, laughing.

Happily, I walk out the door and across the parking lot to Cole's dorm. I text him when I arrive and wait on him to come down to the commons room with his parents to meet me.

He's hobbling a bit as he moves toward me. He did shave his head, just as he said he might. It's a low buzz with an angular line cut into the back and along the sides. He's wearing large diamond stud earrings that really stand out. He gives me a big hug.

"Good to see you, Landry," his dad says. "We're happy you can join us this evening."

"We thought we'd go to the steakhouse. Is that okay with you?" his mom asks.

I smile and nod, then we move outside and make our way to their car. Cole and I get into the back seat. He reaches for my hand to hold. I give him a shy smile and squeeze his hand.

Dinner is light-hearted and fun. His parents ask me about going to Mardi Gras and the times to see the best parades. Their anniversary is coming up, and they may go to New Orleans to spend the weekend. I give them a run-down on hotels and some of the top restaurants and must-see places they would want to visit. I show them how to pull up the parade routes and schedules on their phones and how to use the parade-tracker app.

Afterward, they drop us off in front of Cole's dorm. He tells me we can go to his room since his roommate won't be back until tomorrow morning. His room is clean and smells musky like aftershave. His bedspread is red and black like the Natchez color scheme. He has two oversized black pillows that lean against the headboard. He sits down, leaning back into one of them as he pulls me on top of him. Snuggling up to his chest, I lean in and kiss him along his neck just under his ear. We kiss for a few minutes, then I slide off of him but scoot in close, with my head partly on his shoulder and partly on the large pillow behind my back.

"I missed you," he whispers.

"I missed you too."

"So, you had a quiet day today. Church this morning. No afternoon practice. You feeling well rested on this beautiful Lord's day?" he asks, leaning toward me. He reaches for my hand and brings it to his lips.

"I talked about you the whole break," he says grinning at me. "My brothers got so sick of me. They even started teasing me, making up silly songs, inserting our names into the lyrics." He chuckles.

His comment makes me smile. "That's funny," I say. "I told Jordan about you." I glance at him, giving him a nervous smile, while rolling my eyes at the same time. "I saw him, actually."

"How did that go?" He looks at me with apprehension.

"Good. He has a girlfriend. I met her, kinda. I was over at his house talking to him about something that happened earlier that day, and she found us talking in his room. He smoothed everything over with her later and told her I just needed someone to talk to. She was okay with it once he told her what had happened. We both know we can move on now. He's still a good friend. He's someone I know I can trust."

Cole squeezes my hand. "You know you can trust me too if you need someone to talk to. I'm a really good listener."

"Thank you, Cole. I know. There are things about me I haven't told you about yet. I wasn't sure I wanted to tell you. I don't want you to think less of me."

"Not a chance." He shakes his head. "I'm all ears. I can keep a secret." He lets go of my hand to make an X over his chest. "Cross my heart."

We stare into each other's eyes, smiling sweetly for a beat. I bite my lip and glance up at the ceiling before speaking.

"Have you ever been so angry with someone you wished they were dead or wished something bad would happen to them?" I pause and take a deep breath. "When my dad left, I didn't know much about the situation that lead up to him leaving. Then I talked to my mom about it when I was around thirteen. She told me they had decided to get married when she found out she was pregnant with me. Mom was twenty, and my dad was twenty-two. They were married for about eight years before they separated. He cheated on my mom several times, then right before their divorce was final, he left. He moved across the country with another woman to start a new life." I sit up a little straighter and tilt my head back on the pillow. Cole's thumb slowly traces circles on my hand.

"When I was home," I say, "I found out he's back in town. He showed up at my house on Christmas Day wanting to see me. I ran out of the house and called Jordan to come get me. I was so mad at my mom for allowing him to come into our home. I don't understand why she thinks I'd want to see him." I glance at Cole, and he lifts my hand to his lips and kisses it reassuringly. "His wife died of cancer, and they have a son. He's almost seven." I pause and swallow hard. "I have a half-brother." I bite my lower lip, fighting back tears.

Cole wraps his arms around me and holds me as I tell him more. "I was hoping I'd never have to see my dad again. It was painful when he left. I was only ten. We moved in with my grandmother, and that was great. I pushed the hurt way down deep and closed up that part of me. My mom started working two jobs, and I was with my grandmother a lot, which was fine. She's had a stroke recently, and now she only speaks a little, but she still understands us. She has a hard time walking too. My mom and her sister, Aunt Jackie, help with taking her to the doctor and she stays with Aunt Jackie some if Mom is gone." I toe my shoes off and flip them onto the floor. "The other night at the New Year's Eve service, the message was about forgiving others because God forgives us. But I don't know." I dab at the corners of my eyes where tears are pooling.

Cole pulls me into a strong hug and holds me tight. I sob softly into his shoulder as he gently strokes my hair. After a few minutes,

I sit up, lean my head back onto the pillow, and sniffle. Cole goes to his desk and brings back a couple of tissues, which he hands to me. He sits next to me and gives my shoulder a squeeze before he responds to what I've just shared with him.

"It's normal to feel the way you do," he says. "It's hard to forgive someone who hurts us deeply. I haven't been hurt by a family member like you have, but I've been cheated on by a former girlfriend. I've been cussed at and told things like 'I'll kill you' by players on opposing teams I've played. I've always gone to my mom or dad and talked it out when something was really bothering me, and they'd pray with me. It always helped. Can I pray with you, Landry?"

I nod, and he reaches for my hand and leans his head next to mine. I look up and notice that his eyes are closed. I close my eyes as well and bow my head so that it's lightly touching his. Then I listen quietly as Cole prays for me.

"Precious God," he begins. "I want to lift sweet Landry up to you. You know she means a lot to me. I think she's a great girl, a sweet friend, and I'm happy that you've brought her into my life. She's hurting, Lord, and you know her heart, and you know her struggle. Please give her your peace and allow healing in her life. Speak to her heart. Give her the reassurance she needs to feel your presence in her life. Give her the guidance she seeks. All these things I ask in your name. Amen."

A peacefulness and sense of calm wash over me. Cole presses his lips to my forehead and leaves them there for a few seconds.

I whisper, "Thank you. Thank you for not making me feel stupid or horrible or weird." I wrap my arms around him and revel in his strength. I feel his shoulders and his muscles as I let my fingers run up and down his arms. It's not just his physical strength I feel, it's emotional and manly and protective, and it feels so good I could melt into him right now.

"You mean a lot to me. I'm here for you anytime," he says as he lifts my chin, looking into my eyes. His brown eyes are shinning, and I can see myself in them. I lean in and kiss him softly. He kisses me back with passion then pulls away, smiling. He rubs the stubble on his chin.

"I should probably walk you back to your dorm," he says.

I realize that Cole must have a lot of self-control. With his roommate gone until tomorrow, and with us being alone in his room, *and* with the way I'm feeling about him right now things could have gone a whole lot further. I appreciate how respectful he is and how he's often told me he wants to take things slow.

We walk slowly, hand in hand, across the parking lot over to my dorm. The boot on Cole's right ankle makes it a slow walk, but I'm glad because it gives us time to laugh and catch up with each other, and because I love being wrapped in his strong arms. We stop just inside the door, and he pulls me to him. Slowly, he leans in and kisses me softly and sweetly, his forehead pressed into mine. With one hand on my butt, he slips his other hand under my shirt, caressing the skin just above my jeans.

"Good night," he whispers. "Sweet dreams. I'm praying for you, babe. I'll be thinking about you until I see you tomorrow."

My eyes are closed tightly. Feeling his breath on my lips as he whispers his good night, I drink in his words as a feeling of love swells inside me. Softly, I whisper, "Cole, I . . ." I pause. "Good night, Cole." I say instead, catching myself.

The Letter
27

Things are getting serious. Eyes on the prize------winning the NCA championship in Daytona. The choreographer returns to work with us on a new dance routine for the competition. We spend all day doing nothing but practicing the dance moves. Next Saturday will be our first full-out, then we'll finally move into the month of February.

When practice ends, Coach calls us into a huddle on the mat for announcements.

"Next Saturday is our last Saturday in January, and we plan to do a full-out, so we'll plan on a two-hour practice that day. We'll go back to an all-day practice on the first Saturday in February, then the final two Saturdays in February will also be all-day practices. Since Valentine's Day is on a Saturday this year, we will have a short one-hour practice that day as my gift to you." She smiles.

We silently applaud because we are all too tired to move.

"The dates for the showcase will be sent out in an email and posted in the GroupMe," Coach continues. "Look for those tomorrow. We'll do a showcase of the routine for the students, staff, and your family and friends. Then there will be a private showcase at the cheer gym for alumni. You'll want to make sure your parents and family members get the showcase dates as well as

140

the dates for the NCA championship in Daytona. The link and passwords to watch the championship live on the Varsity channel will also be included in the email. You'll want to give that info to anyone who won't be able to travel to Daytona Beach." She clasps her hands together and says we're dismissed.

As we're changing clothes and gathering our things in the locker room, KK says, "I'm so glad next Saturday is a regular two-hour practice. Maybe I can get my social life back." I laugh along with her.

"I feel ya. Maybe we can finally do that double date we were talking about before the holidays?" I give her a nudge and throw my backpack over my shoulder. She stuffs her cheer shoes into her bag and zips it closed.

"Yeah," I agree. "I saw where there's a dance on Valentine's. I think the SGA is putting it together, and there's going to be a band."

"Mmm. Maybe I'll get asked."

"Maybe we'll both get asked." KK smirks, as we walk out the door into the crisp, and cold, late January breeze.

When we get back to the dorm room, I text Mom to be on the look-out for the email from Coach with the information she gave us, hoping she'll be able to take a few days off work and come to see the showcase and maybe even go to Daytona for the competition.

The next morning KK and I ride to church with Cole and Jared in Jared's truck. I've started taking notes in a journal during the service, and it's really helping lesson my anger toward my dad or at least I'm not as focused on it anymore.

After church we go to a local barbecue place for lunch.

"Finally, on a double date," I announce once we're seated at a booth. The guys chuckle, and KK rolls her eyes at me.

"I'll take anytime I can get with this one," Cole says, leaning into me, and making me giggle.

"I'm up for a double date any time, myself." KK glances at Jared. "By the way, did you hear there's going to be a Valentine's dance?" KK asks, batting her eyelashes at him.

"Oh, when is that?" he asks.

"On Valentine's Day night." KK says, with an eye roll.

"I got you. I'm just kiddin' whit you, girl. I may have a little something up my sleeve. Jus' you wait." Jared gives KK a knowing look and a sexy smile to get her to relax. Cole and I look at each other and snicker. Cole gives me a sweet peck on the nose as our waiter arrives to take our orders.

When they drop us off at the dorm after lunch, Cole takes both my hands in his and intertwines his fingers with mine. I step closer to him so our noses almost touch.

"I'm coming to see you cheer at the basketball game tomorrow night," he says in a soft, sexy voice.

"I'll be looking for you then." I smile and move in closer, pulling him toward me. He wraps his strong arms around me as he leans down to kiss me. I drink in his kiss and give his lower lip a tug with my teeth. He lets out a soft moan then pulls away, shaking his head.

"You have no idea what you do to me, girl," he says, as he waves and turns to walk out the door.

Walking into our dorm room all smiles, I pop onto my bed and say, "Cole Collins is so freakin' hot I can barely stand it."

KK bursts out laughing and throws a pillow at me from across the room.

"Chill, girl. Keep your head in the game."

"I know. I have homework to finish tonight. He's coming to the basketball game tomorrow."

"Jared is, too." She waggles her eyebrows suggestively.

"I'm glad you guys are getting along. And I'm glad Cole and Jared are good friends too," I say, pulling out my desk chair to get a little homework finished.

The next evening KK and I are excited about cheering at the basketball game knowing that both Cole and Jared will be there. I'm glad our boyfriends are good friends.

As we warm up along the edge of the court, I see Cole, Jared, and a few more football players making their way through the crowds into the stands. When they get to their seats, I watch as Cole searches for me. Our eyes meet, and a grin breaks across his face as he waves. I wave back, and butterflies take flight from my stomach all the way up to my throat.

During halftime, our team moves out to center court to perform. When we make our way back to the edge of the court, Cole has made his way down to the gym floor. He walks over to me.

"Hey, you wanna hang out with Jared and KK after the game?" he asks.

"I'd love that," I say, smiling back at him before moving into place to begin the next cheer.

The game ends in a win with everyone converging on the players at center court. Soon, the students have flooded the arena floor with rowdy cheers and celebration. Cole finds me in the crowd, and we walk together toward the exit, stopping first to get my cheer backpack. Reaching down, he grabs it, slinging it over his shoulder, then takes my hand in his.

With plans to go to Pop's, we walk out of the gym to meet up with Jared and KK in the parking lot. We find them leaning against Jared's truck making out. Cole clears his throat to interrupt, and Jared opens the door to the back seat so we can squeeze inside. Playfully, the four of us laugh and cut up with each other. Jared turns up his stereo and gives us a disco show with the LED lighting he has inside his truck. The lights change colors, dancing with the beat of "Element" by Kendrick Lamar.

Later out of breath from laughing and dancing in the back seat, Cole takes my hand and helps me hop out of the truck. Walking into the pizzeria, I wave to my teammates as we make our way through the restaurant.

The guys grab a table across from where the rest of our team is sitting, and KK and I head into the bathroom. Walking back toward our table, I notice Cole's diamond earrings sparkling when the light catches them. Tonight, he's wearing tight black jeans and a football T-shirt with a thick gold chain around his neck. His arm muscles flex as he lifts his glass of water to his mouth. Uh, I know how I feel about him for real. The chemistry between us is off the chain. I'm in love, but I don't feel comfortable telling him, yet.

When we get back to campus, KK and Jared stay in his truck getting cozy while Cole walks with me to the dorm. Since I know KK will be a while, I ask Cole to come into my room with me. Walking inside, he takes it all in as he looks around.

143

"This is my bed." I walk over, plop down on it, and kick my shoes off. He glances briefly at the framed photos on my desk then looks admiringly at me. Reaching up, I take his hand and pull him on top of me. When he lands, his shirt rides up over his stomach, and I get a peek of his abs. My breathing quickens at the sight of his rippled six-pack----or maybe eight-pack. Yeah, probably eight-pack. I move to raise his shirt over his head, but he stops me.

"I want to, but we can't, Landry," he says as he moves my hands towards his back. I place them on his butt as he slowly kisses me.

"I want to. I really, really want to," I say, kissing him along his neck.

Just then the door flies open and KK bounces into the room. When she sees us, she stops mid-stride.

"Oh, my gosh. I am so sorry, you guys. I can go to the commons room and hang for a while."

"No, that's okay. I've got to go back and work on homework anyway," Cole says, standing.

"I'll walk with you to the door," I say, sitting up.

I get off the bed and take his hand in mine, leading him down the hall toward the commons room. When we get there, he walks over to the couch and sits, patting the spot next to him.

"I have something I want to give you." He reaches into the back pocket of his jeans and pulls out a red envelope with my name written on the front. "I wanted to write down some things that were important for me to tell you, and I thought with Valentine's being a week away, it would be kinda like a love letter." He gives me a shy smile as he hands me the envelope.

"Thank you. Should I read it now?"

"How about you read it later before you go to sleep." He pulls me toward his chest, and I lean in, looking up into his eyes.

"Okay," I say teasingly.

"I really do have homework to finish tonight. I better get going." He stands.

I take his hand and walk with him toward the entrance. When we stop, he leans down and kisses me. It's short and sweet, but he presses his forehead against mine and whispers my name. Goose bumps form on my arms.

"Good night," I whisper as he turns to walk through the door.

Back in the room, KK is apologetic about walking in on us.

"It's okay," I say, getting my PJ's and slippers out, ready to head to the shower.

"Well, if you ever need me to be away from the room, just let me know. I've heard some people put a sock on the door." She laughs, cracking herself up. I roll my eyes.

"That's probably just in the movies," I say. "I'm going to take a shower, goofball."

After toweling my hair dry, I pick up the red envelope off my desk and slip under the covers and click on the lamp by my bed. Opening the envelope, I find a cute Valentine's card with a hand-written note on a folded page torn from a notebook. I unfold it and begin reading.

Dear Landry,

I want you to know that you're not just another pretty girl that I'm dating. You're special to me. I do think you're beautiful, sexy too. The first time I saw you that day in the parking lot, I noticed your beautiful long hair and those amazing toned, long, tan legs of yours. The kind of legs that would stop traffic. Then when I saw you tumbling across the football field, I was like. . . whoa! This girl's got mad skills and I knew you had me. I'm more than glad we met. I love your smile and the way you laugh. I love that you didn't care that I was a star quarterback. I know things like that don't matter to you, and you're not about superficial things and status. I like that you are humble about your own talents and abilities, too.

I know how I feel about you, and I don't want to just have sex with you because we can or because I want to. I've done that in the past, a long time ago, and I didn't like how I felt afterward or how it changed the relationship. I prayed about it back then, and I feel that God wants the next time to be with the woman he has chosen to be my wife. I want to wait, and I know it's hard and that a lot of self-discipline and self-control has to be involved.

I can only be as strong as the girl I'm dating is. I don't want this to turn you off or upset you in any way. I hope this is something we can talk about and come to an agreement on. I don't want to lose you. I want our relationship to grow stronger because

I know I'm falling in love with you. Will you be my date to the Valentine's dance next Saturday?
Yours, Cole

I fold the letter, place it back inside the card, and hold it to my chest. He's falling in love with me too. He's poured his heart out to me in this letter and told me about some true, raw feelings. Personal things about what he's done in the past and how he wants this relationship to be better. He revealed his soul to me. It's like something out of a Jane Austen novel. I need to tell him about Jordan and me------what happened between us the night before I left. I need to be honest, too.

A smile falls across my lips as turn off the lamp. I lie down, pull the covers up to my chin, and fall asleep with the letter on my chest.

The Dance
28

Standing beside Jared, Cole watches me as I walk down the hall in my dorm to meet him. He's wearing a black suit, and white button-down shirt with a red polka dot bow tie. He has a shiny black dress shoe on his left foot, the other still has the boot.

KK and I went shopping earlier in the week and I found a white flowy dress. It's knee-length with sparkly rhinestones sewn onto the spaghetti straps. I borrowed Christa's silver glittery pumps and Gracie's silver rhinestone clutch. I've curled my hair and clipped one side up with a large pearl-embellished barrette, letting the rest hang down my back in loose curls.

Cole lets out a loud whistle when I get closer. KK follows behind me, and Jared hands her a single rose. Cole pulls a rose from behind his back and thrusts it in my direction as he steps closer to me.

"Will you accept this rose?" he asks.

"I will," I say, taking it from him.

Gracie and Christa have followed us out to take our pictures. They've decided not to go to the dance and instead are doing a "Galentine's event" with some other girls from our team at Coach McKaye's house. And they seem excited about the plans Coach has made------something about watching a movie starring Matthew McConaughey called *How to Lose a Guy in 10 Days*, baking cookies, cupcakes, and giving themselves homemade facials. Anyway, I think I'll have way more fun with Cole.

"Ya'll get close together." Gracie directs, taking my phone from me for the photo. She takes one of all four of us before we ask for couples' photos.

"You guys have fun tonight," Gracie says, waving to us as we walk out the door.

It's a short walk to the arena where the dance will take place. The night air is cool but not cold. I can tell spring is getting near. Daffodils are popping up in and around all the flower beds on campus, and the once-brown grass is green again.

The band is loud, but the music is good, and we dance for a while before taking a break to catch our breath and get something to drink. The event tonight is in two-parts. First, a one-hour concert and dance then a buffet dinner and short play put on by the theater students. The SGA has come up with a unique idea, combining a typical dance with dinner and a theatrical performance----with both the music and the play performed by Natchez students. Cole says he knows some of the guys in the band. One of them is in his biology class. He points him out as we're dancing.

When the band finishes their final song, a crew rushes in and sets up round tables and folding chairs. They quickly add plastic tablecloths and tea lights. In just a few short minutes, the dance area is filled with thirty tables. Jared and KK make their way over to us, and we grab a table with four chairs. When the line opens for the buffet along the far wall, we wander over to check out the food.

"Mmm, this smells amazing," KK says, lifting the lid on the chaffing dish filled with steak tips.

"They even have fried shrimp," I add.

With our plates filled and bottled water in hand, we make our way back to our seats. A few minutes later, a theater professor appears on stage and introduces the play. The lights dim and the curtains open. It's a short two-act play one of the theater students has written, set in the days just after World War II. It's a sweet love story about a young soldier who falls in love with a nurse after he's wounded in the war. The plot follows his later search for her and their reunion after the war ends. The curtains close, and the applause dies down. Cole asks if I'm ready to walk back. We say good night to Jared and KK, leaving them to their own romantic ending for the evening.

Just as we walk into the night air, Cole takes off his jacket and helps me slip it on over my dress.

"I was thinking we could go somewhere to talk for a while," he says, glancing at me.

"Yes, I'd like that."

"I know the gym is open. The basketball team had practice earlier, and one of my buddies is on the team. I asked if he could leave the rug in the door to catch it so it wouldn't close all the way before he left," Cole says, with a sexy smile.

"You are so funny. I love the way you plan things so we can be alone."

We wander over to the practice gym, and sure enough, one of the doors has a piece of the rug keeping it from closing all the way. After we slip inside, Cole takes my hand, and we walk to the gym floor. The only light is coming from the moon shining through the upper windows. A hint of moonlight glows brightly, forming a shimmering circle on the gym floor. All the bleachers are pushed in, and we sit with our backs against them. I reach down and take my shoes off, placing my feet across Cole's out-stretched legs.

"Coach is driving me to Dallas tomorrow afternoon. I have an early morning appointment with my doctor on Monday. I think I'll finally get the boot off," he says, gesturing at it with his hand. "I've only been able to do curls and to bench press at the gym for weeks now. It'll be good to be able to do leg lifts and squats. I need to get you to come to the gym and work out with me sometime when you don't have practice," he adds, running his fingers across my leg, stopping at the edge of my dress. When his hand stops, our eyes meet and we lean toward each other, lips softly touching before the kiss grows passionate.

He's such a good kisser. I melt into him, wrapping my arms around him as he places a hand at the back of my neck, pulling me closer. When our kisses slow, we stare, transfixed, into each other's eyes for a brief moment.

"I love you, Cole." It pops out of my mouth without any warning.

"I love you, Landry," he replies, cupping my cheek in his palm.

"The letter you wrote me was beautiful. I know I texted you after I read it, but I guess we should talk about what was in it." I pause for a beat and with my legs still draped over Cole's, I stare at my red painted toenails. "I had sex once. It was with Jordan. I don't really even know why I did it. At the time, I just thought I'd show him that I cared, you know. He never put pressure on me or anything. It was the night before I left to come here. I don't even know how I felt afterward. I was in love with him, or at least I knew I loved him. With you . . ." I stop speaking and gaze into his eyes. "With you, it's different. Everything feels different. I want to . . ." I take a deep breath, wondering how much I should say and a bit embarrassed to go further.

"I feel the same way. That's why I've tried to back off and take things slow with you. It's because of how you make me feel. It's different with you too. The feeling is more intense. And believe me, I want to. I just don't want to do something I don't feel is right. I pray about it a lot, asking God to give me the courage to be strong and wait and be respectful of you." He picks up my hand and brings it to his lips, kissing it gently.

"I'm new to the whole church thing, Cole. I kinda get what you are saying, and I want to understand, especially knowing how important it is for you to want to be intimate only with whoever your wife will be. I should try praying for clarity."

"My parents fell in love within a few weeks of meeting each other and got married a few months later. They didn't wait too long." He laughs. "Back in biblical times, people were getting married at, like, fifteen, and seventeen. That's crazy, but times were way different back then." We both laugh.

"Yeah, I cannot even imagine that. I remember my grandmother telling me about when she got married. She said she was twenty-four and was almost considered an old maid." I shake my head. "Now, for a lot of people, careers are more important. I'm not even supposed to be in college right now. That's another thing I haven't told you the whole story about." I lean back against his chest, and he puts his arms around my waist. "I stole some things from the local drug store the day we got out of school for Christmas break my junior year. Jordan and I had been running with a pretty wild crowd, and they dared me, and I did it. The group of girls I was with left me in the store. When I ran out after them, they were already in their car. I was caught and arrested, and I got kicked off my all-star team. But you know about all the good things that came out of all the bad stuff, and I am really thankful for second chances." I lean in pressing my nose into his neck. "Being here is helping me figure out who I really am and what's important to me." Looking up, I meet his eyes, and we stare at each other, fixated, before Cole breaks the silence.

"I'm really thankful for second chances too," he says, pulling me into a slow, intimate kiss that lasts several minutes, leaving me feeling woozy and very turned on. I sigh when we pull apart. Cole stands and helps me up off the floor.

"We should probably head back."

"I wonder what time it is." I open my clutch to check the time on my phone and notice a text that came in from Mom a few hours ago. *I forgot to tell you to check your mailbox I sent you something yesterday.* "There's a text from my mom telling me she mailed me something. Let's walk over to the mailboxes if you don't mind." I reach down to slip on my heels before we walk out of the gym.

Cole is careful to make sure the rug is back in its normal position when we scoot through the door. We walk hand in hand across campus to the student mailboxes. I punch the code on mine, and the tiny door pops open. There's one envelope inside, and I slide it out.

"Do you need to check your box while we're here?" I ask.

"Nah, I'm not expecting anything."

Stopping at the entrance to my dorm, Cole, kisses my hand and whispers, "Good night, my sweet valentine."

Smiling at him, I say, "I love you."

He steps closer, leans down, and says, "I love you."

I slip off his jacket and hand it to him, then he turns to walk across the parking lot toward his dorm. I watch him for a minute before I walk inside and down the hall to my room.

KK's not back yet. I set the long-stemmed rose and my bag on my desk and pick up the envelope. I slide my finger under the flap to pop it open. Inside is a letter, but it's not from my mother. Instead, it's from my dad.

The Response
29

I drop down onto my bed to read what he's written to me. My eyes are filled with tears. I strain and blink, trying to read the words on the page.

Dear Landry,

I know I don't deserve or expect your forgiveness. I hurt you and your mom very badly and acted selfishly. I am sorry for hurting you and your mother. I understand if that's hard for you to believe. I also understand why you don't want to see me. I feel it necessary to ask for your forgiveness and tell you why I'm asking for it now ------but wishing I had asked for it sooner. I also wish I had tried to keep in touch with you over the years instead of letting almost eight years go by without a word.

You know that I was married to the woman I left your mom for. And you know about our son, Todd. He will turn seven in April. His mother was diagnosed with breast cancer when he was four, and she had a full mastectomy and was on chemo for a year. The cancer returned after six months, and she was back on chemo again. She fought bravely for two years until it reached her brain. She was in a lot of pain and she died from an overdose of pain medication. She had made a video for me and one for Todd a few months before she died, and I watched those a few weeks after her funeral.

Basically, her message for me was that I should find you and restore our relationship, because time is so short. She also wanted Todd to know his sister and grow up with a family. So I returned home to Louisiana to work with my brother at the family seafood market. I also came back to apologize to your mother and to you in hopes of re-connecting and restoring our relationship as much as I could.

I want you to meet Todd. He's a great kid. He's smart and funny. He's sad now since his mom died, and his personality has changed.

I don't take what I did lightly. I know how wrong it was. Before Paula died, we had been attending a church in Seattle. She wanted Todd to be raised to have faith in God. She found God before she died, and I know she's with him now. It's a comfort for me to believe that. If you can find it in your heart to let me apologize in person and introduce you to your brother, it would mean more to me than you could ever know. I know I don't deserve a second chance, but I felt the need to ask.

I love you, Dad

I fold the letter in half and let it drop to the floor. I fall face down onto my bed and cry my eyes out. I don't even hear KK when she walks into the room and places a hand on my shoulder, asking me what's wrong. After she gets my attention, I sit up and show her the letter from my dad. After she reads it, she sits next to me and puts her arms around me.

"Oh, Landry. I think you should write him back. He wants to see you so badly. I haven't seen or heard from my mother since I was two years old. My dad is re-married and has a new family. I've only been able to find peace in my heart recently from praying. I've asked God to help me forgive those I would never be able to forgive otherwise."

I nod but don't say anything. I just silently cry and lay my head back on my pillow. She moves off my bed, goes to my dresser, and pulls out a T-shirt for me to slip on. I slip out of my new dress, letting it fall to the floor, slip the T-shirt on, and crawl back under the covers.

The next morning, KK tries to wake me up to go to church with her and the other girls. I mumble something then lie back down. I think about running across the street to find Cole in his dorm so I can fall into his strong arms and let him hold me. But he's going to Dallas with his coach today since he has an early morning

153

appointment tomorrow. I should get up and go with the girls, but I don't feel like moving.

KK leaves with Gracie and Christa and says she'll pick up some lunch for me on their way home from church.

"Thanks," I mumble and fall back under the covers.

When she gets back, she sets a McDonald's bag on my desk and offers me the drink she brought.

"I got you a chocolate milkshake too."

Sitting up, I take it from her.

"If you need me for anything, I'm always here to talk," she says.

"I've been thinking about what you said last night. Maybe I will write my dad back. It won't hurt to pour my feelings into a letter and mail it back to him." I move to the dresser and pull out my practice clothes. "I wonder if my mom knows he wrote me?" I shrug and zip my cheer bag closed. "I suppose she's the one who gave him my address. It looks like the letter was written several weeks ago. It might have been in my mailbox for a while. My mom texted me yesterday to remind me that she sent something for Valentine's Day. That's the reason I went to my mailbox on the way back to the dorm last night. I thought the letter was from her." I grab a chicken nugget and pop some fries into my mouth. Then I pick up my milkshake and my cheer bag, ready to head to practice.

On the way to practice, KK is chatting about her date with Jared last night, telling me how much fun they had with us and how much she likes Jared's sense of humor. I'm barely listening, but occasionally I respond. As we're walking into the locker room to put our stuff down, a text from Cole pops up on my phone.

Hey, I'm on my way to Dallas. Miss u. Since I'll miss class. I'll need to get some work done at the library when I get back tomorrow. Want to meet me there after your practice ends?

Yes.

Awesome. I'll text u on my way home tomorrow. He sends a kissy face emoji. I send back a smiley face, but there's nothing smiley about me today.

When we get back from practice, I sit at my desk and pull out the journal I've been using to take notes at church for the last few Sundays. I read through the pages, gathering inspiration while deciding what to say to my dad. I pick up a pen and pause, staring at the blank page before me. How do I start? Do I start with Dear . . .? What do I call him? He hasn't even been in my life for eight years. Do I know this person anymore? I guess he is still my dad, no matter how I feel. It might be weird if I wrote, 'Dear Mr. Woods, thank you for your kind letter.' I chuckle, remembering the last Jane Austen movie I watched. I thought it was funny how the people in the movie used Mr. and Mrs. in their everyday speech. Oh, well, here goes . . . something.

Dad,

I don't really know how to respond to your letter. I've felt hate for you for so many years. I've pushed down any and all feelings I had for you over the years and tried to forget you. It was the only way I could move on with my life. I was happy, mostly. I may have done things to cover up the pain,----drinking, smoking, just trying to be numb.

When I got a second chance to start over at Natchez College, my life changed for the better. I've made some real friends here. I feel like my teammates are friends for life. I've even started going to the church where my coach and her family go. Some of my teammates also attend. I have a new boyfriend, too. His name is Cole. He's the quarterback for the Natchez College Chiefs football team.

Your letter made me cry, but it also made me think about things. Since I've been going to church, I've learned about forgiving people who've hurt you. It may not be about trusting them again, because trust has to be earned, but I've learned that forgiveness is a free gift, and because God wipes our slates clean, he expects us to forgive those who've done us wrong too. I'm trying to learn how to do that with a lot of prayer right now. I may even be open to seeing you and meeting my brother at some point. Not sure when.

Landry

I tear the pages from my journal and fold them in half then open my desk drawer and take out one of the stamped envelopes Mom left with me when I moved in. I remember thinking, *I'll never use these.* I slide the paper inside. I copy his address from the envelope containing my dad's letter then lick and seal the envelope.

Reaching for my coat, I stick my letter inside the pocket and walk across campus to the mail drop.

On my walk back to my dorm, I say a silent prayer. *Okay, God. I wrote my dad a letter and I mailed it. It's a start, I guess. Please help me to know what you want me to do from here.*

Bae's Birthday
30

My scans went well. I'm all healed up and out of the boot. I'll be back on campus at 3. Meet at the library after ur practice is over?

Cole's text pops up on my phone as I'm walking out of my last class for the day. Then a text from Mom pops up. *Did you get the Valentine's card I sent?*

Sry Mom. I forgot to text u back. I got distracted. I did check my box the other night and it hadn't come yet. But I did find a letter from Dad. I opened it, thinking at first it was a letter from you. I read it and it was a very long apology letter. I wrote him back. I guess you had given him my address.

After mom's reminder, I wander over to the student center and punch in the code for my mailbox. The door pops open, and there's a card inside. Checking the envelope, I see it's definitely from Mom. Sliding my finger under the seal, the envelope pops open. Inside is a Valentine's card and a twenty-dollar bill.

I just got the card and the money. Thx. A few minutes later she sends a reply.

Your dad asked me for your address on Christmas after you ran out of the house. I guess he decided to write to you since he didn't get to talk to you while you were home. I'm glad you read his letter. I hope you can eventually find the ability to forgive him. I love you!

Love you too, Mom. Then I reply to Cole's text.

Can't wait to see u.

Later, when practice ends, KK and I meander into the locker room to change.

"Cole's back from Dallas," I tell her. "I'm meeting him at the library." I pull a T-shirt over my head.

She nods. "That's great. See you back at the dorm later."

Flinging my bag over my shoulder, I make my way out of the gym and over to the library. Cole's sitting alone at a table next to the book stacks. Weaving my way through the rows of books, I come up behind him and stop. Pressing a shoulder into a bookshelf, I watch him, as I bite my lower lip. All the emotions I've been feeling over the past two days have lodged in my throat, and the tight lump of emotion chokes me. Closing my eyes, I take a few deep breaths, which calm me enough to whisper his name.

"Cole."

He turns around. When he sees me, he stands and walks over. I lean my back into the books as he places a gentle, soft kiss on my lips. My arms reach for him, pulling him toward me. Burying my face in his strong chest, I breathe in his scent.

He kisses the top of my head.

"Landry, you okay?"

I shake my head but don't say anything. Instead, I slide down onto the floor and sit with my back against the shelves.

Cole sits next to me and reaches for my hand.

"Talk to me, babe."

As I look up at him, his eyes search mine, and a look of concern moves across his face.

"The other night when I got the letter from my mailbox, it wasn't from my mom," I say. "It was from my dad. He wrote me a long letter asking me to forgive him. He wants to introduce me to my brother." I stare at my feet then turn and hide my face in Cole's neck as he puts his arms around me. He holds me for several minutes as I catch my breath.

"I wrote him back and told him that I was angry with him, that I even felt hate toward him. I told him I was happy here. I mentioned you and my teammates and about going to church. I said that I'm learning about forgiveness and that maybe at some point I would see him--------but not sure when."

Cole kisses the side of my face.

"Landry, that's an answered prayer." He's smiling at me, and we stare into each other's eyes for a beat. Then, I put a hand around his neck and pull him in for a long, slow kiss.

"Thank you," I whisper, looking into his soft brown eyes. "My feelings toward my dad may be changing. Your support means a lot."

He offers his hand and helps me stand.

We move to the table and sit. I pull out my homework, and we chat and laugh while studying. His presence gives me strength. I feel it when I'm close to him. It's the reassurance I needed. I feel safe with him, loved, and even cherished. There's uncertainty about where things are going with my dad, but I feel a change within me. I'm not always confident in my decisions or choices ----the past is proof of that. Becoming who I want to be and holding myself accountable are my goals for the future.

Later that evening, back in my dorm room, everything is quiet. Wondering where my roommate is, I set my bookbag on my desk just as KK walks in carrying a bowl of ice cream.

"Where did you get that?"

"Christa and Gracie went to the store. They just got home. There's some left. I don't think it will fit in their tiny freezer. Go get you some."

I mosey down the hall to Gracie and Christa's room and knock on their door. Christa answers with a spoon in her mouth and a bowl in her hand.

"Hey, want some ice cream?" she asks, spinning around. She points to a container sitting on top of their fridge.

I pick up a paper bowl from the desk and scoop up some ice cream.

"Have a seat," Gracie says, making room on her bed for me.

"Where were you tonight? We went down to y'alls room before we left for the store," Christa says.

"I was at the library with Cole doing homework. He got his boot off today," I say, smiling.

"That's awesome. You are so lucky that Cole Collins fell for you," Christa says, with a dreamy look on her face.
I laugh. "Yeah. I know, girl. I know. His birthday is less than a week away. He'll be nineteen. He gave me such an *amazing*

surprise back in November on *my* birthday. I want to do something cool for him, but I don't have a clue. I need help thinking of something." I set the ice cream bowl on Gracie's desk. "I know I want to create a playlist of my favorite songs to give him. He made that special playlist for me on my birthday."

"Yeah, I remember you telling us about it. It was so romantic and really thoughtful. Do you have anything else in mind that you want to do?" Christa asks.

"I don't know. It's hard for me to think of things like that. I want it to be really thoughtful and special. His birthday is on a home basketball game day, though, so it would have to be something we do after the game, of course." I shoot the girls a frustrated look.

"You could surprise him with a cake," Gracie suggests.

"Um. What? Am I supposed to whip that out of my backpack after the game?" I crack up laughing. Gracie and Christa laugh so hard they snort.

"I know," Christa says, her eyes growing wide. "What if we talk Paul into letting us into the training room at the cheer gym? He's got the keys. We could set everything up in there before practice. No one would be in there after practice ends. Everyone would be at the game. We could put up the decorations and leave the cake on the table." She stands up and walks over to me. Her smile is radiant. She nods at me, trying to get me excited about her idea.

"I love it," Gracie adds.

"It does sound like a good idea. We'll need to go shopping next week and get some balloons, cake mix, ingredients, and some plates," I say, looking from Gracie back to Christa.

*****

The following week, the girls and I go shopping at Target to buy supplies to decorate the training room at the cheer gym for Cole's birthday. We buy a box of cake mix, icing, eggs, and a small bottle of vegetable oil, making sure we have the ingredients listed on the box. I plan on making the cake in the commons-room kitchen tomorrow night. The day after is Cole's birthday and the last day of February. Wow! This month really flew by.

The next evening, after finishing my homework, I gather the cake mix and ingredients then wander into the kitchen next to the commons room, ready to bake a birthday cake. After making the cake, I set both pans on a placemat to cool, leaving a note beside them that says, "DO NOT TOUCH," hoping people will keep their sticky hands off. I set a twenty-minute alarm on my phone, thinking that should be long enough for the cake to cool. In the meantime, I get out the birthday card I bought for Cole and begin writing a note to him on the inside. When the alarm beeps on my phone, I place the card inside the envelope, and write his name on the outside and wander down to check on the cooling cake.

Tapping the cake gently, I check to see if it feels cool to the touch. It does, so I peel back the lid on the chocolate icing and stick the butter knife inside, scooping up some icing and spreading it across the center of one of the layers. Gently lifting the other layer from the pan, I place it on top of the iced center and smooth chocolate icing along the sides adding sprinkles to the top. I unwrap the candles shaped like a number one and a number nine from the package, and center them carefully on my creation before wrapping plastic wrap around the plated cake. Gingerly, I slide my hands under the plate, lifting it from the bottom. I tap on the door to my room, hoping KK will hear me.

"Wow, that looks amazing, Landry," she says, opening the door.

I place my plastic-wrapped masterpiece on my desk and stand there for a minute, admiring my handiwork then I pull out my phone and take a pic.

"This is the first cake I've made by myself."

"I know Cole is going to love it."

"I hope so. I'll send a quick text to Paul, reminding him about the plan to meet us in the training room an hour before practice so we can set up."

When I wake up the next morning, I text Cole '*HaPpY BiRtHdAy*' and add confetti and balloon emojis. He responds with *I love you* and a heart emoji. My day is starting off great, and I know it will end on a high too.

Paul is waiting on us in the training room when we arrive at the cheer gym. We quickly and quietly move into the room. I set the cake down on a table. Then I open a bag of balloons, and we begin blowing them up. Paul helps us tape up streamers on the ceiling and around the room. We hang the balloons upside down from the streamers. Then we blow up more balloons and leave them scattered all over the floor. I carefully unwrap the plastic wrap from around the cake and set the lighter and the plates, forks, and napkins next to it. After taking out the birthday card, and placing it beside the cake, I step back and look around at the scene.

Clapping my hands and feeling thrilled with the surprise I've created, I give my friends a thumbs-up. "It looks great in here. Thanks, guys."

Paul hands me the keys and shows me which one opens the main door to the gym. He tells me the code to punch in for the alarm, and says he'll leave the training-room door unlocked. Reeling from excitement, I give Paul a quick thank you, hug then bounce over to the mat to begin practice with my team.

Practice is only an hour tonight since it's a basketball game day. After changing into our uniforms, the girls and I walk giddily over to the main arena for the game. On the way to the gym, I send Cole a text. *I have a surprise for you after the game. Meet me at the cheer gym.*

As soon as the buzzer sounds, signaling the end of the game, I give KK a glance. She's supposed to distract Cole for a few minutes while I sneak off to the cheer gym. As planned, she walks over and snags his attention, giving me the opportunity to sprint across campus.

Arriving at the gym door, I unlock it then dart over to the wall and punch in the alarm code. As soon as it says, "Unarmed," I run into the training room and grab a pack of colored sticky notes, quickly writing messages on the pages. The first one says, *Hi Cole.* On the second I write *follow me. . .* the next one says. . . *Keep going,* then. . ., *you're getting closer.* The notes lead all the way into the training room, where I'll be waiting with the lights off. As soon as he's near the door, I'm going to pop out and kiss him.

My foot taps nervously while I wait, then I hear Cole come in. I know he sees the notes because he starts laughing, and it sounds like he's getting closer to the hall leading to the training room. When he gets almost to the doorway, I pop out, grab him, and pull him inside, pushing him up against the wall as I press a firm kiss on his lips. Slowly, he moves his arms around my waist, pulling me closer. As I drink in his kiss, my tongue slowly moves with his. When I pull away, I whisper, "Happy birthday."

I reach over and flip on the light. Cole's face lights up when he sees the balloons and the streamers hanging around the room. He looks down and sees the balloons covering the floor.

"I made you a birthday cake," I say, walking over to show it to him.

"It's perfect, Landry. I can't believe you did all of this." Happiness glows on his face.

"I had some help. But I made the cake all by myself."

Flicking the lighter and touching it to light the candles, I announce, "Make a wish." Picking up the plate, I lift it into the air then slowly bring it down in front of him.

He leans down, closes his eyes, and blows out the candles. I set the plate down and open the box of plastic utensils. "What did you wish for?"

"If I tell you, it might not come true. And I really want it to come true," he says, leaning down and kissing me. "I love you."

Breathless, I whisper, "I love you too." I pull away and take out a plastic knife to cut the cake. I place a piece on a birthday-themed plate for Cole.

"Mmmm. This is good," he says as he takes a bite. "I love chocolate." He picks me up and sets me on top of the training table.

After we feed each other cake, I reach for my phone and pull up the Spotify playlist I made for him.

"I made a playlist for you of all my favorite songs. I titled it 'Favorites for Cole.' The first song says, 'Happy birthday to you' in the lyrics. It's kinda funky, and it's from the eighties. I used to listen to my mom's old CDs when I was little. She would play them sometimes when she was cleaning house. It's by a group called Duran Duran, and the song is "Come Undone."

"Cool. I've heard of that group. My mom and dad must be about the same age as your mom. My mom may even have that same CD." He laughs.

I hop off the table, flip off the light, and pull him close as we dance to the playlist playing softly on my phone. The second song is "Dissolve" by Absofacto. When "Pony" by Ginuwine comes on, I pull away from our slow dance and start grooving to the song.

"No. Stop. Uh, uh." Cole is laughing but shaking his head at me. "Hand me your phone, girl. I'm gonna need a cold shower after this if you don't stop. You already make me crazy."

I realize the way I was dancing was a little sexy, and the song is way sexy too. I hit pause on the music.

"Sorry."

"It's all good. But watching you dance to that song, is like, *whoa*. A man can only take so much." He's smiling at me, so I know he's not mad. "I love that you put your favorite songs on a playlist just for me. And I promise I will listen to all of them, but later. It means a lot to me that you set all of this up and even made me a birthday cake." He reaches for my hand and pulls me close, leaning down and touching his nose to mine.

I giggle. "Even if it's in a tiny training room inside the cheer gym."

"That's what makes it so perfect." He gently kisses my lips, parting mine with his tongue.

"You're perfect," I whisper.

"Same, girl. Same. There's nothing better than this-----right here, right now."

"Don't forget I also got you a card. I want you to read it later once you're back at the dorm."

"As you wish," he says, kissing me again.

Photo Shoots & Showcases
31

Big wigs from Rebel Athletic are on campus today to do a photo shoot promo for their catalog and social media accounts. Coach also wants photos to promote the showcase we're performing this weekend. Since it's showcase weekend, I'll get to see Mom. The cheer gym is a buzz with photographers and directors waiting on us to get started. We're in the locker room putting our uniforms on when my phone rings.

"Hey, Mom," I answer.

"Hi, hon. Aunt Jackie and I are looking forward to seeing you this weekend. I needed to call you to let you know your dad called and asked about coming to see you. Would it be okay if he and Todd came, too?"

I'm frozen listening to her voice then there's only silence. I don't know how to answer.

"Landry, are you still there?"

"Yeah, Mom. I'm here. I guess it's okay. I don't really want him to hang around with us. I don't want this to be, like, we all go out for a family dinner one night and I introduce him to my boyfriend. I might say hello to him and hi to Todd after the showcase. But please make sure he doesn't expect anything more than that."

"I'll let him know. They'll drive up separately. Bye, hon. Have a good rest of your day."

"Thanks, Mom."

I walk to the mirror to check my hair and makeup. I tease my hair and add my sparkly bow. Then I pull out my lip gloss and dab the shiny red onto my lips, making them look fuller than they are. I can hear Coach in the background telling everyone to hurry and move into our places for the photos. I set my lip gloss next to my phone and notice a text from Cole. I pick it up to read it really quick.

I've been wanting to see you all day. I could hardly sleep last night after reading the birthday card you gave me. I love what you wrote. When can I see you?

Tonight. I'm at a photo shoot then we have a three-hour practice. Text ltr. Love u.

I set my phone inside my bag and run out of the locker room to find everyone but me in position for the photo. I give Coach an 'I'm-sorry-face' then ask where they want me to stand. After the photo shoot, the Rebel marketing director passes out all-new practice wear and new shoes for the whole team. After changing out of our competition uniforms and into our new practice unis, we gear up for our three-hour practice.

Once it's over, I plead playfully with the others. "Someone scrape me off this mat. I'm dead." I fall back on the mat and stare at the gym ceiling. When no one answers me, I start looking around. "Seriously, you guys are making a Tik Tok right now?"

"Come on, Law. Get up we're all going to Pop's." Jaz leaves the Tik Tok group and hovers over me.

"Not moving," I say, looking up at him. He reaches down and grabs my hand and pulls me into a sitting position.

"You are part of this team. NCFFU. Am I right? Come on, girl." He reaches under my arms and picks me up and carries me a few feet before he lets go.

"Landry, you comin'?" KK asks, stopping at the gym door with her bag already in hand.

"Be right there." I grab my stuff, throw on my jacket, and quickly get into the back seat of Gracie's car with KK.

On the way to the restaurant, I pull out my phone and suddenly remember I told Cole I'd see him after practice.

"Shhhhhh . . ." I cover my mouth, not wanting to cuss out loud. "Grrrrrrr" I growl instead. I start to text Cole when KK interrupts.

"What's wrong?"

"I totally forgot I was supposed to meet up with Cole after practice. He texted me, like, five hours ago and asked to see me. Something about how he really wanted to see me and he couldn't sleep last night after he read what I'd written on his birthday card. Ugh. I suck."

"Text him now and just let him know something came up with the team. He'll understand. What did you write on his card? Was it steamy?" KK asks, giving me a look.

Christa turns around from the passenger seat. Her eyes are wide, and she has a huge smile on her face. "Was it juicy?" She cups a hand to her ear, waiting, like I'm going to spill some hot tea.

"Do you remember what you wrote?" KK asks.

"I wrote it all out in a notebook first, then I wrote it inside the card. I have the notebook with me in my backpack. It's just stuff that I like about Cole. Nothing that you guys would be interested in."

"I'm interested in whatever it was that kept him from sleeping last night. Probably, something like, . . . 'I want to lick you all over like the icing off this chocolate birthday cake.' If he were my BF, I'd have a hard time keeping my hands out of his pants," Christa says, then bursts out laughing.

"Christa, shut up!" I punch the seat in front of me.

"JK," she says, glancing back at me.

"You don't need to share it with us." KK looks sympathetic.

"Here's the page I wrote it on," I say, pulling the notebook from my bag. "It's really just stuff that I've noticed." I clear my throat and begin reading. "Cole. . ., I love to listen to you play guitar and sing. Your smile is radiant. I love your dimples. You totally had me the first time I saw those dimples and every day after that. I love how positive you are. Even when things don't go your way, you give off positive vibes and can light up a room so fast. I love how strong you are. Not just your physical strength, which is obvious and very sexy, BTW, but you're strong emotionally too. I love how I feel when I'm in your arms, like nothing could ever hurt me. I feel loved and cherished with you. I am totally and completely, madly in love with you."

No one says anything. We've already pulled into the parking lot, and the girls are silent. Then I hear a sniffle coming from the front seat. Gracie and Christa turn around and face me at the same time. They both look teary-eyed. KK reaches out and hugs me.

"I'm so happy for you," she says, releasing me from the hug.

"Oh. My. God. Landry. Nicholas Sparks vibe, much?" Christa says, her tone drips with sarcasm.

"He sounds like one in a million. Hang on to him," Gracie says, getting out of the car.

"He definitely is," I say while stuffing the notebook back into my backpack.

"If I can be serious, though, I'm really sorry, Landry." Christa says as she steps out of the car. "I didn't mean the things I said about Cole. I was just joking. The love letter you wrote to him is, like, the sweetest thing I think I've ever heard in my life." Christa looks solemn.

As I slide out of the backseat, I glance at Christa but don't reply, instead I press Cole's number to see if he'll answer.

"Hey, babe. How did practice go?" He asks.

"It was long. The team wanted to go to Pop's after practice tonight. I'm sorry. Maybe we can meet up in the morning and see each other before class?"

"I really want to see you tonight. Even if it's just for a few minutes. When you get back to the dorm, just text me. I'll come out and meet you in the parking lot. I love you."

"Okay. Bye, I love you, too."

When we get back to the dorm, it's raining. I'm sure Cole will just want to see me later, and I don't really want to be out in the rain. But I promised him I'd text him when I got back. He answers my text quickly and says he'll be right out. The girls run into the dorm, and I give my bags to Christa and KK to carry inside for me. I'm standing next to Gracie's car with my jacket up over my head scrolling through my Instagram when Cole pops up next to me. He's grinning like a Cheshire cat and he's dripping wet.

"Hey," he says.

"Hey. Maybe we should go in . . ." Before I can finish my sentence, his mouth is on mine, his hands cupped beneath my chin. And suddenly I don't care that I'm standing in the rain. I move my jacket from off my head, stick my phone inside the pocket, and let the jacket fall to my feet. Throwing my arms around Cole's waist, I pull him in tight. When the kiss slows and we pull away, he searches my face, and his eyes pierce mine. I watch as the raindrops slide down his face and one hangs on the end of his nose.

"You. You are my person, Landry Ann Woods," he says.

"You *are* my person, Cole Jay Collins." My cheeks burst with a smile, and we both laugh. We can't take our eyes off each other. I'm sure we'd look ridiculous to anyone who might see us standing in the middle of the parking lot in a rainstorm without umbrellas, staring into each other's eyes, completely oblivious to the rain.

"The words you wrote on the birthday card you gave me last night. . . no one has ever said those things to me before. Not like that. I love you. I *love* you." He picks me up and twirls me then puts me back down.

"No one has ever made me feel the way you make me feel." I lean in and press my face into his chest. A car horn honks, and I'm shaken from my dazed state.

"We should probably get out of this rain," I say.

"We probably should, but I don't want to. But I don't want you to get sick either. I know you've got a long week of extra-long practices ahead, and it's only Monday."

"Yeah. I should go in," I say, keeping my eyes on Cole's face, and those dimples. I reach up and kiss him on the cheek then turn and run toward my dorm.

He watches me go inside before he jogs to his dorm.

When I get back to my room, KK's in bed, with the lights off. I tiptoe around the room, gathering a towel for my hair and quickly change into PJ's. As I crawl under the covers, my phone dings with a text from Cole. *I miss you already.*

*****

The day before our first showcase, we are all on edge as we start the third full-out for today's practice. I hope after this one, Coach will feel confident enough to let us go. When we end the routine, she sets down the iPad she used to film us. She looks around at us, and smiles, then she starts to clap.

"You guys are ready for the showcase tomorrow," she tells us. "Plan on being here at one-thirty for a run through and warm-up.

After everyone is in full makeup and uniform, we will walk together, partnered up, to the arena as if we were walking into a competition. After the showcase, you will be able to hang around and speak to your family and friends. Rebel Athletics will also have a photo station set up for fan photos afterward. We'll have the same schedule on Saturday but, of course, the alumni showcase will be here in the cheer gym. Ya'll are dismissed."

The next morning I'm a bundle of nerves when I wake up. I have a hard time focusing on what's going on in class. But when I get a text from Cole, my nerves vanish.

Can you meet me after class at the cafeteria for a quick bite?

Yes. But I'll only have 20 minutes before I have to get ready to go to the cheer gym for warm-ups.

I grab a salad and a fruit punch and find Cole sitting at a table with a large plate full of food and I scoot in next to him.

"Someone's hungry," I say, with a laugh.

"Wow, that's all you're going to have?" he asks, looking at my salad.

"I can't eat too much before a performance. Just a few bites. It's really easier to perform on an almost empty stomach. Lots of sugar and lots of caffeine work best," I say, grinning.

"I can't wait to see the performance this afternoon. I'm sure it's going to be amazing."

"I hope we pull off a good show with no drops, no busts, and no mistakes." He gives my hand a squeeze and leans in giving me a sweet kiss on the cheek.

"It will be great. You'll be great."

My phone chimes with a text from KK. *Are you coming back to the room or did you take all your stuff with you this morning?*

I have everything with me. I'll see you at the cheer gym in a few minutes. I'm eating a quick bite with Cole.

Once we've stretched out, the flyers warm up with backflips to cupies, then we gather in a circle, arm in arm, at the center of the mat. Someone starts off the chant very quietly. "We can." It gets louder as we go through the words of our pre-performance chant with our arms around one another and our heads bowed. "We will." Together, we continue as the chant grows even louder. "We can, we must, we will." After we've repeated it over and over about twelve times, Jaz screams, "Welcome to the ring of fire!" We repeat it after him. "The ring of fire!"

Partnered up and hand in hand, we walk in a line across campus to the main arena. When we walk through the doors, Coach Zack stops us in the hall and hands us each a candy-filled Pixy Stix straw. I tear open the top, tilt my head back, and let the sugary powder fall sweetly onto my tongue. Coach Zack gathers our empty wrappers, and we form a circle with our heads bowed and our hands clasped together. He says a quick prayer and some words of encouragement.

We can hear the roar of the crowd as they watch the opening performance by the band and the Chiefs mascot, who's in full headdress with a flaming steel ring of fire in his hand. He runs round the arena floor with it above his head doing a war dance. He performs this same routine opener before each of our home basketball games. Usually, it's all done with the lights off, but it's only three thirty in the afternoon, so this time it's less dramatic.

The adrenaline rush I feel right before a performance is like nothing else, I've ever felt. It's scary and exciting. I'm pumped up, feeling like a rock-star, and ready to take the mat.

We move out of our circle and partner up again as we get ready to run to the edge of the mat and take our places. They've set up the smoke machines for us, just as they do for the basketball players when they enter the arena for home games. When the smoke machines start going off, we take off, running into the arena. We stop along the edge of the mat, facing the seats usually designated for fans of the home team. Unfortunately, the audience on the other side of the arena will be looking at our backs during most of the routine.

We wave to the crowd with energetic smiles then take our opening positions on the mat. The music begins, and we hit our first stunts. The level-7 basket tosses go off without a hitch, and our tumble passes are clean. When we get to the pyramid portion, of the showcase, there's a slight bobble on KK's side, but she manages to reposition herself and correct it. When the routine ends, a deafening explosion of applause and screams erupts. We embrace each other, filled with joy that we've just completed the first showcase of our competition routine for the NCA championship in Daytona.

The Introduction

32

When the cheering dies down, Coach asks us to move into the foyer, where Rebel Athletics has set up a photo station for fans wanting to get pictures with us. As we're taking photos with locals and kids from near-by cheer gyms, I see my family near the entrance. My mom, my aunt, and I guess my little brother, Todd, are standing around chatting. Then my dad takes Todd's hand and they move into the line for souvenirs and candy. My mom catches my eye and waves. After the last picture is taken, I slide out of the photo area and make my way to Mom and Aunt Jackie.

"That was incredible," my aunt says. "I'm so glad I was able to see your competition routine. I filmed it all on my phone. I'll show it to Uncle Joe and the boys when we get home tomorrow." She says, touching me on the arm.

"Your dad and Todd sat with us," Mom says, watching me cautiously. "I watched your dad out of the corner of my eye during the performance. He was crying during most of it but trying really hard not to let it show. I think Todd was awe-struck by the whole thing, maybe even more so by the Indian Chief with a flaming ring of fire." She laughs. "They went to see what kind of souvenirs your dad could buy for Todd." Mom looks in the direction of the pop-up shop across the way.

Cole and Jarred walk up to us from behind. Cole gently places a hand around my waist, startling me. I jump. When I realize it's him, a huge smile breaks across my face.

"Guys, this is Cole, my boyfriend, and his friend, Jared," I say, gesturing to them.

Cole and Jared reach over to shake hands with Mom and Aunt Jackie.

"It's very nice to meet you both," Cole says. "I'm glad you could come to see the showcase today. She did a great job, as always." He gives me a grin, taking my hand in his.

I lean my head on his shoulder.

KK wanders over to say hi, and Jared gives her a hug. Then as we chat some more, I hear a youthful voice, "There she is, Dad."

Todd runs toward us with a plush Indian mascot in one hand and a tomahawk in the other. My dad in tow, is carrying what looks like a shopping bag full of T-shirts. Todd looks tall, considering he's only six. He has the same color hair I have, mousy brown (or had before I lightened it over Christmas break.) He stops in front of me and looks up. "Hi. You're Landry, my big sister."

I bend down to his eye level and hold out my hand. His eyes, like mine, are light brown with flecks of amber and green. When he smiles at me and shakes my hand, I notice he's missing one of his front teeth.

"You must be Todd. I've heard a lot about you," I say. "I'm glad you came to see me today. It looks like you have some cool things there." I point to what he's holding.

"Yeah. The Indian was cool. He was dancing with a fire ring. But I liked your team. It looked like the girls were flying into the air. When they did the splits and then the back flip in the air, it was cool."

We all laugh at the excitement bubbling out of this little boy with the cute voice and slight lisp. Cole offers his hand to my dad and introduces himself. This whole thing feels awkward, and I guess I should have been the one to say said hi to my dad. But I'm glad Cole took the initiative, because I don't even know if I would have acknowledged my dad standing there. They shake hands politely. Todd starts telling dad he's hungry, and we all shuffle nervously.

"I'd like to go back to my dorm room and change clothes before going anywhere," I say in a rush.

Nervously, my dad says, "We don't have to join you. I don't want to infringe on any plans you have. Todd and I drove up separately."

Mom butts in. "We haven't made any plans with Landry yet. What would you like to do, dear?"

Everyone's eyes seem to land on me, and I glance at Cole.

Jared says he and KK are going to head out, and they wander off. The rest of us are left looking at each other and down at the floor.

Finally, I say, "There's a casual barbecue place in town. We can all go there after I change. Maybe we could meet you guys there?"

That seems to break the tension. Mom and Aunt Jackie look pleased. My dad looks a bit relieved and Todd asks, "Can we go now?" He tugs his dad's sleeve.

Mom asks the name of the place and says they'll see us there. Then I walk hand in hand across campus to my dorm with Cole.

"I don't have to go with you guys," he says. "I don't want to encroach on family time."

"I want you to be with me. I feel more comfortable when you're around. I haven't been near my dad in almost eight years, and I need you there for support. Please go with me. I think they were kinda expecting you to go anyway." I say, with a bit of pleading, giving Cole my best puppy-dog eyes impression.

When we walk into the dorm, I ask Cole to wait in the commons room.

"I'll change really quick," I say, jogging down the hall toward my room.

Arriving at the restaurant, Cole parks his truck near the entrance. He quickly jumps out and runs over to open my door for me. He takes my hand and helps me step down out of his jacked-up truck. Walking into the restaurant, we can see our group near the back, chatting casually with each other. We wander over and take the two seats they left for us near the end of the table.

"I like the old rustic look of this place. It looks like it's been here since the fifties," Aunt Jackie says, looking around at the dollar bills stapled to the ceiling, walls, and support beams. One wall is filled with framed photos of past football players and cheerleaders from Natchez College.

174

"Have you eaten here before?" she asks.

I nod. "I believe it probably has been around that long. It's owned by a local family in town."

Our waitress arrives and asks Cole and me what we'd like to drink. Then she wants to know if everyone is ready to order. Once everyone has placed their orders, she leaves, and quiet descends around the table. Todd is busy coloring on his kids' menu and is oblivious to the awkward silence.

"Cole, tell us about yourself. Landry has told us that you are the starting quarterback this year," Mom says, giving Cole a pleased smile.

"Yes, ma'am. I'm glad I earned the position. There was a sophomore in line for it as well."

"Landry tells us you come from a football family," Aunt Jackie adds.

"That's right. A family of four boys." He laughs. "We all played football in high school, and we all received scholarships to play in college, but my oldest brother has had the longest football career so far." He pauses and glances at me, and we share a smile. "Chris, my oldest brother, plays for the Atlanta Falcons."

Dad looks impressed. "What position does he play?"

"Running back," Cole says, looking in Dad's direction.

"We'll be interested in watching more football next season now that we know who to look for," Mom says. Everyone chuckles.

"Well, not everyone in my family is big on football. My dad had to learn it after he had four sons." Cole grins. "He's more of a soccer guy. He's originally from the island of Trinidad." He takes a sip from his water. My mom and aunt ooh and aah at the mention of the tropical island. Cole sets his glass down and continues.

"My dad is a pastor at a church in Tyler, Texas, which is just a little over an hour north of here. My mom and dad met when she was doing mission work at my dad's home church in Trinidad her senior year in college. They ended up getting married, and my dad started seminary at a college near Fort Worth called Trinity Valley. It's the same college my mom was attending when she went on the mission trip. She grew up near Fort Worth in Grand Prairie, Texas. After they were married, my dad got a job at a church nearby.

Then he was asked to be the lead pastor at the church in Tyler. He's been there since my oldest brother was born."

A few moments later, our food arrives, and everyone focuses on the meal. Mom and Aunt Jackie update me on the latest happenings in Lacombe, including an election for mayor and other bits of town politics.

Dad asks about the classes I've taken this year and I tell him about my math and English courses as well as my interest in both sports marketing and sports medicine. It's the first time I think I've actually spoken directly to him since I've been in his presence.

When dinner is over and we begin our walk out to the parking lot, my dad stops me, taps me on the shoulder, and gets my attention. I turn around and look at him.

"Landry, can I speak to you for just a moment?" he asks.

I nod then glance at Cole, who gives me a reassuring smile. Aunt Jackie gets Todd's attention and points to a bird sitting on a branch in a tree. The group moves in the direction of the tree and I can hear Cole laughing and high fiving with Todd.

"I'm glad I was able to come and see your performance and meet your boyfriend. Thank you for allowing Todd to have the chance to see you. He's known about you all along. I had a few photos of you at the house back in Seattle. You've never been a secret to him. It means a lot that he was able to meet you. He asks about you often." His eyes move from my face to the ground. He pauses a beat then continues. His voice is filled with emotion as he tries to choke out the rest of what he wants to say.

"I'm so sorry, Landry. I'm sorry for everything. I'm sorry for the hurt I caused your mom and the way I've hurt you. I'm just so, so sorry." He's sobbing now, and I'm not sure what to do. I reach over and put a hand on his shoulder.

"I may not understand it," I begin. "And it still hurts me a lot. But I want to forgive you. It's something I've been praying about a lot lately. I do think I can get to a place where I feel I can forgive you and give you another chance."

He leans toward me and puts his arms around me, and we embrace.

"Thank you," he says, blinking away tears.

When we walk over to where Mom and Aunt Jackie are, I don't see Cole or Todd. Then suddenly Cole comes running around the corner with Todd up on his shoulders. Todd is laughing, and Cole looks like he's having fun. Mom whispers into my ear, "Cole is a really great guy. And I can tell he loves you."

I smile and blush. Her comment warms my heart. "I love him, too, Mom," I say, softly.

Cole takes Todd off his shoulders and sets him down. Then my half-brother runs to me and wraps his arms around my legs, squeezing them tightly.

I bend down and embrace him.

"I'm glad you came to my showcase. I hope you had fun. Maybe I'll see you again soon." I give him a peck on the cheek.

He looks up at me, smiling, then wanders over to his dad and takes his hand.

My dad waves goodbye and opens the car door so Todd can climb into his car seat in the back. After he's buckled in, Dad gets into the driver's seat. We watch as they back out. Todd waves at us as they drive away. *That's my brother.* I bite my lower lip, holding my emotions in, and fighting back tears as a painful lump forms in my throat. *And my dad is back in my life,---but for how long?*

Spring Is in the Air
33

We have two more weeks of practice before we leave for Daytona. We're counting down the days. It's T-minus fourteen days before NCA Nationals.

Logan sprained his ankle on a tumbling pass yesterday. We think he's going to be able to come back and join us for the competition, but in the meantime, we're using one of our back-ups in his position. He's been sitting with his leg propped up on a chair at the edge of the mat, cheering us on as we practice.

Coach announces that practice is over and gathers us in a huddle for announcements.

"We have two all-day-practice Saturdays left. I know we've been practicing long hours. I'm going to let you guys out early on Friday. We'll have a short one-hour practice so you can have the night off."

Applause breaks out. Happily, I hop off the mat and rush to gather my bags from the locker room. I snatch my phone from my backpack and quickly text Cole the good news. *I have a short practice on Friday. So pumped.*

By the time I get back to the dorm, he's texted me back. *Awesome. There's a luau event on Friday at the lake. Campus Club is putting it on. It starts at 7:00. Want to go with?*

Yes, babe. Of course. Sounds fun. What do we wear to a luau?

Anything you want. I'm wearing a swimsuit and a tropical shirt. I think I have a couple of leis in my closet. I'll bring those too.

Cool. I'll see you tomorrow afternoon before tutoring. I add a kiss emoji.

I set my phone on my desk and toss my bags onto my bed. Then I kick off my shoes and stretch out on my bed, getting comfy as my head settles on the pillows. KK opens her closet and starts changing out of her practice wear.

"Hey, KK, did you hear about the luau on Friday night at the lake? Cole just invited me to go with him. Do you want to see if Jared and Gracie and Christa want to go too?"

"I think I saw a flyer about it posted on the announcement board. It sounds like it would be fun. Are you going to wear a bikini? I only have one. We could go shopping before practice tomorrow."

"I can't. I've gotta save the rest of my money for Daytona. Also, I have to meet with Paul for tutoring before practice tomorrow anyway. I've still got the bikini I wore to the pool parties back at the beginning of the year. I think I'll wear the top from that and cut-off shorts. I'll go down to Christa's room and see if she and Gracie want to go with us on Friday. Be right back."

I knock on their door, and Christa answers with "Come in. We're naked."

Christa cracks me up. She has an odd sense of humor, and she's a total goof. Wearing a T-shirt and Nike Pros, she's lying on her bed, working on homework. Gracie's talking to someone on the phone about an upcoming photo shoot for Varsity.

"There's a luau event at the lake on Friday night," I say. "I'm going with Cole, and KK's going to ask Jared. Do you guys want to go too?"

"Sounds fun. Can we bring other people with us?" Christa, asks.

"Yeah, I think so, as long as they are students at Natchez. It's sponsored by Campus Club. Why? Are you going to bring the baseball player I saw you eating lunch with today?" I ask in a teasing tone.

"Maybe. Nosy much? How do you know I was having lunch with a baseball player?"

"Come on, Christa. You've made your way through almost every team on campus. You briefly dated a football player during football season. Then you were flirting with that basketball player last month. Now that it's baseball season, you've been talking to the pitcher."

She smirks at me and rolls her eyes. Then she goes back to writing in her notebook.

"Not all of us are as lucky as you have been, you know. You found your perfect guy. Maybe I'm still searching for mine," she says quietly, almost in a whisper.

When Gracie gets off the phone, she goes over to her desk and pulls out a chair for me.

"Here. Have a seat and stay a while."

"You have another photo shoot coming up?" I ask, sitting down.

"It's the day after we arrive in Daytona. It's at eight in the morning. Gross." She sticks out her tongue. "They want me and Brodi to do a shoot on the beach for the cover of their new catalog."

"That's cool."

"I guess. Sometimes I get sick of all the fuss. But my parents expect it. They think it's good for my career," she says, rolling her eyes and putting finger quotes around the last four words.

"I just came down to see if you guys wanted to come to the luau on Friday night. It's at the lake and starts at seven. It's sponsored by Campus Club."

Gracie picks up her calendar off her desk and reads it aloud.

"Let's see. It's Monday night. Nothing on Tuesday. Test on Wednesday." She slides her finger all the way across and says, "Works for me. I'll ask some of the guys from the team. Brodi, Jaz, and Donte may want to dress in hula skirts."

The three of us burst into laughter.

*****

The weather on Friday night turns out to be perfect--------only a slight breeze and the evening feels warm as the days get longer with the approach of spring. Cole and I walk along the lake toward the dock, where the luau party is just getting started. There's a stage set up on the floating dock, and people are gathering near it, laying down blankets and towels in the grass along the water's edge. Cole pulls a towel out of his bag and spreads it on the ground, and we sit. He reaches into the bag again and pulls out his ukulele. He leans over and gives me a quick kiss on the cheek, then he bounces onto the dock. I grin at him and clap softly, excited to hear him play and sing again.

The sun is setting along the horizon, and tiki lights are being lit by students as they stroll up and down the shoreline. KK and Jared plop their blanket down next to ours, and I point to Cole, who's sitting on a barstool, about to begin his performance.

When he begins to strum, people settle in to listen. His tone is slow and bluesy as he sings "At Last," which was made famous by the incredible Etta James. Cole's eyes find mine as he sings. KK nudges me, and I'm grinning so big I might burst. After he ends that song, he starts in on a new one with an upbeat tempo. "Yours is the heart that is beating inside us," he sings. "Yours is the kingdom, forever you reign." Then he shouts, "Hands up!"

Everyone around me stands, and I join in, hands pumping the air, bouncing to the beat and singing the praise song loudly into the night air.

When Cole finishes the song, he asks us to bow our heads with him as he prays a short prayer. When he's done, he introduces the Campus Club leader then makes his way from the floating dock to me. As he sits next to me, he reaches for my hand. I intertwine my fingers in his, feeling so much love. I'm so very proud of my boyfriend. I lean my head on his shoulder then turn my eyes to the speaker. Everyone gathered around us is listening with their eyes fixed on the stage.

"So, here's this man who completely ignores most religious protocol," the speaker says. "He claims to have the authority to forgive sin, and he was very comfortable with unrepentant sinners. And he was hated by the Pharisees, who saw themselves as the keepers of the holy law. They asked him why the heck he'd want to hang out with sinners and tax collectors and why he was touching people with leprosy." He laughs. "Reasonable question, right? So, he's asked the question, but do you remember what his response was? Sometimes we may even use the phrase today." He pauses a beat then looks out into the crowd gathered along the shoreline. "He said, 'It's not the healthy that need a doctor but the sick. I have not called the righteous, but the sinners.' The Pharisees were so busy finding fault in him for healing people on the Sabbath and eating with sinners that they couldn't see the forest for the trees, so to speak." He opens his Bible.

"In Mark, chapter eight, Jesus asks, 'Who do you say that I am?' To this, Peter answers, 'The Messiah, the son of the living God.' He closes the Bible and places it on the stool next to where he's standing. "Let me ask you . . ., who do you say that he is? What is your relationship like with God? What do you believe? We'll pick up here next Wednesday evening at our regular time and location. We've got some fun stuff planned for you guys tonight. There are fruit kebabs, mini key lime pies, water, and soda on the far table. And now I think it's time for a little limbo." He wiggles his hips then breaks into a cha-cha. "Let the festivities begin."

Caribbean music begins playing from giant speakers that are set up behind us. People pop up off their blankets and towels to join the line that has begun to form. Cole and I quickly move in that direction. I can see Brodi, Gracie, and Jaz dancing to the limbo beat as they cheer on Donte, who's squatting and leaning back as he makes his way under the limbo stick. By the time it's our turn, the stick is only a few feet off the ground. Cole makes it through, and I follow, almost falling over as I ease under the stick. Cole takes my hand and helps me stand up straight.

"You want to get something to eat?" he asks.

"Sure."

We glide to the food table and fill our plates with sliced watermelon, fruit kebabs, and key lime pie. Once we're situated on the blanket with plates in hand, I look at Cole with a serious expression on my face. "Do you know how awesome I think you are?"

He grins, shly. "I think you may have mentioned it. I think you are pretty great too." He gently rubs his hand over my knee.

"I'm serious, Cole. You make me a better person. I've grown so much in so many ways since meeting you." Shifting my eyes away from him, I laugh, thinking about how I must sound. "It's corny to say, but you complete me. I don't think I could ever not want you in my life." He looks at me.

Our eyes fixed on each other. He lifts my hand to his lips, kissing it gently.

"I'm not going anywhere, babe."

Later, hand and hand, we walk toward the field where Cole parked his truck. He opens the passenger door for me to slide in. So many drivers are trying to leave at the same time, that it's caused a long line to form along the dirt road that leads us to the highway and back to campus.

"I think I know another way back to the main road." Cole looks back over his shoulder as he backs out slowly, hoping to squeeze through the mass of jumbled cars pushing their way toward the road.

We exit the field along a dirt path and follow it until we see an embankment and a bridge. But it looks like the hill up to the bridge is blocked. There are huge rocks covering the path. Possibly the rocks were washed downhill from the last hard rain. Cole looks over at me and gives a reassuring smile.

"Don't worry. I have four-wheel drive."

He brakes then shifts gears, and the truck slowly but surely makes its rumbling way over the stones. The truck rocks back and forth as it churns up the embankment to the top. Bracing myself, I place one hand on the dashboard and the other on Cole's leg. He smiles at me, showing those to-die-for dimples, and I relax. Once we make it across the bridge, I let out a sigh of relief. Cole shifts out of four-wheel-drive and back into regular gear.

Laughing, I release my grip on the dashboard. "That felt like something out of one of those truck commercials."

Cole lightly pounds the dashboard. "Ford F-150, gotta love it."

Just a short drive down the dirt road takes us back to the main highway toward campus.

As we're driving along, we hear a pop, then the truck begins to swerve. "Shit," Cole says under his breath as he works to get the truck under control. He slows and we pull to the side of the road.

"I think I blew a tire." He hops out and rushes to the back of the truck. I get out and follow.

"Yeah. I must have gotten something in the tire when we came over those rocks or over the rickety bridge, but I have a spare."

Cole moves to open the door to the backseat of his truck and gathers some tools from under the seats. Then he crawls under the truck bed to loosen the spare. Following along beside him, I use my phone flashlight to help him see. After he pulls the spare tire out, he pauses, running a hand across my cheek.

"I'm sorry about this, Landry. I was trying to avoid sitting in a line of traffic for thirty minutes. I know changing a tire on the side of the road late at night is not the best ending for a date."

He looks crestfallen. I give him a reassuring smile then lean in and kiss his cheek.

"I wish I could be of some help. But I've never changed a tire before, and I don't even own a car."

"It's not that hard." He gently tugs my hand and we squat next to the back right tire. He explains how to use the jack and how it raises the truck enough to remove the old tire. Then he shows me the tool he will use to remove the tire and replace it with his new one. Once the new tire is on and Cole carefully lowers the jack, he tosses the old tire into the bed of the truck. He gathers his tools and goes about placing them back under the back seat. I hop back into the passenger seat just as blue lights flash behind us. I glance at Cole, who was just about to hop in.

"He showed up a little too late to help," I say with a grin. Cole glances my way but doesn't return the smile. Now the officer is walking toward Cole, shining his flashlight.

"Good evening, officer. I just flixed a flat. My girlfriend and I are heading back to campus. We're students at Natchez."

The cop flashes his light into Cole's face then toward me in the passenger seat.

"Let's see some identification------driver's license and college IDs," the officer says, still shining his flashlight in Cole's direction. "It's a little late to be out. Where are you two coming from anyway?" he asks, taking Cole's ID from him.

"We were at the Campus Club luau. There was a lot of traffic leaving and we left from a back road. I must have gotten something caught in my tire when we left. It blew out right as we hit the highway heading back toward campus."

The officer ignores Cole's last statement and looks to me for my ID. Then he walks back to his car, but before he gets in, he tells Cole to put both hands on the back of his truck and to stand with his legs spread. The officer watches Cole carefully then slides into his car and goes about putting the information from our IDs into the system. I think this whole thing seems really strange. We were just changing a flat tire. I thought the officer stopped to see if he could lend a hand. A minute later he gets out of his squad car and hands Cole his driver's license and school ID.

"You guys have a safe night." The cop gives me my school ID then tips his hat. Once in the car, he speeds past us.

"Cole, don't you think that was really weird? I thought he was going to see if we needed any help," I say, looking miffed.

Cole slowly moves the truck back onto the highway before speaking.

"It's not weird for me. Stuff like that happens to people like me. Black men are stopped by the cops all the time for no reason. I'm sure once he looked up who we were and called it into the station, someone told him who I was. Being an athlete helps my situation. My parents had a tough time of it when they were first married. People were always looking at them strangely. That was thirty years ago. You'd think things would have gotten a lot better by now, but not much has changed." He glances at me with sad eyes. I move closer and place my left hand on his leg as he drives.

"After my dad got the job at the church in Tyler, they would find beer cans and dog shit on their front stoop. One time they even had a rock thrown through their front window in the middle of the night. They had to install cameras, although they never pressed any charges against the people who did any of it."

The truck rolls into the parking lot and we pull into a spot in front of Cole's dorm. Unbuckling my seatbelt, I move next to him, leaning my head on his shoulder. He turns to face me.

"My mom and dad did a lot of volunteer work in their community, and my dad's congregation grew. Things got a little better for them but not a hundred percent. When my older brothers started playing football and showing talent, things really changed, especially when my oldest brother led our team in rushing stats and touchdowns, taking us all the way to state, where we won that year. After that we were destined to play football. It's a good thing we had talent."

Cole lets out a short laugh then takes my hand in his, bringing it to his lips.

185

"It doesn't seem fair but that's how it is. I'm the star quarterback and I've been able to gain respect by playing a game I love. But in the long run, I want to show other kids like me that you can make it to the NFL with talent while also maintaining a reputation for being a good person, a Christian, and someone that kids can look up to. My parents taught us it's not just talent but who you are as a person that really matters in the long run."

His eyes meet mine. My heart aches at what he's just shared. I want to shout his praises from the rooftops. Still focused on his eyes, I try to give him some encouragement.

"It's my wish that one day everyone will be able to see exactly what an amazing person you are. I really want that for you. Fairness, equality, courtesy, and respect. No one should be treated differently just because of the color of their skin," I say, bringing my face close to his, our lips almost touching.

"Me too, babe. That's my wish too," he says as his lips close on mine in a tender kiss.

Daytona Beach
34

"I'm going to be thinking about you the whole time you're gone, babe," Cole says, nuzzling my neck. We're holed up on the third floor of the library the night before the team leaves for Daytona. I have to finish two assignments and get them turned in since I'll miss a few days of school.

"I wish you could come," I say, feeling disheartened.

"You know there's a slight possibility I will be able to make it out there, maybe not in time for your performance but maybe before you come home," he says, trying to be cheerful.

"It just depends on what time Coach ends practice on Friday. Since you guys perform both days, don't rule it out just yet. I may surprise you. I'm glad your family is able to come out and see you."

"I know my mom has taken off a lot from work this year, but she hasn't taken a vacation in years, so it's good for her. And it makes me happy that they'll be there. Even my dad. Ugh. I've got to get this assignment finished, so we can do something else tonight."

"Oh, what else are we doing tonight?"

"This. Lots and lots of this," I say, pulling his face to mine and giving him a sexy kiss. Then I plant three more quick kisses on him before I turn my attention back to my assignment.

The next morning, my phone alarm goes off at the crack of dawn. KK and I begin moving about the room in a zombie state as we list everything, we're supposed to take with us. "Did you pack two pairs of cheer shoes and two bows?" I ask.

"Yes. Got that. Did you pack a phone charger?" she asks.

"Yep." Looking down at the bags I'm about to take, I mumble a list to myself. "Okay, socks, uniform, dress for dinner out, T-shirts, warm-ups, practice clothes, swimsuit, makeup, hairspray, toothbrush. I think I'm ready," I say, picking up my duffel and my cheer backpack.

KK, Gracie, Christa, and I file out of the dorm with our backpacks on and our duffel bags in hand to meet up with our coaches and teammates at the cheer gym. The sun is starting to rise, lightening the sky in a pink hue as we walk along half-asleep, I'm half-listening to music, with one earbud in, while also listening to birds chirp as the day awakes.

A charter bus is waiting at the entrance of the cheer gym when we arrive. Walking into the gym, we find our teammates gathered around our coaches, who are passing out plane tickets and boarding passes along with last-minute instructions. With tickets and schedules in hand, we load onto the bus for our two-hour drive to the airport.

Later on the plane, I send a quick text to Cole and one to Mom. Once the plane is in the air, I fall asleep then wake to KK shaking my arm, telling me that we are about to land. Once we're off the plane, I pop into the bathroom. While waiting in line I read and respond to my texts from Cole. After we have all exited the bathroom, Coach leads us to the bus that will take us to our hotel. By the time we get there it's almost four p.m. and I'm exhausted, it's been a long travel day. When the girls and I get checked into our room, I fall face-down onto the bed.

"What time do we need to be ready?" I ask, my voice muffled.

"We need to walk to the convention center and pick up our badges and bags by no later than seven tonight," Gracie answers.

"Great. It's nap time." I crawl under the covers, set the alarm on my phone, and drift off to sleep.

When my phone beeps me awake, I switch it to off and quietly sit up, trying not to disturb KK, who's sleeping next to me, and

Gracie and Christa, who are also still asleep. I tiptoe around the room, using the restroom, brushing my hair, and checking my phone messages. Gracie wakes up and asks what time it is.

"It's five after. We have at least forty-five minutes to get over to the convention center to pick up our stuff."

She nudges Christa. "Come on, Christa, wake up." she whispers.

I walk over to KK and tap her shoulder to wake her. Once everyone is back among the living, we head out of our hotel and over to the convention center to pick up our competition badges, our free backpacks, makeup, and other freebies that Varsity has for us.

"Someone text Coach and let her know the four of us have picked up our stuff," KK says, throwing her new bag of swag across her back.

"What do you guys want to do now?" I ask.

"Text the rest of the team in the GroupMe and see what everyone else is doing. I'm hungry and I'd like to go eat now," KK says.

"Jaz, Donte, and some of the other guys are at the Crab Shack. That's on the beach. It's not too far away. We can walk down the beach to get to it," Christa informs us.

"According to the replies in the GroupMe, it looks like some of our team is on their way here to pick up their badges and those that already have, are planning to stay at the hotel," Gracie adds.

"Are ya'll up for hanging with the guys at the Crab Shack for dinner?" I ask.

"I'm down," KK says.

"Yep," Christa responds.

"Sounds good to me," Gracie chimes in.

When we get closer to the Crab Shack, we can see that the guys are down on the beach kicking a soccer ball around. We wave and yell their names, and Jaz looks up, and waves. As he does, the soccer ball goes past him toward the water's edge. Donte chases after it. Brodi, Logan, and Mark are screaming, "Don't let the ball touch the water!" The four of us freeze, watching in horror to see if they can get to the ball before it touches the water. It's one of our team's weird and crazy superstitions: none of us are to go in or touch the ocean until we've hopefully won the national championship. I know the boys know this; Jaz was the one who mentioned it to me as we were boarding the airplane. I feel like I'm watching in slow motion as Donte and Jaz run toward the ball. Jaz scoops it up just before a wave comes up, almost touching it. He lifts the ball above his head, signaling victory.

"I saved it!" we hear him scream.

Everyone breaks into applause. The girls and I run over, meeting the guys in the sand.

"That was a close one," Christa says, while fist bumping Jaz.

"What are you guys doing playing soccer on the beach? I thought you were saving us a table at the Crab Shack," I ask, wondering what the deal is.

"We were just waiting until they paged us. When you guys texted us, we went back to the hostess and told her to make it a party of nine. I think that made the wait a little longer. We bought the soccer ball in their gift store," Donte says, laughing.

"Well, you guys just about gave us a heart attack. It looked like Jaz was heading straight for the water," I say with a hand over my heart.

"Nothing to worry about. I got the ball just in the nick of time. No water touched me or the ball. We are all good," Jaz says confidently.

"We should emphasize to the other new team members about not going into the water until after we win," Gracie suggests.

We look at one another and nod in agreement as we hear Donte's phone buzz.

"Our table's ready, guys," he says.

Once we're seated with menus in hand, we discuss the schedule for the week.

"Breakfast at our hotel ends at ten a.m. I heard Coach say that when she handed out room keys," Gracie says, setting her menu down.

"We have practice tomorrow through Thursday in ballroom C. And our team dinner is at five-thirty tomorrow night," Christa adds.

"Who else has our schedule memorized?" Jaz laughs.

"Like, the most important part would be, what time do we compete on Friday and Saturday? And what do we get to do on Wednesday and Thursday nights since we'll be done with practice by one and we won't have a team dinner to go to?" Brodi asks in his most sassy tone.

"My family will be in town on Thursday and I'm planning to go out with them Thursday night," I add, glancing at Brodi.

"My family will be in on Wednesday, so I may be with them Wednesday and Thursday night," Gracie says.

"Same," Christa adds.

"My grandparents are going to watch both days of competition by streaming the Varsity channel. I gave them my code," KK says.

"Just stay out of the water," Logan says, high fiving Jaz, Donte, and Brodi

"Stay out of the water? Has there been a shark attack?" our waitress asks when she walks up to take our order. We all burst out laughing.

When we regain our composure, Jaz shakes his head and explains.

"We're competing at the NCA college cheerleading championship on Friday and Saturday. We can't touch the water in the ocean until we've won the championship. Then we all run into the ocean with the trophy."

She nods and smiles at us. "Awesome. Best of luck to you guys. Are you ready to order?" We nod, as she begins writing down our selections.

"While we're eating, Jaz asks, "So, does anyone remember our times for Friday and Saturday?"

"On Friday we're supposed to meet Coach outside of ballroom C. She posted a pic of the schedule on the GroupMe. We warm up in ballroom C, then we ride the tram to holding. We take the mat at three forty-five. On Saturday, the schedule is similar. I took a screen shot of the schedule," I say, munching on my fries. "The awards are at six-thirty Saturday night."

Jaz and Donte nod in my direction, acknowledging my comments. Then Jaz asks, "Is Cole coming?"

I glance at Jaz and give a shrug, finish chewing then take a sip of my tea and set my glass down.

"I'm not really sure. He said he might be able to come. It all depends if the football coach lets them out of practice early enough on Friday for him to catch a flight. I'm not going to worry about it. I don't really expect him to fly all the way to Daytona Beach from Texas just to see me compete. I gave him the Varsity code to stream the competition live. I know he's rooting for us even if he can't be here in person. I think Coach said the school is planning to show the competition on a big screen in the aux gym both days, so anyone who wants to can watch it live."

The guys give me a sympathetic look. KK puts her arm around my shoulder and gives it a squeeze.

"It'll be fine it he's not able to come. We know the entire school will be rooting for us and sending positive vibes from home," I say with an upbeat tone.

"We got you, girl," Jaz says, reaching for my hand across the table.

"You guys are my family," I say, lifting my glass in a toast.

We tap our glasses together in a toast, and in unison say, "To the ring of fire."

The Championship
35

Our plane just landed. We'll get to our hotel at 3:30. Will you be available to go out to dinner with us? Mom's text comes through just as we're wrapping up practice for the day. After reading her text, I toss my phone into my bag while reaching in for my hotel key card. Then I make my way to the hotel room to change. KK, the rest of the girls, and I plan to hang at the pool and sunbathe for a few hours today. We hung at the pool for a while yesterday, and I got a little bit of sun. I'm glad. I hate spray tanning. The smell is weird, and I can never get it to look right on my hands or around my toes.

Walking into the room, I set my bag on the bed, and retrieve my phone to text Mom back.

Can't wait to see you guys. Text me what time I should meet you. I add a smile emoji.

We can pick you up at your hotel at 6:00. We're staying at Tropical Winds. We have a rental car. It's me, Aunt Jackie, your dad, and Todd. Today is Todd's birthday so we are planning to celebrate that at dinner.

After I change into my suit, KK and I make our way to the pool to meet up with the girls. After getting comfy in my chair, I text Mom back. *Your hotel is not far from us. We're at Grand Seas. I could walk down the beach and meet you somewhere.* I check the time on my phone then set a timer to wake me if I fall asleep.

I glance at KK, who's thumbing through the *People* magazine she bought at the airport.

"I'm going out to dinner with my family tonight. Mom will text me after they get to their hotel and let me know where they want to go."

"Okay. I'm just planning to hang by the pool for a while."

"I was going to ask if you wanted to go with me."

"I don't know. Do you think I should? It's your family. Your dad came, right?"

"Yeah, but I don't think anyone would mind."

"Do you feel you need backup? I know you had Cole with you the last time you were with your dad."

I tilt my head. "I guess. I don't know. Maybe I should go by myself, but in a way, it still feels a bit awkward."

"I'll go if you want me to." She fist bumps me.

I smile at KK. She knows me too well. I lean my head back in my lounge chair and drift into a nap while the warm Florida sun kisses my skin. After my phone alarm goes off, KK and I make our way back up to our room to get ready for dinner with my family.

"Where did they make plans to go tonight?" KK asks while turning off the blow-dryer.

"They picked a place called Landshark. They wanted to go to a casual place on the beach," I say, slipping on my sandals and buckling them.

KK and I head out and down the beach toward the Landshark restaurant.

"I think I see it up ahead," KK says, pointing.

"Yeah. I think that's it with the bright yellow Adirondack chairs facing the ocean."

As we get closer, I can see my dad and Todd throwing a frisbee back and forth. Todd sees us, and runs toward me, with the frisbee in his hand.

"Hey, Landry," he says, smiling up at me. "I remember you, but I forgot your name," he says, pointing at KK.

"Hi, Todd. I'm KK, Landry's roommate and cheer teammate." She rumples Todd's hair.

"Cool frisbee. Can I try?" I ask. He hands it over. "Step back a few more feet," I say, "and I'll toss it to you."

"The guy in the restaurant gave it to me because I told him it was my birthday," he says, jogging backward.

I fling the frisbee in Todd's direction, but it goes a little over his head, and my dad steps up behind him and catches it.

"Hi, girls," he says. "We were just hanging out here on the beach for a while, waiting on our table to be ready. Your mom and Aunt Jackie were more interested in shopping at the restaurant's gift store. She said she'd text when our table is available."

"Come on, Dad. Throw it again," Todd says, jumping up and down. He doesn't have any shoes on. But my dad is still wearing his tennis shoes in the sand. KK and I sit in the Landshark-themed Adirondack chairs and watch as they toss the frisbee a few more times.

Then Dad announces, "Our table is ready. Todd, go get your shoes. You left them next to that chair." He points just to the left of me.

Todd runs over and sticks his bare feet into his tennis shoes, wriggling his feet around until the shoes are on. KK and I stand and follow them up the deck stairs and into the restaurant, where we have a corner window table. A balloon bouquet and a stuffed shark grace the center of the table.

"Wow. Look, Dad," Todd says, picking up the tiny shark from the table, and holding it up in the air. "This restaurant is so cool." He plops down in his seat, grinning.

Dad gives my mom and aunt a look as if to ask . . . *Did you have anything to do with the party centerpiece?*

Mom and Aunt Jackie glance at each other and shrug. *Busted.* I think my mom likes playing second mom to Todd. I know she must feel bad he lost his mom at such a young age, although I haven't spoken to her about it. She's the one who's back in the same town with them, more involved in their lives than I am. I guess it's good for Todd-----and maybe even good for my dad to have someone familiar around who can offer help and give them some support.

"Happy birthday, Todd. I almost forgot to tell you. You turned seven today, right?" I ask.

He nods. "Tell me all the cool stuff you got for your birthday," I say. "I already know about the shark and the frisbee." I laugh.

"This morning before we had to leave for the airport, Dad went and picked up Dunkin Donuts. I got to eat two chocolate donuts with sprinkles for breakfast, and Dad gave me three birthday presents that I opened before we left." He holds three fingers up. "He told me that I could bring one of them with me if I wanted to."

"Oh, cool. Which one did you bring with you?" I ask.

"I brought the Nerf football. Dad said we could play with it on the beach. We did that today after we got to the hotel. Our hotel is on the beach."

Our waiter arrives and says, "Someone's having a birthday. Let me guess which one it is." He looks around then points to Todd, who nods frantically like he's waiting on another surprise to pop out.

"Great," the waiter says. "I'll bring the treasure box over and let you pick something out. First, let me take your drink orders."

When he returns with our drinks, he brings along another waiter, who is carrying a small treasure chest. He lifts the lid and holds it out in front of Todd, who chooses a Hot Wheels car. Dad nudges him to say thank you. He does, and the waiter closes the lid, wishing Todd a happy birthday before he walks over to another table where some kids are waiting.

During dinner I try to keep the conversation light and friendly. I still feel a bit awkward around my dad, but I'm trying really hard to let go of old hurts and raw feelings from my past.

"How's Grandma?" I ask.

"I took her to the doctor yesterday morning before I went to work. They changed her blood pressure meds, but everything else looked good. Uncle Joe and the boys are staying with her until we get back home late Saturday night," Mom says.

"Is your family in town to watch the competition?" she asks KK.

"My grandparents have a large farm in Oklahoma, and they can't be away too long. They're going to watch it live on the Varsity channel on their computer."

"We'll be leaving on Saturday night for the airport," Mom says. "It was the easiest way to get a really cheap flight. We'll end up missing the awards ceremony, but we will be able to see both performances live and up close," she smiles.

After dinner, a huge piece of chocolate cake arrives with a candle on top and two scoops of ice cream on the side. As our waiter goes to set it on the table, we all burst into the "happy birthday" song.

"Thanks for dinner, Dad," I say, later as we stand to leave.

"Thank you, Mr. Woods. I hope you had a great birthday, Todd," KK says, leaning down toward my half-brother. Todd's hands are full with the Hot Wheels car, frisbee, shark, and balloons. He nods at her then looks at me expectantly.

"I'm going swimming in the ocean tomorrow before we go see your competition. Did you go swimming in the ocean already?" He looks up at me, expectantly.

"No. Our team won't get in the ocean *unless* we win the competition. Then we'll run in together with our uniforms on and our big trophy in our hands. We think it's *really* bad luck for anyone on our team to touch the water until after we've won. It's one of our crazy superstitions."

"What's superstitions?" he asks, looking from me to his dad.

"I'll explain it in the car," Dad says. "Landry, we can give you and KK a ride back to the hotel. If you don't mind holding little guy on your lap."

"Sure. We'd appreciate a ride back even though we're only a few blocks away."

Shortly after that, Dad pulls in front of the hotel. KK and I get out of the back, and Mom jumps out with us to give me and KK what she calls her 'good-luck-hugs.' She crosses her fingers, holding them up as she gets back into the back seat.

We wave as they pull away.

"That was fun," KK says, on the way to the elevators.

"Yeah, it's getting easier to be around him. And I know he's got a lot on him, being a single parent now."

"I can't understand how that must feel for you. I've tried to imagine how it would be for me if my mom came back into my life. I think I'd be glad if she did." KK looks a bit sad.

"You are such a good friend," I say, giving her hand a squeeze.

Back in the room, the girls are playing cards with Sherry.

"Hey, guys. How was dinner?" Gracie asks, looking up at us as we walk in.

"Fun," KK says, sitting down on the edge of the bed. "It was Landry's little brother's birthday."

197

"Aww. That's sweet. That was probably fun for him to have you guys there." Gracie adds.

I nod and start taking off my sandals, kicking them into the corner near my suitcase, just as all of our phones go off with texts. I open mine since no one else seems to care about the simultaneous messages.

"Coach wants us to meet in her room in fifteen minutes," I say, looking over at the girls.

"It's the night-before tradition," Sherry says, smiling. "You'll see once we get there. Come on." She motions for us to follow her out the door.

We squeeze into Coach McKaye's hotel room. All of us smoosh together, including the team subs who didn't make mat this year. Coach asks us to circle up, and we each take the hand of the person next to us, criss-crossing our arms in front of us. Then Coach begins talking about how important teamwork is and how proud she is of us.

"We have a special tradition for the night before we compete. Each person on the team says something to compliment a teammate. We go around the circle, then after everyone has had their turn, I'll wrap up. Whoever would like to begin can start."

Logan is the first to speak. "You guys know I love all of you. This is my fourth year on this team and my fourth year to make mat. I'm going to miss it more than any other cheer team I've ever been on my entire life. Jaz, you are like a brother to me, and you've always had my back. Donte, you are legit a cheerleader with your positive energy and enthusiasm. Your vibe is contagious, man." He chokes up a bit, fighting back tears. "I'm considering sticking around after graduation to coach." He sniffles, and we all put our heads down, hands clasped, waiting on whoever wants to speak next.

"Gracie Brown, you are not only my friend and my roommate, but now I feel like you are my sister," Christa says, "I deeply respect you. You are a strong competitor, and you have no fear. You make the hardest stunts look easy. You make me not only want to be a better cheerleader, but your positive, hard-working, caring, nature and your talent make me want to be a better friend, a better student and an all-around better person too." Christa is full-on crying, as most of us are now.

"Landry, I'm so glad we were put together as roommates," KK says, going next. "I liked you from the first day I met you. You were chill and seemed down to earth. But over the last few months, I've really gotten to know you. We've shared our goals, our fears, and our heartbreaks with each other. You have grown so much as a person this year. Just being around you on a daily basis has helped me to grow as a person and in my faith in a way I never knew was possible. I know you would never feel like you were a role model to anyone, but let me just say, you are. I love you."

Tears are dripping from my nose. I breathe in deeply and sniffle, then clear my throat before I can speak.

"Jaz, you have had my back this year in more ways than one. You are a tough cookie, but you are genuine and a great friend. I know I can count on you to be honest and fair, and you are one of the best cheerleaders I've ever met. Thank you for being you and for helping us to see each other as equals on the team."

Once everyone has had a turn to speak, Coach prays over us then reminds us to get a good night's rest. "Remember to eat a good breakfast in the morning. I'll see you guys tomorrow. I love you guys."

We take turns giving each other hugs while wiping tears from our cheeks. Right before we leave the room, Coach Zack breaks into one more pre-comp chant. "Guts, glory, and glitter. Let's leave it all on the mat!"

The next day, we ask Logan to come down to our room to help with our hair. In addition to being the best at making the 'poof' look perfect, he is our good luck charm. With our backpacks packed, makeup on fleek, hair styled, uniforms straight, cheer shoes tied, and bows in place, we get on the elevator and make our way down for warmups. After stretching out, we do warm-up tumbling and stunting before we run through the routine. Coach Matt gives out our pre-comp Pixy Stix straws, and Coach Zack gathers us in a circle.

"Hard work beats talent when talent doesn't work hard," he says. "You guys have heard that quote a thousand times over the years. You've got both and you've got this!"

Hand in hand and partnered up, we walk to the shuttle that takes us to the venue. Hopping off the shuttle, we partner up again to make the walk to the backstage area. Coach McKaye stops us before we go in, and we gather in a circle. As we stand with arms around each other's waists, and our heads bowed, the chant starts off soft and slow.

"We can, we must, we will." It gets louder and louder until we are screaming it. "NCFFU," collectively we chant.

Jaz shouts, "Welcome to the ring of fire!"

Donte yells. "Guts, glory, and glitter. Leave it all on the mat!"

Coach Matt tosses a large bottle of red glitter into the air, and we take turns tossing it to bring the glitter down in sprinkles. Coach Zack pulls out a makeshift "hit zero" sign he's attached to a paint stick that's been painted red and black. Each of us slaps the "hit zero" symbol, the term on the score sheet that means we've hit without any deductions. Then after a round of fist bumps, we partner up again and make our way to the "on deck" area. My adrenaline is pumping hard and fast. My heart is beating like crazy.

The announcer calls our team on stage. Smoke explodes from the entrance as we bounce onto the stage and into place to begin our performance.

Two minutes and thirty seconds has never meant more to me in my life. This moment is everything. The music starts, and we begin. Everything is hitting. No tumble busts, no bobbles, the pyramid lands with perfect timing. We end with the dance, strike our final pose, and the music stops. We jump into each other's arms, proud, and grateful. When Jaz comes to me with a hug, I notice his face is bleeding. The blood has started to run down his neck. Once we're backstage, I ask him about it.

"Are you okay, Jaz? Your cheek is cut." One of the staff notices as well and sends the trainer over to take a look.

"KK kicked me going into the pancake flip," he says, pausing to let the trainer examine his injury.

"He's going to need a few stitches," the trainer reports. "We'll get him stitched up. Let's go to the training room. I'll need to clean it good then give you some Lidocaine." He leads Jaz to the training room while the rest of us huddle together, waiting on the coaches to meet us backstage to watch the replay of our performance.

The coaches come running into the backstage area with hugs and cheers. Then we turn our attention to the TV screen and watch our performance back.

"You guys hit zero. No deductions, I'm sure," Coach says, smiling, and glued to the screen.

After watching ourselves perform, we know she's right, we hit. Now we wait on our score, so we'll know how we rank against the other teams going into tomorrow. Jaz returns and says he has three stitches in his cheek. A Band-Aid is covering his wound, and he's holding a bag with more bandages inside.

Before we make our way into the crowd to watch the rest of the teams perform, we stop to pick up our backpacks. I open mine, taking out a Natchez cheer T-shirt to throw over my uniform. I slide my phone out of a side pocket of the backpack to send Mom a quick text and that's when I notice I have a text from Cole. *That was amazing, babe. We got here just in time to see your performance.*

Wait. What? He's here? Or does he mean he watched it at the aux gym?

You Made It!
36

Hey, you. Did you watch it at the aux gym? I type the text quickly then hit send.

No, Jared and I are here. Coach had us watch game film at 7 then we left and headed to the airport. We had an Uber drop us off at the venue, and we got here just in time.

OMG! I rush to KK, smiling, and grabbing her in a hug. She already knows why I'm acting so hyped.

"Yeah," she says. "They are actually here. Jared texted me too."

Both of us are now bursting to find our boys. Another text pops up from Mom. She'd texted me while we were watching the replay and with all the excitement, I forgot to look at it. I read her texts to find out that they have all gone down to the beach to hang out and are wondering if I'm able to sneak away and join them.

Hey, Mom. We think we did good. We are waiting for our score sheet so we'll know where we stand going into tomorrow's competition. Guess what? Cole and his friend Jared got here today. I need to find him. I'll try to get with you guys later.

My phone rings as soon as I hit send on the text.

"Hey, babe," Cole says when I answer. "You guys did amazing. Jared and I stepped over to Sloppy Joe's. We wanted to grab a bite. Long flight, no food, two guys, you know." He laughs. It's so good to hear his voice and know that he flew all the way from Texas to surprise me.

"I'm so glad you made it. KK and I are waiting for Coach to give us today's score. It should be just a few minutes. My family is hanging out down at the beach right now. KK and I can meet up with you in a few minutes. We can walk over to Sloppy Joe's and meet you there."

"Okay. We don't have to stay here. We can go wherever. We can hang with your family if you want."

"Let me call you back. Coach is about to make the announcement." I hang up.

I turn my attention to the coaches as Zack reads our score aloud. "Zero deductions. And so far, we are in first place out of the four teams in our division. The last team will hit the mat at five-fifty-five tonight. Coach Matt, Coach McKaye, and I will stick around to watch them. You guys are dismissed. Remember you have a curfew again tonight. Be back in your rooms by eleven. Eat a good breakfast in the morning. And we'll leave one hour earlier tomorrow." He waves, and the coaches walk away to make their way back to the viewing area.

"Are you guys catching the shuttle back to the hotel?" Gracie asks.

KK and I look at each other and grin. We haven't had a chance to talk about our plans yet. I shake my head.

"Actually, Cole and Jared flew in, and they came to see our competition. They're at Sloppy Joe's right now," I say in an excited rush.

Gracie's eyes get big. "Holy cow. That's cool. I guess we'll see you guys later. Have fun." She turns to leave, and KK and I walk over to Sloppy Joe's to find the boys.

"I'll send Jared a text letting him know we're walking their way now," KK says, pulling out her phone. As we get to the entrance, she gets a reply. "They're coming out to meet us."

Seconds later, Cole and Jared step out of the restaurant, waving to us. Both are wearing Natchez College football T-shirts, Nike basketball shorts, and tennis shoes. Cole's diamond stud earrings sparkle when the sunlight hits them. He's grinning from ear to ear. I run toward him and jump into his arms. I kiss him all around his face before landing on his full lips.

"I'm so very glad to see you," I say, softly.

"I wouldn't have missed this. I was going to make it somehow. When we found out that we would just be watching game film on Friday morning, we knew it was going to be easy for us to make it to the airport."

"Does your coach know you guys skipped class on Friday? And I guess you guys don't have practice tomorrow?" I look at him skeptically.

He looks at me with a sheepish grin. "We didn't tell him. But he gave the team the weekend off. The coaches are planning youth camps for the last two Saturdays in April, so they're in a planning meeting tomorrow morning. And since we had practice over spring break, same as you guys did, well, you know . . ." He grins. "We decided we needed a little break in our spring." The four of us giggle.

"Oh my gosh, I'm sooooo happy!" I wrap my arms around his waist and squeeze.

"So is your family still down on the beach?" he asks.

"Uh oh. I feel kinda bad. I told Mom I'd get back with her. I'll call her now," I say, pulling my phone from my cheer backpack and pressing Mom's number. After hanging up, I nod.

"They're still down there. You want to walk with me?" Cole grins and takes my hand.

"Landry, Jared and I are going to head to the hotel," KK says. "I want to change out of my uniform. I think we're going to hang at the pool for a while. Text us later." She and Jared wave as they turn to leave.

Cole and I make our way down to the beach. Mom and Aunt Jackie are sitting near the edge of the water. Todd and my dad are throwing a football back and forth a few feet behind them.

Todd sees us first. He runs with the football over to Cole. Before he gets to us, he yells, "Hey, Cole. Catch." He throws the ball. It's a little short, so Cole runs up to catch it. Then he high fives Todd, who looks like he's just found his long-lost best buddy. Todd obviously thinks Cole is cool, which I think is adorable. When Mom sees it's us, she and Aunt Jackie stand and walk over. Dad tells me the performance was excellent, and we exchange pleasantries while Mom, Aunt Jackie, and I greet each other with hugs. Todd is busy goofing around with Cole and doesn't seem to notice me.

"We didn't know if you would be able to make it. It's great you're here. I know it means a lot to Landry," Mom says to Cole. I blush and grin.

"Yes, ma'am. I knew I wanted to do everything I could to try and be here for this."

"Where are you staying? Did you fly down by yourself?" Mom asks.

"Can we get some ice cream?" Todd asks, tugging on his dad's hand.

"I haven't figured out where I'm staying yet. Jared and I flew in a few hours ago. I guess we thought as long as we made it down here, that was the most important thing. I'm sure we'll find somewhere to stay."

Todd walks over and looks up at me and Cole. "Do you want to get ice cream?"

Cole looks down at him, smiling. He gives him a fist bump.

"I'm going to let Landry decide," he says, turning to me.

"Sure. Then I want to go back and change out of this uniform."

All of us troop up the steps from the beach to Zeno's Boardwalk Sweet Shop. Cole takes my hand as we're walking.

"You guys really didn't make a reservation at a hotel? You just flew out here?" I ask, glancing at him. We stop outside the shop, allowing Mom, Todd, Dad, and Aunt Jackie to walk inside first.

"The main thing we wanted to do was make sure we got here. We figured we could find a hotel after that. There's, like, hundreds up and down the beach." He lets go of the door as we step inside.

We wander around the sweet shop and marvel at the magnitude of flavors of homemade taffy lining the shelves. Cole selects a pineapple-flavored soda from the drinks-on-ice section.

"Pineapple? I don't think I've ever tasted pineapple soda before," I muse as Cole hands the attendant behind the counter a bill to pay for the drink.

"Here." He offers me the bottle, and I take a sip.

"Oh, wow. That is really good. I think I'll get one too." I reach for another bottle, and Cole offers to pay for mine. We tap our bottles together in a toast and find a table. Mom and Aunt Jackie, Dad, and Todd are busy sampling taffy.

"If you want some ice cream, you need to go look at the flavors they have. It looks like Aunt Jan and Aunt Jackie are going to buy enough taffy for everyone," I hear my dad say to Todd, shepherding him toward the ice cream counter.

I suppose it's good Mom is going by "Aunt Jan." It probably makes Todd feel more comfortable and not like a group of strangers have all of a sudden shown up in his life.

After Todd has his ice cream and Mom and Aunt Jackie have purchased two large boxes of salt-water taffy, we move back outside.

"We haven't made any dinner plans yet. But it's about that time," Mom says, looking in my direction.

"I need to catch the shuttle back to the hotel to change. And, honestly, I may just stay there," I say. "We have curfew at our hotel since we compete again tomorrow. And Cole just got into town." I don't want to say I don't want to go to dinner with them again, but I hope they pick up on the hint that I'd rather hang out with Cole.

"We understand, hon," Aunt Jackie says, leaning in to hug me. After hugs all around and high fives and fist bumps for Todd from Cole, they decide to pop into a restaurant close by before heading back to their hotel. Cole and I walk to the tram pick-up spot so we can head back to my room.

"I bet you and Jared could stay with Jaz and Donte in their room or with Josh and Logan. Or any of the guys on our team," I say once we're seated on the bus. "Coach probably won't mind. I mean, you did fly all the way out here to see us perform. She may even have an extra coach's badge to give you guys so you can hang out with us during warm-ups. Then you can stand at the front of the stage with them during our performance too."

"Maybe. You know, I'm good with going with the flow."

We get on the elevator at the hotel, and when we get to my room on the third floor, I knock to see if anyone is in the room. I hear Christa say, "Come in," so I slowly open the door and peek my head in. Jaz, Donte, Mark, and Christa are playing UNO on one of the beds.

206

"Hey, ya'll," I say, stepping into the room. "Guess who came to Daytona?" Cole steps in behind me.

"No way. I knew you guys would be here one way or the other. Didn't I tell you that the first night we got here?" Jaz says, laughing. He gets up and gives Cole a cool-guy handshake.

"I'm going to change really quick," I say, tossing my backpack onto the floor and pulling a pair of cut-off jean shorts and a tank top from my suitcase before popping into the bathroom. When I come out, I slide my feet into a pair of flip-flops.

"Cole, you want to go hang out on the pool deck or somewhere?" I ask, smiling at him.

"Yeah, I do." He stands and picks up his backpack.

"Oh, you know what, guys? Cole and Jared need a room to crash in tonight and tomorrow," I say, looking at Jaz and Donte.

"Yeah, it's fine with me if they stay in our room. Or they could stay in one of the coaches' rooms. I think Matt and Zack have individual rooms. Do you want to ask Coach?" Jaz asks.

"I can ask her later. I guess we'll go down to her room before curfew again tonight?"

"Yes. We'll go down there for a few minutes. She'll want to talk to us about the schedule for tomorrow," Donte says.

"Where's your luggage?" Christa asks, looking at Cole. He turns around and shows her his backpack. "That's it?" she asks. "A backpack?"

"I've got everything I need in here. A couple of shirts, shorts, a swimsuit, slides, a toothbrush------traveling light." He laughs.

I take his hand in mine and wave to the group as we make our way out the door to finally be alone.

The pool deck isn't as crowded as I thought it would be. We find an open cabana. The sides of the cabana are draped with flowing fabric along each side, creating an almost secluded space for us. We sit on the double chaise lounge. I kick off my shoes, then lie on my side facing Cole. One of the pool staff members stops by to tell us the cabana bar will be closing in ten minutes if we want to place an order. He offers us a menu, and we order loaded nachos and Cokes. A few minutes later, our order arrives, and we get comfortable again, setting the plate between us and sharing the meal.

"It looks like things are still going good with your dad," Cole says. "Todd seems to be having fun too." He cocks his head to the side to look at me as if to ask if his assessment is correct.

"It's going okay, I think. I haven't really spoken to my mother about it other than telling her about his letter and that he apologized again when they came to the showcase. I have no idea what they've talked about, but my mom seems very taken with Todd. And he's calling her Aunt Jan. I think she believed Dad when he returned and told her about his wife's death and how he wanted to turn things around with me. I think she may even feel sorry for Todd since he lost his mom the way he did at such a young age." I let out a deep sigh and wipe my fingers on my napkin, then I take a sip of my Coke. "I don't think I'd be talking to him at all if it hadn't been for the New Year's Eve event we went to at Coach McKaye's church. Between me hearing that message and you being such a positive influence, I've really been able to let go of a lot of the hurt, and I'm learning to forgive. I get that he's trying to raise a son alone, and I know he's sorry for what he did to me, just dropping out of sight and out of my life. I think he wants to make up for that mistake. He's making the effort, and I appreciate that." I pick up another chip and take a bite.

Cole's eyes follow me like he's searching for the right thing to say.

"I'm glad," he says. "You know, I think your dad coming into your life was an answered prayer. Maybe it was one you hadn't prayed for yet-----because you didn't know he would be back until he was. And even with the sad circumstances that brought him back, something positive has come from that. Now you're actively seeking God's help and direction through prayer, and that's another positive. There are more positives than negatives." He smiles, and his dimples make my heart melt.

I move the plate of finished nachos to the table next to me and scoot in closer to Cole.

"You are the most positive thing to come into my life," I say, pulling him into a slow, soft kiss. "Actually, two things: you and knowing that God has my back."

Cole taps the end of my nose with his finger. "Mm-hmm. I know I can't take all the credit. You've got to give credit where credit is due. I'm all right with playing second fiddle to God for sure."

"Hey, guys." We both turn to face the voice interrupting our quiet convo. KK and Jared are standing in front of our cabana.

"Hey. What's up?" I ask, sitting up a little straighter.

"It's almost curfew, so we're going to go up to Coach's room," KK says. "I'll let her know that Cole and Jared want to crash in one of the boys' rooms."

"Yeah. Thanks. We'll be up in a few minutes," I say before they turn to go.

The guys hang out in our room until we return from our pre-comp traditions and announcements from Coach. When we get back to our room, Jared and Cole grab their backpacks, and we walk them down to Jaz, and Donte's room to say good night.

"I usually wander down to breakfast around nine thirty." I say, covering a yawn.

"I'll meet you there," Cole says, leaning in and giving me a kiss on the cheek. "Good night, beautiful," he says, stepping inside the room.

The next morning while eating breakfast with Cole, I give him the details on meeting up with us to take the tram to the competition venue for warm-ups. Coach has two extra coach's badges, and she gives those to Jared and Cole after we get on the tram. I whisper to Cole that he and Jared can't be in our circle when we do our pre-comp rituals. He laughs and says he understands because of playing football for so many years.

"Each team I've been on has had their superstitions and rituals. One year in high school, we came off a losing streak after our team ate Chick-fil-A nuggets in the locker room. We had all eaten the sauce with our nuggets. So from that game on, we had to at least have the sauce in the locker room. We all kept packets of Chick-fil-A sauces in our lockers, and we kept winning game after game after that."

I crack up laughing at his story.

"When one of the guys would have a good play or we'd score, we'd yell stuff like, "You got the sauce!"

I laugh harder and start snorting. Cole and I are still laughing as we step off the tram.

After warm-ups, we walk outside before going backstage to go "on deck." Coach tells us to circle up, and Logan starts looking around suspiciously.

"I think Cole and Jared should walk away and wander into the crowd, then they can meet the coaches at the front of the stage," Logan says, nodding in Cole's direction. "We need to have everything as close as we can to the way it was yesterday before we walked on deck." Logan says, loud enough for everyone to hear.

I give Cole a look, but I know he understands. After they walk away, we get into our huddle.

"Make sure you are standing next to the exact same people you stood next to yesterday," Donte says. We all look around, and Christa and Sherry switch places. Brodi and Josh do the same. "Okay, everybody good?" Coach Zack asks. We look around and nod.

The chant starts off slow and soft, "We can, we will, we must." It gets louder and louder. "Guts, glory, and glitter. Leave it all on the mat." We repeat it, shouting it again. Then Coach Zack pulls out the bottle of red glitter and tosses it around. We each take a turn sprinkling some into the air.

"Welcome to the ring of fire!" Jaz yells.

Then Zack pulls out the "hit zero" sign, and we all slap it on our way backstage, where we wait to be called on deck. Pixy Stix straws are passed out and we tip our heads back, letting the sugary powder pour onto our tongues. The coaches leave to make their way to the front of the stage, and our team is called to the "on deck" position. Adrenaline is pumping heavily in my veins, and my heart is beating rapidly. I'm ready to take the stage and kill this routine. We were in first place heading into today, and as long as we "hit" victory is ours.

Smoke explodes as our team is announced. We bounce onto the stage and take our positions for the opening. The music begins, and our routine starts with the impressive level-7 basket tosses and double downs. Everything is going smoothly. We make it through the jumps, the stunts, and they all hit. Then on the last tumble pass, I notice Logan wince in pain. He must have come down wrong on his bad ankle, but he keeps going and is able to hop into position for the pyramid. We do the dance and we pose, freezing in place as the music stops. We've done it. We jump up and down and go nuts. Logan is hopping around, definitely in pain. Once we're backstage, he collapses onto the ground. Coach Zack picks him up and carries him over to the TV as we watch the replay. Coach McKaye is beaming.

"That was beautiful, ya'll," she says. "It was perfect. Now, ya'll know at awards, whatever place we get, we congratulate all the other teams." She nods at us. "Ya'll have free time until six. Then meet back here so we can walk to awards together."

Cole scoops me into his arms. "I'm so proud of you," he says then kisses me.

Coach Zack calls for a trainer to take a look at Logan's ankle. "I'm so glad it happened near the end of the routine and he was able to make it through," I say, looking in Logan's direction. "Let me text Mom and see if we can see them before they head to the airport." Cole hands me my backpack, and I pull out my cell.

Cole and I meet my family at Sloppy Joe's and eat a quick meal with them before they have to leave to return their rental car and catch their plane home.

"Thank you, guys, for coming. It means a lot to me that all of you came to Daytona for this competition," I say, giving hugs to everyone.

"I guess the next time I see you, we'll be moving you out of your dorm to head home?" Mom asks.

"Yeah. I only have four more weeks left," I say, glancing at Cole.

Cole and I watch as they walk across the street to the parking lot. Mom turns around and waves one more time before she disappears into the car.

Water, Waves, & Winners

37

"Let's go back to the room and hang for a while. We have a little over an hour before we have to be back for the awards," I say, taking Cole's hand as we walk to the shuttle that will take us back to the hotel.

Back in the room, I kick my shoes off and plop down on the newly made bed. "I love coming back to a clean hotel room with fresh towels and a perfectly made bed," I say as Cole snuggles up next to me.

"I love coming back to the room to be alone with you," he says, placing a hand under my chin, and pulling me in for a passionate kiss that lasts several minutes.

"What time do you guys have to leave for the airport tomorrow?" I ask.

"Our flight leaves at seven-fifteen tomorrow night. I guess we would need an Uber to pick us up around five-thirty."

"Oh, that's good. We'll get to spend the whole day together hanging at the beach. By the time you and Jared have to leave for the airport, it will be time for our team to get ready for our second team dinner."

"When was your first team dinner?"

"It was on Monday night, the night after we arrived. It was at Bubba Gump. But I heard Coach splurges and takes her team somewhere fancier if they win. So the location will be a surprise until the day of the dinner. But we'll still go out for dinner as a team the night before we leave even if we don't win."

"Oh, so if you come in second or third you have to go back to Bubba Gump?" He laughs and starts tickling me.

"I'm going to find out if you're ticklish too." I slip my hands under his T-shirt and gently run my fingers up and down his sides, just under his arms. He squirms a little.

"I'm not going to complain about that one bit. You can work as hard as you want to find out if I'm ticklish," he says, kissing me along my neck up to my ear.

"I was thinking . . ." He pauses. "When your mom said something about moving you out of the dorm, it gave me an idea. I'm planning on going to Georgia to train with my brother at the Falcon's training camp in May. Maybe I could take you home. The back of my truck will hold all of our stuff."

"Yeah. I think I'd like that. Maybe you could spend the night on your way to Georgia. And maybe you could come through again on your way back to Texas?"

He nods. "Definitely sounds like a good plan to me."

A few minutes later, my phone alarm goes off, alerting me it's time to head back to the venue to meet up with the rest of the team for the awards ceremony.

Soon the moment has arrived. Our team walks onto the stage together, although Logan is now on crutches with an ice pack wrapped around his ankle. We hold hands and keep our heads down as we listen and wait. The announcer begins with fourth place then moves on to third. My heart is in my throat. After second place is announced and that team takes their award, we know we've won. There's a short pause as the announcer continues. "And your NCA National Champion College Coed small D1 team iiiiiiiis . . . Natchez College."

We explode with screams. KK and I fall to our knees in tears. Logan, Mark, and Sherry meet the announcer at center stage to take the huge four-foot trophy and banner from him. They lift it high in the air before setting it down and engulfing the rest of the team in celebratory hugs.

As we move off the stage and down the stairs, our coaches, our team alternates, and Cole and Jared come running toward us. Everyone is crying and hugging. It's surreal. It's the best feeling in the world. This moment in time is the culmination of hard work, struggle, long practices, pushing to be the best, and giving up other things to make this moment, this *very* moment, a reality. No one can take this from me-----ever. If it never happens again, I will still have this. I will always have this moment, this feeling, this championship.

Our team takes off toward the beach. I take KK's hand in mine and we run into the waves, jumping, splashing, cheering, completely exhilarated. The guys lift Coach McKaye up over their heads before putting her down in the water. We each take photos with the trophy as the waves splash us in the face. Gracie jumps on Jaz's back and holds the banner up high for a photo. Our alternate teammates stand at the water's edge filming the entire thing. Cole and Jared have pulled out their phones and are filming too.

I move back to shore and stand just out of the waves' reach. Pausing, I catch my breath-----a permanent smile is plastered across my face.

Cole steps up to me. He's radiant. Then slowly my teammates emerge from the water, greeting their family members and friends. The rest of our teammates and our supporters who've made it down to the beach come forward to congratulate us. I reach my hand out to take Cole's, and he leans in and kisses my cheek. Someone snaps a photo of us. Cole offers to take one of me holding the trophy in the air, the waves crashing in the background. The photo session continues until we've gotten multiple team photos with the trophy and the banner. Everyone gets a photo by themselves with the trophy, and we all pose for a photo with the coaches. As the photo session wraps up, the coaches head to the shuttle bus with the trophy and the banner to go back to the hotel.

Most of us decide to walk back along the beach. I slip my cheer shoes off and stuff my socks inside, tie the long strings together, and drape the shoes over my shoulder. Cole takes my hand, and we walk slowly along the water's edge as the waves lap at our bare feet.

"I don't know if it's possible to feel happier than I am right now," I say, glancing into his eyes.

"Me and you both," he replies.

By the time we reach The Grand Seas hotel, the sun is starting to set. Cole and I, along with several of my teammates, sit in the sand, taking in the moment as the setting sun casts a glowing orange on the best day of our lives.

"How do you hit the pause button?" I ask, letting out a sigh, and leaning my head against Cole's strong shoulder. He searches my eyes as he considers the question. He's never in a rush to answer. It's like he waits until he's found the right thing to say-----one of the many reasons I fell for him. He's soft-spoken and smart. Physically strong and emotionally strong. And he's on a spiritual level that I'm slowly striving to meet.

"I don't think you hit pause," he says. "I think you ponder. I think you can ponder things in your heart. Hold them dear and treasure them with gratitude, knowing that there will be more. There will always be more-------more to hope for, more to pray for, more to be grateful for, more to do, more to feel. Life is going to be about moments, some of them perfect and some of them not so perfect, and some of them will be awful. God doesn't promise perfection until we get to heaven. Until then, we take the bad and the ugly along with the good and the mediocre." He squeezes my hand while his eyes pierce mine. "And as we go through this life we've been given, I hope I work hard not only in my sport and for my team, but as a human------a human who has limits but who loves and gives to the best of my abilities, thankful for the grace, love, and forgiveness I've been given."

"That's a quote to live by. I'll ponder it in my heart." Smiling at him, I tilt my head just enough to touch my lips to his. His arms are folded around me. I snuggle closer to him as we hold each other, his chin resting on top of my head. My mind and my heart are at peace, as I stare into the glow of the setting sun.

After it gets dark, we walk up to the room to find Jared and KK cuddled up watching Netflix.

"Where are the girls?" I ask.

"They are with their families at dinner," KK says, hitting pause on the TV.

I pop into the bathroom to change out of my uniform and into shorts and a T-shirt.

"Coach ordered pizza for everyone," KK says when I come out. "If you guys want some, it's in her room. Everyone's been going in and out, getting a few slices then carrying them back to their rooms. Jared and I already had some.

"Sounds great. Cole, you want some pizza? Then we can find a cozy place to hang near the pool."

Cole and I walk to Coach Mckaye's room and fill two plates with pizza, and we each grab a bottle of water. We get cozy in our favorite cabana-enclosed chaise lounge and spend the rest of the evening wrapped up in each other, talking and laughing.

The next morning after breakfast, we head out onto the beach to hang out with Jared and KK. We enjoy the day lounging in the sun and tossing around a tennis ball we found in the sand.

After eating a leisurely lunch poolside, we gather our things and head up to our rooms to shower and change. KK and I are excited about our team dinner at Chart House, where Coach has reserved the entire deck overlooking the ocean. I slip on the sundress I bought for the occasion and run a brush through my hair, leaving it down and letting it fall past my shoulders. I slide my feet into my sandals. KK pulls her long blonde hair into a messy bun, slips into a pair of wedges, and says she's ready. We meet up with Jared and Cole in the lobby as they wait for their Uber to arrive.

When it does, we walk with them out to the car, stopping on the curb. I turn and face Cole. He lifts my right hand to his mouth, brushing it across his bottom lip while lovingly staring into my eyes. Then the tranquility is broken when Jared gets into the back seat and says, "Let's go."

Cole and I share a quick kiss before he slides into the car. I turn to KK. "It's time for a celebration. Let's not keep the team waiting."

Night to Shine

38

The boys on our team take turns carrying our giant trophy through the airport and onto the airplane------an event in and of itself. We felt like rock stars rushing through the airport, and even though it only lasted a few minutes, it was a cool feeling. We received cheers from other teams as we passed them on the way to our gate. Now we're loading onto the bus that will take us from the airport in Fort Worth back to campus. I'll be back in my dorm in about two hours, then it's back to class tomorrow morning.

Things will go back to normal this week, but the joy from my time in Daytona will stay with me. Tryouts for next year's team are being held this week. The coaches recruit from around the country from big-name teams like Top Gun in Florida, Stingrays in Atlanta, Smoed in California, and Cheer Athletics from Dallas. Some recruits come from teams as far away as Hawaii or Canada. But the recruits don't have to try out, only the people coming from smaller, more random teams do. Only the fourth years have to help with tryouts.

Since I won't be involved, I'll get to watch Cole at practice. Watching Cole Collins at football practice is easy on the eyes, let me tell you. I quickly type out a text to Cole. *I'm on the bus back to campus now*. We text back and forth for the remainder of my ride.

As we approach the school, I see that a huge banner has been placed across the entrance sign   ----"Welcome Home 15 Time NCA National College Coed Cheerleading Champions" -----

Applause and cheers fill the bus as we pass the sign. The bus driver lets us out in front of the cheer gym. The trophy and banner are taken inside, and we grab our duffel bags and backpacks and head toward the dorms. When we walk through the dorm entrance, the girls hanging out in the commons area turn to look our way. Cheering breaks out, and they run over to congratulate us.

When we reach our room, I'm glad to be back. As we walk inside, I take a deep, cleansing breath and toss my bags onto the floor then flop backward onto my bed, letting out a loud, exhausted sigh.

By Wednesday afternoon, I'm feeling more in the groove, having recovered from homework overload. I have three more assignments to finish in the library, then I'm hoping to go to the field to see Cole before his practice wraps up.

An hour later, finally caught up on my assignments, I check my phone for the time. *Yikes, I need to hurry.* Quickly, I stuff everything into my backpack and toss it over my shoulder then hustle down the library steps and out the door, walking fast as I can toward the football field. By the time I get to the fence, I can see the team at center field in a huddle, surrounded by their coaches.

I move to the bleachers and take a seat in the lower stands. As I sit, I notice a van from the local TV station parked across the way. A camera crew on the opposite side of the field is filming the practice. When the huddle breaks up, the camera team rushes to Cole and stops in front of him. A microphone is shoved into his face, and he stops to talk with them politely. I stand, craning my neck to watch with my hand shielding my eyes from the sun. When the interviewer moves onto another player, Cole looks around and sees me.

I wave, and he jogs over to me. He sits next to me in the bleachers, placing his helmet at his side. His arms and his forehead glisten with sweat. He looks sexy, beautiful, masculine, and strong. There are many times I've melted into a pool of mush from just being close to him. This is one of those times.

"Hi," he says. He grins, putting those to-die-for dimples on display.

"Hey," I say, radiating vibes of *Oh-my-god, I think you are so incredibly hot.*

"You must have gotten caught up on all your homework," he says.

I nod. "I did. Looks like you've just been interviewed by the local TV channel," I say, teasing.

He chuckles. "They've been filming practice the last few days. I guess they're putting together some hype for the upcoming spring scrimmage game this Saturday."

I nod again, smiling, feeling silly, and still taking in the sight of him. He starts to say something, but I stop him with my lips, pressing them into his, and kissing him with an undeniable passion.

He moves his hands around me, pulling me in close.

"I should go take a shower. Then maybe we could go somewhere." He stands, taking my hand as we walk toward the edge of the field. Then he lets go of my hand and jogs backward into the locker room. "Be right back," he says, keeping his eyes on mine.

I lean against the building, waiting for him to shower and change. As players emerge from the locker room, they give me the nod, acknowledging me in their cool-guy-way. Finally, Cole comes out, wearing a cool-looking pair of ripped jeans, a Natchez T-shirt and he smells fresh like soap and citrus with a hint of sandalwood. He takes my hand and we walk to his truck, where he opens the passenger door for me, and I climb inside. Leaving campus, we head toward the lake. He drives down a dirt road and stops at a clearing. We get out and walk through the grass to the edge of the lake. We sit together in the grass with our legs stretched out and, his right-hand resting on my thigh. The warm spring wind blows in our faces. The sun, glowing and orange, has begun to set in the sky.

"It's so beautiful here," I say, taking a deep breath.

"Yes. God blessed Texas."

"With his own hands. Yeah, I've heard that." I laugh. "The lakefront where I live has beautiful sunsets and ancient oak trees dripping in Spanish moss. I live about a mile from Lake Pontchartrain. We call it the North Shore. There are no beaches, just a short sea wall holding the water back and grass and trees along the shore. It's a great place to hang out and walk your dog. There are a few really good restaurants near there too. We'll have to go when you're in town. I need to let Mom know that you'll be staying with us on your way to Atlanta and will take me home from college." I look at Cole and smile.

"I'm looking forward to seeing your hometown," he says, tilting his head to the side, his eyes shining.

"I'm looking forward to showing you around."

He moves to stand, pulling me up with him, then he bends down on one knee and looks up at me. I suddenly feel faint. What is he about to do? He takes my hand in his and holds it gently.

"Will you go to the prom with me?" he asks.

"What?" I ask, confused.

"Night-to-Shine. It's a prom-like dance for special needs kids, and they need volunteers to help with the event. I helped with one back in high school. Campus Community Church is sponsoring one on Saturday night, and I signed up to volunteer. And I'm hoping to take a beautiful date to volunteer along with me if she'll go." His smile is huge and contagious.

"Oh, right. Coach McKaye told us about that. I didn't pay much attention to the information she sent out about it." I kneel, and gaze into his eyes. "Yes, I'd love to go to the prom with you, even if we are there to work."

"It will be a lot of fun. I promise. Some of the kids will need a lot of help some may be in wheelchairs. Some are high-functioning, and they come with dates, and others need someone to dance with and talk to. It's a really special night."

"It sounds like it will be. Thank you for thinking of me."

"I'm always thinking of you." He leans in slowly, and our lips barely touch before the kiss becomes very sexy.

Back at the dorm, I walk down to Gracie and Christa's room to look through their dresses. Gracie says she and Sherry have signed up to help at the event too. So, I look through Christa's closet and pull out a black sequined sleeveless dress. I hold it out for Christa to see.

"Can I borrow this one?" I ask.

"Yes. That's the dress I wore to prom last year. Is KK helping out at Shine prom night too?" she asks.

"She and Jared are going to the Azalea dinner thing that night. He was asked to be an escort for one of the Azalea girls. That's at the country club. There's a lot going on this weekend with try-outs wrapping up on Friday night, the spring game on Saturday afternoon, and the Azalea parade that morning. Then we have to perform at the town square after the parade, and there's the Night-to-Shine prom and the Azalea club thing," I say, folding the dress over my arm.

"Yeah. End of the year stuff gets crazy quickly. But only three more weeks and it's summer break," Christa, says, waving both hands in the air, to a silent beat.

Gracie huffs. "I won't have much of a summer break. I'm spending most of June doing cheer clinics around the country." She turns back around to finish typing something on her computer.

"What are you doing Saturday night, Christa?" I ask, closing her closet door.

"I have a date with Carter Moss," she says, with a huge grin.

"The baseball pitcher you've been talking to and having lunch dates with?"

"That's the one. We're going out to eat then to the movies. Can't wait. I really like him," she says beaming.

On Saturday morning our team falls in line marching behind the band in the Azalea Club's parade featuring each rainbow-costumed Azalea girl in full antebellum dresses, matching picture hats, and matching umbrellas. Our team is set to perform at the town square just after the parade. Our competition routine draws a roar of applause when we finish. Cole is with his parents, and they wave me over to them.

"That was an incredible performance," his mom says. "I can see why your team has won so many championships. Cole has tried to explain it to us. We've always been a football family since we have four boys." She laughs.

"Thank you, Mrs. Collins," I reply.

"We're also looking forward to watching you cheer again at the game this afternoon." His dad, adds.

After spending a few minutes casually chatting with Cole and his parents, I smile shyly before saying goodbye. Wandering back toward my teammates, the girls and I head back to campus to change into swimsuits. The plan is to hang out at Sherry's apartment-complex pool since we don't have to be at the football field util much later.

After spending a few hours at the pool, KK, Christa and I go back to the dorm to get back into our uniforms for the game. The scrimmage game is shorter than a normal football game giving us plenty of time to change into formal wear for the events going on tonight.

I Take a step into Christa's black sequined dress, and she zips it for me. Then she touches up the ends of my hair with the curling iron.

"Guys, I've got to rush out. Jared is here to pick me up, and we can't be late since he's presenting on the Azalea court tonight." KK leans toward me, giving me an air kiss.

"You look amazing, KK," I say, glancing in her direction. She's wearing the fitted lavender satin gown I wore to the homecoming dance. Her long blonde hair is braided and hanging over her left shoulder. She pops through the door, making her exit.

I step back and look at myself in the full-length mirror we have propped up on a chair. My skin is tan from being at Daytona Beach last week and from being at the pool earlier today. My arms are slim and muscular from many years of cheerleading. The sequined dress fits my slim figure well, and its deep V-neck shows off a bit of cleavage. A deeper V-shape on the other side exposes my lower back.

I haven't thought much about my appearance before or even about what Cole might see in me. I'm tall and slim with a shapely, athletic body. This is the first year I've worn long, fancy dresses and the first time I've been asked to dances, parties, and even prom. I'm actually attending a prom tonight. So many positive things have happened to me this year, and I'm not sure I deserve any of them. I step away from the mirror and slip on the black sequined Van's I got for Christmas. No one will notice my flat slip-on tennis shoes under this long dress. And, I want to be comfortable all night. The night is about these special kids, and I don't have time to worry about my feet or a fancy pair of heels. My phone pings with a text from Cole letting me know he is walking over to get me.

"Have fun on your date with Carter tonight," I say to Christa, who nods and gives me a teasing smile.

"I promise to," she says, wrapping the cord around the end of the curling iron.

I pick up my black wristlet and wave as I walk through the door to meet Cole.

"Wow," I say when I see him. "You look dashing and handsome." He's waiting for me near the entrance of the dorm, wearing an all-black suit, black tie, white button-down, and shiny, black shoes.

"Never more beautiful than you." He lifts my hand into the air, twirling me around. Then he lets out a loud whistle. I blush, embarrassed by the attention. He gestures toward the door then holds it open as I walk through. Outside, he helps me into his truck, and we head to Campus Community Church.

In the parking lot, we see the news truck, from the station that sent a crew to Wednesday's spring football practice. As we get closer to the entrance, we hear loud cheers and applause. A long red carpet extends from the edge of the parking lot through the entrance to the building. On either side of the carpet are parents and volunteers, who cheer as each special need student steps inside for the dance. Closer to the entrance the news crew stops and interviews the students briefly.

When Cole and I get to the entrance, the interview team recognizes him. We hear a reporter say as we pass, "Cole Collins is here volunteering tonight along with several other Natchez College students." I can feel the camera following us as we enter the dance.

In the foyer, there are volunteers stationed at tables and passing out sparkling princess crowns for all the girls. Coach McKaye is working one of the tables. I wave to her as we walk past. Cole stops to speak with a boy in a wheelchair. Cole high fives the boy and laughs, telling him to save a dance for him if he can keep all the girls away. A volunteer with Shine greets us and tells us to have fun and just be ourselves around the students. Ask them to dance, talk with them, and enjoy ourselves.

When we get out to the dance floor, Cole speaks to a young girl with Down syndrome and asks her to dance. He gives me a smile as he leads her out to the dance floor. I look around and notice a

223

boy standing next to a lady who might be his mom. I walk over and introduce myself to them. His mom smiles at me and tells me her son is shy but would love to dance. I offer my hand and lead him out onto the dance floor, trying to be as engaging and relaxed as Cole. When the girl Cole is dancing with finds her friends, he joins me, and we dance together in a group.

"Are you having fun?" he asks.

"You are a natural at this. I feel awkward. You're at ease and I'm worried about how to act around these kids." I say, softly.

"You're doing great," he responds. "All the guys here are going to want to dance with you."

I glance around the room. The mom I spoke with earlier is beaming as she watches her son have a good time. Gracie, Sherry, Lisa, and Mark are here now. They had stayed at Sherry's hanging at the pool longer than KK and I did and wanted to get ready for the scrimmage and this event at her place. I watch as they go to the photo booth to pose with some of the kids. As the night goes on, I relax more and find it easier to chat with these kids, who are excited to have a night to dress up, and be at a party, dancing and doing the kinds of things other kids enjoy. I try to meet, and dance with as many of them as I can, forgetting about my own anxieties.

I watch Cole as he interacts with each student. He's so natural, kind, and genuinely friendly with everyone. I wish I were more like him, unconcerned about my own needs, my own fears, or just what people think. Before I came to Texas, I don't think I was a very nice person. I had a lot of hate in my heart. It was hidden for many years, but it was there. I stole things, and it doesn't matter that it was on a dare. I stole from a store. I was arrested, expelled from school, and kicked off my cheer team. I don't know if I really deserve this second chance I've been given, a place on a national championship team, the perfect boyfriend, and a little brother. I may not deserve any of these things, especially someone as nice and charming as Cole Collins.

When the evening wraps up, the students leave with happy smiles, having had the time of their lives. Cole and I, along with the other volunteers, help with the cleanup. We clear cups, trash, balloons, and plastic tablecloths, and we stack chairs and tables.

Whew. I'm glad I wore my Vans under this dress. Gracie, Sherry, and Lisa have shed their heels, and are walking around barefoot as they work.

We say good night to Coach and exit through the main entrance. TV crews are still filming and interviewing students as they leave. As we pass them, one of the crew members stops Cole.

"Can we get a quick interview?" he asks.

Cole nods, and we stop and wait until the camera cuts away from two students and their parents. Then the camera guys turn their attention to us. The bright lights glare, causing me to blink, as I try to focus on where I should be looking.

"Cole Collins, the starting quarterback for Natchez College, is here tonight volunteering with a friend. Cole, tell us about your experience with Night-to-Shine and what it means to you," the interviewer asks. He holds the mic in front of Cole.

"I volunteered with Shine in high school. It's always been a night that I've looked forward to. This year I included my girlfriend, Landry, who's on the national-championship cheer team at Natchez." He looks at me, grinning---- *those dimples*. I beam back at him before he continues with his remarks. "I love speaking to the kids, getting to know them, dancing with them, and letting them teach me some moves, ya know?" He laughs. The camera cuts back to the guy doing the interviews, and we walk on.

As we walk away, we hear the reporter say, "Tonight's Night-to-Shine------ an evening to remember as local volunteers give back to the special needs students in our area. A fun night was had by all. Back to you, Frank."

"We should turn the news on when we get to the dorm. We might be able to catch the end and maybe see ourselves on TV," I say, buckling my seat belt. Cole looks at the clock on the dash.

"If we hurry back," he says, starting the engine.

When we walk into to the commons room at my dorm, I pick up the remote and turn on the TV. Cole and I sit on the couch getting comfy. He takes his suit jacket off and loosens his tie. I snuggle up to him, and his arm is around me as I flip through channels, trying to find the local news.

"Here it is," I say, stopping on the right channel. We watch brief interviews with parents and excited students entering the dance on the red carpet. Then the camera cuts to students dancing.

"Look, Cole, there we are dancing." I pull my phone out of my wristlet bag to get a video of the scene on the TV. But before I can, the camera cuts to more interviews with students and volunteers. Cole's interview is last. I quickly switch my phone to video and film it.

"Got it. I'm going to text it to my mom. Do you want me to text it to you?"

He laughs. "Sure. My mom might want to see it." Then he leans in to kiss me.

"I don't know if I deserve you," I say softly, almost in a whisper. I lower my head, fighting back tears. A lump of emotion tightens in my throat.

"What do you mean by that? You are an amazing girl. Look at me, Landry." He lifts my chin gently with his hand, peering into my eyes, waiting for my response.

I pull away and spring off the couch. Fighting tears, I rush down the hall and fling the door open to my room. Then I lean back against the closed door as the tears flow.

KK's just stepping out of her shoes and rushes over to me.

"Landry, what happened?" she asks with panic in her voice.

"It's me," I say, frustrated. "I just don't know if I deserve feeling happy. For *so* many years I've fought back hurt and pain, and I just don't know if I deserve the second chance I've been given. It's been amazing. Making new friends, meeting Cole. He's so wonderful. I just don't feel worthy." Putting my hands up, I cover my face. "I'm so embarrassed. I almost broke down in front of him. I don't know why, but I jumped up and ran down here."

"You deserve to be happy. You deserve every good thing that's come to you recently." KK brushes a tear from my cheek just as we hear a knock. Startled, I jump away from the door.

"Landry, can I come in?" Cole's asks in a soothing tone.

Feeling unsure of what to do, I glance at KK, who urges me to open it.

"Let him in. Don't start a fight over something silly." KK whispers, giving me a stern, look.

Opening the door, I let him in as KK slips out into the hallway.

"I'm going down to Gracie and Christa's room." She calls over her shoulder.

Cole puts his arms around me and pulls me close. "Talk to me, babe."

I move away from him and plop down onto my bed. Cole sits next to me. Breathing deeply, I pull myself together before speaking.

"You're kind, and always so positive. You're an extremely talented athlete. You're smart, you can sing and play the ukulele, and you love God with an uncompromised passion. I'm none of those. As I Watched you tonight, lighting up the room, dancing and showing those kids a great time, and giving of yourself, it made me wonder what you would want with someone like me. I'm flawed. In fact, I'm beyond flawed. I'm just someone who was given a second chance, and I showed up here and met you, then all kinds of amazing things started to happen. I'm just not sure I deserve any of it." As the last words spew from my mouth, I grow more upset.

Cole stands to face me, looking directly into my eyes. "From where I'm standing, I can tell you that you *are* an amazing girl. Don't be afraid to be happy. Don't let negative thoughts into your head."

His fingers gently touch the side of my head. I look down at the ground, fighting the next round of tears which are sure to come any second.

Cole leans in.

"Thoughts like that are from the enemy, not God. Some of the things that happened in your life were not things you chose. And, yes, we all do bad things and make mistakes, but God loves us and forgives us when we ask. He'll always be there for us, no matter what. You are a beautiful girl with a beautiful soul and a big heart. You give everything you've got for your team and your friends. You've been through a lot, but you've also learned a lot. You're still growing and still learning. Don't let thoughts from the enemy get into your head and mess with you. I love you. Don't forget that. *I love you,*" he whispers, leaning his head in, so that our foreheads touch. I listen to his breathing, feel his breath on my face, drinking it in.

"I love you, too." Tears pool in my eyes, and my breath catches. "I want to feel like I deserve you, along with all these good things that have come my way recently. I want to be positive like you. Even when you got hurt and were in the hospital, you remained so positive. How?"

He takes both my hands in his.

"I was down on myself when it happened. I felt I had let my team down. My parents had come to see the game, and I let them down. We weren't going to end the season with a win or with a championship game. I felt it was my fault. But I also realize that sometimes bad things happen to us. We live in an imperfect world around imperfect people. I pray a lot, and I try to be grateful and thankful every day. And it's not a sign of weakness to ask for help when you need it. I'm not perfect, but I strive to do better every day while I count my blessings, one of those being you."

His smile lights up the downer moment I've created. I focus on the site of Cole, those dimples, his contagious smile, and his shining eyes filled with so much love.

The soft smile he's giving me tugs at my heart, and I smile shyly. "Can I blame this on PMS?"

He chuckles, sits next to me, and takes my hand in his. Softly and gently, he gazes into to my eyes.

Starring back, my look is serious.

"For real, though, I'll strive to do better every day, be more thankful, ask for help, kick enemy thoughts out of my mind, and ponder good moments in my heart. And hopefully always take your advice." I pause and squeeze his hand. "Because I don't want to hurt any more or feel down on myself. I have felt real happiness lately and I want to feel that more and more."

The way he's looking at me right now vanquishes all my negative thoughts. He pulls me in and holds me. I lean into his chest as he wraps his arms around me, more tightly, I feel comforted, safe, and loved.

Gear up! It's the End of the Year
39

After Cole leaves, I walk down the hall to let KK know it's safe to return and that the disaster I was about to create has been avoided.

"Now that you've helped me fix my love life, how was the Azalea Club event? I ask as she slips out of her dress.

"It was okay. I guess." She opens her dresser to get out a T-shirt, pulls it over her head, then sits on her bed, leaning back onto the pillows.

"You don't sound too sure," I say, reaching back to try unsuccessfully to unzip my dress. "Can you unzip me?" I stand in front of KK as she reaches for the zipper. "You want to talk about it?" I ask.

"I think the girl who asked Jared to escort her likes him. You should have seen the way she was smiling at him while they were dancing."

"There was a dance too? I guess I thought the Azalea Club girls were being presented to the senior members like a debutante thing," I step out of the dress, and lay it across my bed, then slip into a T-shirt and shorts.

"Yeah, it's like the campus garden club. The garden club in town helps run the group on campus. The younger members keep the campus gardens up and the senior members keep the town gardens and greenways maintained and then every year around Azalea Trail time, they host a parade then the ball/dance/diner thing--- whatever. The Azalea girls get to ask anyone they want to escort them, and I figured she picked Jared because he's a football player. I didn't really understand until we got there how much was involved, a dance, a formal dinner, and a fancy Azalea-girl-coming-out-presentation. The girl who asked Jared to escort her won an award for raising the most funds for the club this year. They're adding a new park bench next to the quad with the extra funds she raised." KK rolls her eyes.

"Do you think Jared likes this girl, or was he only going to the event with her because she asked him to be her escort? I mean, he did take you with him and you're his girlfriend. That probably sends a message."

"He told me she's in his math class and they sit near each other and they talk sometimes. He just told me she needed an escort for the presentation thing. He asked if I could come, and she said yes. I don't think he thought anything of it. We still danced together at the event, but the girls in the club have the first dance with their escorts. I just thought I noticed something that made me think she likes him."

"Did you ask Jared about it?"

"While we were dancing, I said, 'I think she likes you.' He just laughed."

"It's bothering you, so I'd bring it up with him again and see if you can talk about it. You shouldn't have to go around guessing whether he likes someone else or whether some other girl is trying to flirt with your boyfriend."

"You're right. I'll find time to talk with him more this week. How was prom night, other than the fact that you almost had a meltdown after it was over?" We both giggle.

"It was a lot of fun. Cole was so nice to all the special needs kids. They seemed to be having a lot of fun. Cole's a natural at talking with everyone. I can learn a lot from just being around him. I think he makes me a better person. I can learn a lot from the special needs kids I met tonight too. They were so happy and joyful despite things they deal with. They laughed and danced like it was the greatest event ever. But I get the feeling they're always that happy." I move over to sit with KK on her bed. "We get so hung up on the little things in our lives that we sometimes forget things aren't as bad as they seem. I know I was feeling down on myself tonight, thinking I didn't deserve someone as awesome as Cole."

KK places a hand on my knee. "You should never think about yourself that way. He *is* awesome, and you deserve awesome. Stop beating yourself up over your past mistakes."

I glance up, taking in her soft blue eyes. "Talking to him about it, made me see things in a different light. The same thing goes with the uncertainty *you're* feeling over what happened tonight at the Azalea thing. Don't let something that may be a misunderstanding get you down. If you need to talk to Jared, don't wait."

"Yeah. I feel. I'm going to text him now and see if we can talk."

"Now it's my turn to give you some privacy. I'm going down to Gracie and Christa's. I want to hear all about Christa's date," I say, moving toward the doorway.

*****

Only two more full weeks of school left, then it's finals week. Our team is hosting a clinic this weekend for local all-star teams and local high school teams. Each time we host a clinic, it's a huge fund raiser for our team. There was one right before school started, but since I was new to the team, I didn't have to work it. This weekend, it will be all hands on deck.

The football team is hosting clinics for middle school football players this weekend and next, so Cole will be busy with that. Hopefully we'll be able to spend some time together on Sunday night. I finally had the nerve to call my mom and tell her that Cole will be taking me home from college on his way to Atlanta, which came with the question about him spending the night. She didn't seem bothered by any of it. I'm sure she was happy not to have to take off more work to make the drive, but I also think my family really likes him, which makes things easy.

After helping twelve girls with their standing tucks for an hour, I walk over and pick up my water to take a drink. I touch my phone screen to show the time. Oh, good clinic wraps in fifteen minutes. The coaches announce we're moving to stunts, so I move into my back-spot position. A few minutes later, Coach calls time and asks us to move to the center of the mat for a group photo. When we're done, I see Paul walking over to talk with Coach. I wander over, wait until they're done talking, then get his attention.

"Hey, I guess you won't be our trainer too much longer," I tell him. "Do you know what you'll do after graduation?"

He picks up his medical bag and looks at me. "Yeah, I'm going to get my masters at the University of Texas."

"Awesome. Thanks for being a friend and a great tutor this year." When I stick my hand out for him to shake, he pauses then pulls me in for a quick hug.

He grins. "Who knows? I may come back to work here as the official trainer. Or I may go to work as a sports trainer at a different school. Life can be unpredictable. Good luck, Landry." He holds a fist out for me to bump.

After we say our goodbyes, I wander over to KK and grab my bag so we can walk back to the dorms together.
. When we get to the parking lot, I hear my name. Glancing up, I see Cole looking hot and sweaty. He jogs toward us.

"Hey, you want to walk over to the ice cream shop?" he asks.

"Yes. I'll go change. Meet you back here in ten?" He smiles, gives me a thumbs-up, and heads into his dorm. I scurry into my room, quickly changing into shorts and a cute top, and slipping my feet into a pair of leather flip-flops. I tell KK bye and hurry down the hall and out into the parking lot to find Cole waiting for me on the sidewalk. He takes my hand in his, and we walk across campus and a block over to the ice cream shop which is close to downtown.

Once we have our cones, we walk outside and sit at a table next to the shop's entrance.

"I told Mom that you would be driving me home on your way to Atlanta. *And* she didn't mind when I asked about you spending the night."

Cole nods, taking a lick of his ice cream. "I was wondering if you'd come to my house for a few days, first? It would be the only time I'd have a chance to show you around my hometown. I'll be visiting my brother at the Falcon's training camp then heading to Houston to help my other brother with a Pop Warner camp for two weeks. I won't get back to Tyler until June seventh."

"You're thinking of leaving after the graduation ceremony, right? Then driving to Tyler for a few days, then on to my house in Louisiana before you start your busy summer?"

He nods.

"I'd love to go home with you," I say. "I'm sure that won't be a problem for Mom. I think she really likes you."

Cole leans in and licks the side of my cone, where the ice cream has begun to drip onto my hand. He licks my finger too.

"Hey, you. Mouth on your own cone, please," I say, teasing.

I bite down on the rest of my cone, crunching down on the sugary goodness. Then Cole and I stand to leave. He places his arm around my waist as we walk slowly back toward campus.

"I know you want to get a lot of studying in this week for finals. I'll try not to bug you too much," He says, tickling me near my waist.

"I have two finals on Tuesday, then one each day until Friday. But you can bug me all you want. I promise I won't mind."

When we get back to my dorm, he pulls me into a passionate kiss. I bite his lower lip teasingly. "Bye," I say quietly. Walking slowly backward while staring at him, not watching where I'm going, I bump into the concrete bench that sits next to the front door, almost falling over. "Oops."

Cole shakes his head, laughing at me. "Don't hurt yourself. Maybe you should turn around so you can see where you're going," he jokes.

"Then I wouldn't be able to see you," I say with a bit of a sassiness in my voice.

"Go inside and study." He wags a finger at me.

I turn and pop into my dorm, smiling from ear to ear.

A little later, I see two dorm room checklists being slipped underneath our door. I walk over and stoop to pick them up.

"One of these has your name on it, one has my name." I hand KK hers, and she puts it on her desk.

I proceed to read mine, although packing up and leaving the dorm for the summer is the last thing on my mind.

"It looks like there's not much to it. Just leaving the room clean, and it says not to take any of the furniture with us." I lay the paper on my desk and go back to studying for finals.

"I'm going to miss you, you know," KK says, looking up from her notebook. "I wish you could come to Oklahoma and stay for a few days."

"I know. It sucks not to have my own car to go wherever I want. I'm hoping with having two jobs this summer, I'll make almost enough to buy one."

"I guess you heard that Christa is going home with Carter Moss to Lufkin for a week before she flies home to Florida."

I nod. "Mm-hmm, I did hear about that. I'm happy for her. I know she dated around this year before finding the right guy. I'm glad things worked out between you and Jared too. And he's coming up to get you and take you home with him sometime this summer, right?"

"So he says. We'll see. I still think he's a bit of a flirt." She laughs.

*****

The last week of school arrives faster than I'd like, and now it's finals week. Coach informed us that we're hosting another cheer clinic this weekend after finals end. Then she's hosting a party at her house on Monday for the seniors who graduate on Tuesday. After our senior teammates graduate, I'm looking forward to heading to Cole's hometown in Tyler.

Finally finished with finals, I come back to the dorm and look around. I don't have a lot to pack up, and most of what I have will fit inside my two duffel bags, my suitcase, and my backpack. But I may need a plastic container. I had my bedding in three large Target bags when I moved in. I'm staring at my bed in a daze when KK walks in.

"Finished with freshman year! Can I get an amen? What are you looking at?" She walks closer to me.

"Nothing. I was just thinking about packing. Maybe I need a plastic bin to pack my bedding and towels in since it won't all fit in my suitcases."

"Yeah. I have a couple of plastic tubs that I brought stuff down in. I wish I had an extra one. I'd loan it to you. Have you thought about selling your books back to the bookstore? I definitely don't want to take those with me. We can see if Gracie and Christa need to sell books, too. Maybe after that, we can swing by Target and look for a plastic bin."

"I'll call them and see if they're in their room." I pull my phone from my back pocket.

Walking outside to the parking lot with the girls reminds me of the first time I saw Cole. My friends and I were heading to the grocery store and he, Jared, and a couple of other football players were standing next to a car parked near Christa's. The memory makes me smile as I get into the back seat of Gracie's car to head over to the bookstore.

The cashier hands me my cash and a receipt for the books I just sold. When we're all settled up at the bookstore, we get back into the car to head to Target.

"I can't believe I only got one hundred dollars for all those textbooks. I paid like two hundred and fifty at the beginning of the semester," I say, baffled.

"Same," Gracie says, over her shoulder as she drives.

"It's a total racket," Christa adds.

"Look on the bright side, we now have cash to shop with," KK, says, making the thumbs up sign at us.

Back from Target, I set the large plastic bin inside my closet. I pause and stare, not focusing on anything in particular.

"I need to decide what I'm wearing to the party and graduation. And I need to pack a separate bag to take to Cole's," I say.

"Yep," KK answers. "I have two dresses picked out. One for the party on Monday at Coach's house and a different one to wear at graduation on Tuesday," KK replies.

I pull a few outfits together and push them to one side of my closet.

"What time does the clinic start tomorrow?" KK asks.

"Tomorrow's session starts at ten. Sunday's starts at two. I'll set an alarm on my phone to get us both up in the morning. I'll work on packing Sunday night. I don't want to think about leaving yet," I say, finally shutting the door to my closet.

Parties & Packing
40

The party at Coach McKaye's house is similar to the one she hosted for us at the beginning of the year, although we know this one is mostly for our teammates who graduate tomorrow. There's a feeling of sadness and longing that hangs in the air as we move into the backyard. Music is playing on the outdoor speakers, and the LED pool lights are flashing to the beat of "7 Rings" by Ariana Grande.

Coach McKaye's husband, Brad, stands at the grill, perfecting the ribs. He lifts his tongs in a wave when he sees us walk up. I look around, at the gathered group, my teammates, my family, my friends. Thinking about the seniors graduating and leaving has me feeling nostalgic and melancholy. Logan plans to come back as an assistant coach, and I'm thankful for that.

We'll meet eight new teammates in July. More friends, more family. Every year a few will leave, and new ones will take their places, each one forever holding a special place in my heart.

Coach gathers us in a circle to pray over the meal. This is the last time this team will circle up, hand in hand with heads bowed, and eyes closed, listening intently to Coach's words. When the prayer ends, I wipe tears from the corners of my eyes. I notice others doing the same.

Then I realize it's *not* going to be the last time we will all be together. We have our national-championship-ring ceremony and dinner the first week of August. Remembering this makes me smile. I don't feel so down anymore. We'll celebrate our win one more time together when we get our rings. Yes! I can live knowing we'll be together again in August. My Debbie Downer mood is lightened. Taking a deep breath, I move into the line forming for food.

Once we're all seated at tables Coach rented for the event, she stands near the middle and gathers our attention.

"I love you guys with all my heart," she says. "You are all champions and forever will be. No matter what happens from now until the end of your lives, you guys are national champions. You all will forever be part of the Natchez College cheer family. If you need anything at any time throughout your life, you can always reach me. If you want to come back to coach, to teach a clinic, or just to cheer on our new team, you're forever welcome here. I know we'll be back together for the championship ring ceremony in August, but I want you guys to know how much I love and will miss my seniors." She wipes tears from her cheeks, and the seniors converge on her in a giant group hug.

The rest of dinner is fun and casual as we all sit back and share stories from the year. Donte has us laughing hysterically as he recounts the way we tricked Jaz into thinking practice was canceled on his birthday back in September. He believed us and was out at dinner with a friend when Coach started calling trying to find out where he was. Brodi brings up Halloween night, reminding us about Jaz and Donte's Niki Minaj and Donna Summer costumes. We remember their hilarious fashion show on the bus to an away game the day before Halloween. Jaz makes fun of me, reminding everyone about the night Cole said hi to me at the pizzeria and how I acted like I didn't know he liked me.

Sherry talks about all the nights some of the team stayed up till the wee hours of the morning playing spicy UNO. I only did that with them a few times early in the year. After Cole and I started dating, I skipped most of the UNO nights.

We laugh and joke about the time the flyers were learning a new stunt and KK kicked Jaz in the nose. We bring the talk full circle to our NCA performance a few weeks ago, when she kicked him again, and blood ran down his face when he came off the mat on day one. We laugh about Christa getting pushed into the crowd, at a basketball game, landing on some guy's shoulder, when a player came out of bounds trying to catch the ball.

When the laughter dies down, the tone turns serious. Coach brings out a bottle of champagne and pours everyone a sip. She raises a toast to us, our team, and the memories we've made this year, the ones we laugh about and the ones we've cried over. She toasts the seniors and their futures. We tap our red Solo cups together and sip, swallowing the crisp, bubbling liquid, knowing in this moment that this team and these memories will live forever in our hearts. When the crescendo of the bubbles diminish and our cups are empty, we help Coach clean up before we disperse back to our dorms and apartments to think about packing and tomorrow's graduation ceremony.

The next morning, the four of us dressed in casual dresses, and wedge sandals (sequined black Vans for me), gather in the hallway before walking together across campus to the arena. We meet up with our coaches, who have a row for our team reserved near the front so we can see our teammates as they walk across the stage. We sit, with KK on one side of me, Christa on the other, and Gracie next to her. I look down the row to wave at Jaz. Then my eyes move to a girl making her way to the baby grand piano to the left of the stage. She sits and begins to play "100 Years" by Five for Fighting. The lyrics pull at my heartstrings. I glance at KK, who's tearing up. I reach over and wrap my pinkie around hers and give her a ghost of a smile.

The football team files in on our left. I wave and blow an air kiss to Cole when he glances my way.

"Can you believe this will be us in three years?" Christa asks.

"Three years feels like a long time from now," I say.

"I don't know if I ever want this to end," KK says, twirling her finger in a circle to encompass the friends on our row, and I know what she means. Someday we won't all be together, and I will miss the team, the college, and the friendships.

"Live in the moment," I say just as the president of the college steps up to the podium to begin the service.

When everything is said and done, we meet up with the graduates from our team at the front of the arena and spend the next half hour taking photos in various combinations of duos and small groups before we all pose as a team. After hugging and kissing on all of our grads, we hand Sherry her flowers and say our final goodbyes. Then the four of us turn and make our way back to the dorms. In the hallway, we stop in front of our room. With tear-filled hugs, KK and I say goodbye to Gracie and Christa, promising to keep in touch over the next two months. We pull away, and they walk down the hall to their room.

"I wonder if we could get this same exact room next year," KK says, as we walk into our room.

"We can ask the RA when she comes to check us out later today."

I go about taking the sheets, blankets, and pillows off my bed and folding them into the large plastic container I bought over the weekend. I set my stuffed-to-the-gills duffel bags on top of the container, along with my two backpacks and cheer bag. I roll my suitcase next to the other bags and look around, the room looks so, bare.

KK finishes packing her stuff and snaps the lid on her last container. A knock on our door startles me and I go to open it. Standing on the other side are KK's grandparents and she rushes to hug them.

"Are you all packed up, baby girl?" her grandpa asks.

"Yes. I think so. I have two plastic containers ready to go and two suitcases, my duffel and my backpacks. I'm just going to walk down to the bathroom and look around again. I'll be right back."

While she's gone, her grandparents ask me about my summer plans. I tell them about teaching summer camps at my old cheer gym back home.

My phone dings with a text from Cole asking if I'm almost ready to leave. I quickly text him back. *Yes.*

When KK walks back into the room, I tell her I'll go get the RA so she can check us out. When the RA arrives, she takes a look around and signs each of our papers taking them with her.

"Wait," I say, stopping her before she walks out the door. "Do you think KK and I can have this same exact room next year?"

She smiles at me.

"Yes, of course. Some other girls, Gracie and Christa, asked me the same thing. No problem. I'll put that in my notes. Just make sure that each of you puts a deposit down online by the end of May." She turns to leave.

"Well, I guess we need to start working on getting these into the truck." KK's grandpa bends to pick up a few of her bags. Her grandma takes the large rolling suitcase, and KK picks up one of the big containers. I gather some of my bags and follow them out to the parking lot. Cole is loading his guitar into the back seat of his truck when I walk out. I walk over with my backpacks and two duffel bags.

"Hey," I say, walking up to him.

"Hey," he says smiling at me. "I was just putting the last of my things in here."

Peeking into the cargo area of his truck, I see that he has three plastic containers and a large suitcase. In the back seat he has duffel bags and backpacks. He takes my bags from me and adds them to the stuff in the back seat.

"I have a large plastic container, a big suitcase, and another big duffel bag still in my room," I say.

"I'll go with you to get those." He follows me into my room.

KK's gathering the last of her things when we walk in. Cole picks up my large plastic container. I throw my duffel across my shoulder and grip the handle of my large rolling bag. All of us walk out to the parking lot with the final load.

"KK, have a great summer. I'll see you in July," Cole says, nodding in her direction as he walks to his truck with my plastic bin.

I follow KK and her grandparents to their truck and stop next to it. KK loads the plastic container into the back, and her grandfather adds her two suitcases.

"I guess that's everything," he says, closing the hatch on the back of the truck.

I let go of the suitcase handle and drop my duffel onto the ground. KK and I run to each other. I grab her, squeezing, not wanting to let go. Both of us are sobbing.

"We'll talk every day," I say through my tears.

She nods.

"I love you," she says, choking on her tears, as she tries to get the words out.

"I love you too," I say, loosening the grip I have on her.

KK gets into the back seat of her grandparents' truck. I watch her buckle her seat belt then she waves. I pick up my bags and make my way over to Cole's truck. He lifts my large rolling bag, and places it in the back of the truck, then he takes my duffel from me and sticks it into the back seat. I turn and watch KK's grandparents' truck as they leave the parking lot and turn onto the main road. Then I hop into the passenger seat of Cole's truck.

Summer

41

Once we are on the highway, Cole asks what music I want to listen to. I suggest "Adore" by Harry Styles, telling Cole the song reminds me of him. He smiles and queues it up on his Spotify. The windows are rolled down, and the wind whips through my hair. It feels like summer and freedom and forever. For the next few days, I'll be with Cole, with nothing planned, nothing to do, just being with each other. And right now, that's what I want most, just to be.

In less than two hours, we are pulling up to Cole's family's house. The driveway and carport are empty. The carport is attached to a white-brick ranch-style home. Cole backs his truck down the driveway and parks on the right side of the carport.

"Here we are," he says, shutting off the engine.

"It looks like no one is home," I say, opening the door to get out.

"They knew about what time we would be getting here. So I bet they'll be back any minute. Let's unload the truck. We can leave the containers in the carport and just take what we need inside for now."

I help Cole unload the truck, and we put his containers and bags in one stack and my things in another. He picks up a few of his bags to take inside, and I pick up the duffel bag I packed for my time at his house. He walks up the steps that lead up to the house. He punches in a code to unlock the door and the light turns green. He turns the knob and we step into a large laundry room. Then he slides a barn-style door open to reveal a kitchen. The tile floors are white, and the cabinets are painted an almond color. The granite counters are a mix of light cream and black with flecks of amber. The kitchen is open to a family room and to my right I can see the dining room. A large center island has four barstools underneath.

"Come on. I'll show you around," he says. We head toward the family room and take a right into the foyer, where the front door is. To the right of the front door is the dining room, and on the other side of the front door is a small office. There's a staircase that leads upstairs, but instead of going up, Cole turns around and leads me down a hallway where we pass three bedrooms and a bathroom. At the end of the hall, he shows me the master bedroom. Then we turn to walk back down the hall, and he stops in front of one of the bedrooms.

"You can have your pick of any of these three rooms."

I poke my head into the room that's across the hall from the bathroom. It's a quaint room with gray walls and floor-length black curtains on both windows. There's a full-size bed in the center of one wall boasting a combination of floral-print throw pillows. A leopard-print chair sits next to an antique dressing table.

"I'll take this room," I say, moving to place my bag on the bed.

Cole grins at me. "Let me show you one last thing." He takes my hand and leads me down the hall toward the foyer and up the staircase. At the top of the stairs is one large room. We step inside. There are two large windows facing the front side of the house and two large windows on the side. At the far end of the room is a bathroom sink area with the bathroom door on the left and the closet on the right. Two of the walls are painted red, and the opposite walls are a khaki color. A king-size bed sits in the middle of one wall, flanked by nightstands and matching lamps. A large bookshelf on the opposite wall is filled with trophies and photos. I step closer to the bookshelf.

"This is your room." I turn and face him.

"Yes. I finally got this room after Corbin left for college. First, it was Chris's room, then when he left for college, Colton got it. Then Corbin moved into the room after him, and now it's been mine for the past five years. Before that, I had the room that you are going to be staying in. What do you think?" He sets his bags on the floor and steps closer to me. His look is expectant.

I take a look around and nod. "On, Tuesday, May twelfth I got to stand in the bedroom of Cole Collins, QB1 for Natchez College, who may one day play in the NFL. And I can now say I've been *in* his bedroom," I say in a sassy, teasing tone.

We laugh and he pulls me in for a kiss that at first is soft and gentle but quickly becomes hungry and passionate.

"We're back," someone yells loudly from downstairs.

I jump and pull away from Cole, who looks at me with a shy grin.

"Let's go down," he says.

We hurry down and bounce into the kitchen, where his mom and dad are setting groceries on the kitchen island.

"Hey there, you two." His mom steps over and kisses us both on the cheek.

"We had to pick up a few things from the store," his days says. "Your mom wanted to make your favorite dinner tonight."

"We just got here. I was showing Landry around." Cole leans against the counter.

"Why don't you show her the backyard too?" I'll make some tea and bring it outside to you. Then I'll start dinner," his mom says, walking to a door between the kitchen and the living room and opening it for us to go out. Cole and I walk out onto a deck that overlooks a large backyard. In the distance I can see a tree house in a large oak tree, a playset next to it with a large plastic yellow slide attached, and a tire swing hanging from a branch. We walk down the deck stairs into the grass.

"I like your tree house and tire swing. Your parents kept everything intact."

"Yes. They have one grandson now, and Colton's wife is expecting their second baby in September. I'd practice for hours every day throwing the football through that tire swing. We can even adjust it with the rope to have it hang higher or lower." He takes my hand and we walk closer to the tree.

"The iced tea is ready." His dad calls to us from the deck, two glasses in his hands. He sets them on the table and walks back inside. Cole and I walk back to the deck and sit at the patio table, sipping our tea.

"Mom can sometimes be a perfectionist with dinner when we have guests over. She wants to make the perfect meal," Cole says, setting his glass on the table.

"Maybe I should offer to help?"

"Not right now. I think we'll help with the clean-up. Mom probably wants to use a memorized recipe, and she can get things done pretty quickly. Just sit back and enjoy my company." He picks up his glass, holding it out for a toast. I tap my glass to his and sit back and relax, talking, laughing, and enjoying having time with Cole.

A few minutes later, we take our empty glasses to the kitchen and set them on the counter. Delicious smells fill the room, making my stomach growl. The dining room table is already set, and Cole's mom comes back into the kitchen and pops the oven door open.

"It's almost ready," she says, turning around and facing us.

"What can I help with?" I ask.

"How about filling some glasses with tea or water and taking them into the dining room for me." She walks over and shows me the cabinet with the glasses and points to the ice maker on the fridge. I go about filling glasses, and Cole helps me carry them into the dining room. Cole's dad helps with taking things out of the oven then goes to take a dessert out of the refrigerator. We help move everything onto the table, then the four us hold hands to bless the meal. Cole takes my hand and his dad's while his mom reaches for my other hand.

"Let's pray." Cole's dad bows his head, and we follow suit.

After the prayer ends, we sit down, and Cole's mom begins passing me plates of food.

"Everything looks delicious, Mrs. Collins," I say, filling my plate.

Once everything has been passed around, his dad asks.

"Cole, are you going to show your lovely girlfriend around Tyler tomorrow?"

"I'm planning on taking her to the rose gardens first."

"Perfect," his mom says. "There are fifteen acres and five hundred different varieties of roses there. You will love it."

I nod and smile with food still in my mouth. When I finish chewing, I say, "I can't wait."

"Remember, we'd like for you to be back in time to go to prayer meeting and dinner at the church tomorrow night." His dad motions with his fork toward Cole and gives him an expectant look. "Prayer meeting is a brief gathering of church members of all ages," he explains to me. "Afterward, we have a potluck-style dinner in the lower level of the church. I know you won't be here this weekend for church, so I thought you two could come tomorrow night. Everyone will be glad to see you, Cole."

"Yes, sir. We'll definitely plan to do that."

After dinner, Cole and I take care of all the cleanup while his parents take a break and relax. His dad reads a book and his mom starts a knitting project. When we finish with the dishes, Cole announces that he wants to drive me around downtown.

"We'll be back later. Don't wait up," he says, as we walk through the laundry room to the carport.

"There are a few of my favorite high school haunts, I guess you could call 'em, that I'd like to show you," he says, a little later, placing his right hand on my knee as he drives.

I waggle my eyebrows in response, trying to look sexy. Then I mouth the words "high school haunts," trying not to laugh.

He drives slowly through the downtown area, over old brick roads, and turns the corner at an old-fashioned theater with the name Tyler in lights above the marquee. He pulls into a parking spot behind the building then reaches into the backseat and retrieves a Natchez College stadium blanket from the floorboard.

"Follow me," he says, opening his door and getting out.

I pop out on my side and take his hand. We scoot into a narrow space between the theater and the building next to it. I start to get the feeling we may be in a scary movie and someone could jump out at any moment and start chasing us through the narrow alley. Halfway down the alleyway, Cole stops and points to a metal ladder attached to the brick wall of the theater.

"What? You want me to climb up that ladder? Where does it go?"

"To the roof. Here, I'll squat, and you climb onto my shoulders. You'll be able to reach the lowest rung. You trust me?" he asks with a sheepish grin.

"I trust you." I climb onto his shoulders, he stands up easily, lifting all 118 pounds of me. I place one foot and then the other onto the lowest rung. Then I look down at Cole, wondering how he's going to get up without help. He motions for me to climb, and as I do, he leaps up, gripping the sides of the ladder placing his feet quickly on the rungs. We make it to the top, and I climb over a low wall onto the rooftop.

"Wow. You jumped, like, four feet off the ground. Obviously, you've done this before. Show off!" I say, with a laugh.

"A few times."

He walks to the edge, where the view of the town is best, and spreads the blanket. After we're seated, I cuddle up to him and he wraps his strong arms around me.

"It's pretty, seeing everything at night," I say. "A perfect rooftop view."

"I had a good friend in high school who worked at this movie theater. Sometimes I'd meet him here after work. One night I was in the back parking lot waiting on him, and I saw him bring the trash bags out to the dumpster that used to sit next to the ladder to the roof. He saw me waiting, pointed at the ladder, and asked if I wanted to try to climb up with him after he locked up. We got up here and sat for a couple of hours just talking. We didn't do it a lot, but we did it enough that it became a go-to hang out for us. We spent our last night in town before we both left for college sitting up here talking about stuff."

I lean my head into his chest and wrap my arm around his waist.

"Where does he go to college?"

"He's at Baylor University in Waco, Texas, studying communications. He thinks he may want to go into the ministry and work with youth."

"If you weren't a football player, or maybe if for some reason you don't end up in the NFL, do you know what you would want to do?"

Cole nods. He pauses, the way he does sometimes when I ask him a question that he wants to answer seriously.

"I'd like to be a high school football coach and teacher. Maybe live in a small town, not too far from family. I want my parents to enjoy their grandkids. And I'd try to be a good coach, a mentor, and a good teacher. Maybe make a difference in some kids' lives."

"Cole. Oh. My. Gosh. Do you know how much you make my heart melt?"

He smiles at me then looks away briefly before turning back and looking into my eyes.

"What if *we* had graduated today? Instead of us just finishing our freshmen year of college, what if that had been us up there walking across the stage to graduate? And what if I got down on one knee right now and asked you to marry me? Hypothetically speaking, of course."

"If we had just graduated today, what would I say if you asked me to marry you? I'd say, yes in a heartbeat, no questions asked."

His smile is radiant. With a passionate kiss, he pulls me down on the blanket, and I wrap my legs around him. I like his hypothetical question a lot.

The next day, Cole and I enjoy a day at the rose gardens, then he takes me over to his high school. We sit in the stands and watch his old team and coaches at practice.

"Glory days and Friday night lights," Cole says, with a shake of his head. "I made twenty-four touchdown passes and rushed for almost thirteen hundred yards my senior year. I was a finalist in the regional powerlifting contest for my weight my senior year too."

"I know it's your goal to get picked up by a bigger team. Texas, LSU, Arkansas, Oklahoma. Any of them would be lucky to have you."

"Yeah. If we have a true winning season and make it to the playoffs next year, maybe I'll be eligible for the transfer portal. If that happens, would you transfer schools and come with me?"

"I have thought about that. But I don't think I would. I think I'd stay at Natchez. I wouldn't want to give up a full scholarship. I don't think I'd get anything close to the scholarship I have now at another school. I mean, I love LSU, it's my home-state college, and I have a friend there. She's a cheerleader, so I'm not sure. I guess it's one of those decisions that you have to make when the time comes. And that's if ----and only if ----you end up as the quarterback at LSU. Then it would be a definite maybe."

The whistle blows, calling practice to an end, and the team gathers at center field. Cole takes my hand and leads me down the bleachers to the edge of the field, where we wait to speak with his old coach. When we leave the football field, we head over to Cole's family's church.

Cole parks in front of Bethel Baptist Church, and we walk into the chapel. Cole is greeted warmly by everyone. He shakes hands and receives lots of hugs from little old ladies. He introduces me as his girlfriend. They all smile and gush, telling me how pretty I am and letting me know that Cole is quite the catch, as if I wasn't aware. I can't help but laugh to myself.

We find his brother Colton and his wife, Tracy, sitting with their toddler next to Cole's mother near the front. We slide onto the pew and say hello. Cole's nephew toddles over and gives Cole a high five before going back to sit in his grandma's lap. I lean in and congratulate Colton and his wife on their pregnancy. When Cole's father begins the message, I wish I'd brought my notebook.

He begins with the idea of a vine and how it must be cut back and pruned so it can bear fruit. He references the process to the way we are clipped and pruned as we are shaped by the things that happen in our lives, some of them good and some of them bad. These events might prompt us to reach for God's help, allowing us to become closer to him as he shapes us, prunes us, and gets us ready to bear fruit in order to grow spiritually.

He closes with a final story.

"The farmer plants new grape vines in the early morning one spring day. He grew them from seedlings in his greenhouse all fall and winter. Now that all fifty plants are bigger, taller, he knows it's time to move them into the soil. He's prepared the perfect spot on a sunny, sloping hillside and spends all day from sun-up to sundown planting and fertilizing. The next day he waters them. A week later they are growing, looking beautiful with new buds. Then the frost comes that night. He awakens to find that the frost has killed the buds. He's saddened and tells a neighboring farmer about losing his newly budded grapes to the frost. But his friend, reaches out, gripping the farmer's shoulder and says, But there's always a second bud."

Home

42

The next morning Cole and I load my stuff from the carport back into his truck. I hug his mom and dad as we say our goodbyes, and I thank them for their hospitality. We head to I-20 and make our way into Louisiana then head south to bayou country. We stop in Baton Rouge for lunch, finding a place next to the LSU campus to eat. We spend a few minutes wandering around the campus taking pictures and selfies, carefree, happy, and in love. After the six-hour drive, we approach Lacombe at last. We drive along the lake front as the sun is starting to set, and before long, we're pulling up in front of my house.

"Mom should be home from her job at the dentist's office by now. She's got to work tomorrow evening at the restaurant, but we can have dinner there tomorrow night if you want," I say, gathering my bags from the back seat. Cole takes one of my bags, his large duffel, and the rolling suitcase as we walk toward the steps leading to the front porch. I open the screen door and check to see if the front door is unlocked. It isn't, so I knock. The cat rushes up the stairs to the door, wanting in. She must have been out all day and looks a bit panicked and desperate for her food bowl. Mom comes running to the door, flings it open, and hugs me before taking one of my bags.

"You guys made pretty good time," she says, ushering us into the living room.

"We stopped for lunch in Baton Rouge and spent some time looking around campus." I say, setting my bags down.

251

Grandma is sitting in her chair in the living room. She smiles at me, and I pad over to her. I lean in and kiss her cheek.

"Grandma, this is my boyfriend, Cole Collins. We met at the college I go to in Texas. He's on the football team."

She nods and smiles and lifts a hand to wave at Cole. Cole walks over to speak to her, and Mom goes about moving my bags into the bedroom.

"Is this everything?" she asks, walking back into the living room.

"No, there's actually a container in the back of my truck. I'll go get it." Cole pops out the front door and comes back with the large plastic bin. He sets it on the floor.

"Come on, Cole," I tell him. "I'll show you around, although there's not much to see." We walk down the hallway from the living room past the kitchen. "My room is here. You'll be sleeping in my room, and I'll sleep with Mom. My grandmother's room and Mom's room are both on the other hall across from the kitchen." He steps into my room and looks around at all the cheerleading medals I have hanging on nails around the room. His eyes land on the poster of Harry Styles on my closet door. He chuckles.

I pull him down to sit next to me on my bed.

"The bathroom is across the hall. There's only one full bath. Mom has a half bath in her bedroom. The only room you haven't seen yet is the kitchen. It's just a three-bedroom, one-and-a-half bath home with a living room and kitchen. An older home that hasn't had a lot of remodeling done or anything, but this is home," I say, gesturing around the room.

"Now, *I* can say that on May fourteenth, I've been in Landry Woods' bedroom. In fact, *I* get to sleep *in* Landry Woods' bed." We both crack up laughing, and I dissolve into a fit of giggles as Cole starts to tickle me.

Mom pops her head into the room. "I've made jambalaya for dinner. It's ready whenever you guys want to eat."

"Sure, thanks Mom. We'll be there in a minute." After my mom leaves, I turn to face Cole, putting my hand on his cheek, and pulling him in for an intimate kiss. The cat jumps up next to me and begins to purr. "This is my cat, Rocky. I think I told you about her. She always curled up on my pillow when I was talking with

252

you on the phone. Just so you know, I can't remember how much I've told you, but Grandma had a stroke a year ago and can only speak a few words at a time. She gets around okay with a cane, and we think she understands everything we say. I don't want it to freak you out or anything."

"Nothing can freak me out. I do remember you telling me about her having a stroke a year ago. I also remember you telling me you found Rocky when she was a few months old. You told me that she looked like she'd gotten into a fight. You said that's why you named her that."

"A lot of those long phone conversations took place right here." I pat the floral-print bedspread then stand, taking Cole's hand, and lead him into the kitchen. We sit at the small kitchen table. Mom passes Cole the bowl of jambalaya and the basket of french bread.

"This is the best jambalaya I've ever had, Ms. Woods."

"Thank you. It's Mom's recipe." She glances at my grandmother.

"My mother's," Grandma says, smiling.

"Yes. Great-Grandma Landache," Mom says, nodding. "You know your dad and Todd will want to see you."

"Where are they living now?" I ask.

"He's living at his dad's old fish camp on the bayou."

"That old place. I haven't been there since I was eight or nine. That was probably right before Grandpa died."

"He's been fixing it up. From what he's told us, he's remodeled the bathroom, and had new carpet put in, and he's updated the kitchen. He's done a lot of the work himself. In addition to working at the family seafood market, he's also been running the shrimp boat again."

"Maybe we'll stop by there tomorrow before we go to the restaurant. I'm going to show Cole around town. When we were in Tyler, he took me to his old high school, and we went to a beautiful fifteen-acre rose garden. Did you know Tyler, Texas, is the rose capital?" Mom looks impressed.

"Sounds like you had a great time. I'm glad you're able to stop by and visit with us too on your way to Georgia." She smiles at Cole.

The next morning, I text Cole before I get out of bed. *You up?*

He texts back. *Yes. You want to get in the shower first?*

Sure. I reply. I set the phone down and grab a change of clothes out of my suitcase. Stopping at my room, I tap lightly on the door.

"Hey," I say, poking my head inside.

Cole looks at me with a sleepy smile on his face.

"Hey, you," he greets me. "Don't use all the hot water."

"Okay," I say, closing the door. I get in and out of the shower quickly then go back to Mom's room to dry my hair. When I hear the shower turn off, I figure Cole is almost ready. I wander into the kitchen to find that Mom has made biscuits and bacon. There's a note on the table. *We've gone to the store, then we'll be working in the garden. Love, Mom*

Cole pops into the kitchen wearing a Natchez football T-shirt and shorts with his Adidas slides.

"There's some leftovers." I point to the biscuits and bacon. Cole picks up a slice of bacon and pops it into his mouth, then he eats one more. I finish off the last of my biscuit and take two bottles of water from the fridge and hand him one.

"Ready?" I ask.

Walking out the back door, we see Mom and Grandma working in the garden. Mom has turned most of our backyard into a garden since I've been away. She has corn, tomatoes, beans, cucumbers, squash, and even watermelon. Grandma is in the middle of the bean row, walking slowly and picking beans. Mom is on her hands and knees weeding around the watermelon plants. She stops and looks up at us, wiping her brow.

"Heading out this early? Did you eat anything?" she asks.

"It's almost ten, Mom. It's not that early. Cole ate the rest of the bacon, and I had a biscuit. We'll be gone most of the day. But plan on us eating at the restaurant tonight around six." We wave bye and walk around to the front of the house, where Cole's truck is parked along the curb.

"Where to first?" he asks, starting the engine.

"Take a right and drive all the way down Lake Road. I'll show you the lake, then we'll drive past my cheer gym. Then we'll go to my old high school. Then down to the lake-front, and we'll eat lunch at Rip's on the lake."

Later that evening, Cole and I go to Sal and Judy's for dinner. Mom is not our waitress, but she stops by our table to say hello. Then the owner comes over to meet Cole. I think he wanted to check out the boy I've brought home. I'm sure Mom has told everyone about Cole.

When we get home, we relax on the porch swing. I take the pillow from the swing, place it in Cole's lap and put my head on it, curling up against him. He plays gently with my hair as we swing ever so slowly back and forth. Casually, we drift in and out of conversations. I hold one of his hands in mine, sometimes bringing it to my lips.

"So, you'll be back next Friday night?"

"I will. Right here, next Friday."

"Where is the Falcons' training camp again?"

"Flowery Branch, just north of Atlanta. My brother has a house in Buford, Georgia, on the lake. I'll plan to take you there sometime."

"I'd like that."

The next morning, Cole leaves for Atlanta. We stand in my front yard for a long time just holding each other. I know he'll be back in a week, but I'm going to miss him like crazy. There's always the chance he'll be leaving to go to another school after this next football season. I feel it, like it's tangible. One day he'll be gone, but until then I'll take it one day at a time.

Faith of a Flyer
43

Summer's coming to an end. It's been four weeks since I've seen Cole, and it will be two weeks and two days before I see him again. Since the last week of May, I've worked two jobs. I taught three weeks of cheer camp at the gym while working at my dad's family's seafood market on Saturdays.

Now I'm working every day at the shop, until mid-July, when I'll head back to school. I've put most of my money into a savings account. As of right now, I have $700 in the bank. But it's not enough to buy a car.

I enrolled my brother in my cheer-camp classes, and now he's throwing a great back handspring. Dad says he can continue tumbling lessons for the rest of the summer and into the fall. He may even let him join an all-star team next season. Even though camp classes have ended, I still spend time with Todd as much as I can. Sometimes he's at the seafood market, and sometimes he's hanging out at my house. And occasionally I go out to their house on the bayou.

The road to the old fish-camp house is down a dirt road. It winds through the woods before you see the clearing and the river. The old house sits up high on stilts, always ready for high water. A concrete parking pad and patio are under the house, along with a porch swing, and a picnic table.

I pull Mom's old Honda into the grass next to the house. She usually lets me take her car for the day as long as I drop her off at work at eight and pick her up at four-thirty from the dentist's office Monday through Thursday.

The sun is bright, and it's already hot, although it's early in the morning. I walk up the stairs to get to the deck where the front door is.

Todd answers, "Landry's here." He calls, and I step into the kitchen.

Dad plans on taking the shrimp boat out this morning, and I'm taking Todd into the seafood market to work with me for a few hours. The old fish-camp house is small with a combination living-room kitchen area two bedrooms, and one bathroom. It works for Dad and Todd, and I get the feeling Dad likes being at the fish camp since it brings back fond memories of family. I remember spending summer days here. My cousins and me would take turns jumping off the dock into the water and swinging from a rope tied to a post at the end of the pier. My grandpa would boil live crawfish over a fire, then he'd dump the huge pot right onto newspaper pages spread out on the long picnic table. Then the whole family would sit down to eat.

"Good morning, Landry," Dad says, walking into the kitchen.

"Can I help untie the ropes?" Todd asks, walking to the door.

"Yes. But don't walk onto the dock by yourself. Wait until one of us is with you." Dad gets a thermos from the cabinet and begins filling it with coffee.

"Come on, Todd. I'll walk down to the dock with you." I take his hand in mine and we walk together down the stairs, and through the grass to the dock. I sit down at the edge. Todd sits next to me. When Dad comes down, he shows an eager Todd which lines to untie. Dad hops onto the boat, taking his thermos of coffee with him. He sets it in the cupholder next to the helm then gets off the boat and walks up to me on the dock.

"Landry, I appreciate you taking an interest in Todd. He's a lot happier, I can tell. I know it has a lot to do with you." He's talking so quietly I can barely hear him. I step a little closer.

"He's going to enjoy staying at the cheer gym with the friends he made this summer at camp," he continues. "And I've signed him up for Boy Scouts. I know you only have a few more weeks left before you go back to school. I've got a sitter lined up to help out the rest of the summer on the days that your mom can't look out for him."

"I wanted to get to know him. It's been good for me too."

He nods then turns his attention to Todd, who's sitting next to the cleat that the boat line is tied to. Dad looks back at me like he wants to say something else.

"Are you ready for me to untie it, Dad?" Todd asks, him anxiously.

"Yeah, buddy." Dad steps onto the front of the boat and watches Todd untie the line. Then Todd quickly runs to the other side of the dock and goes to the next cleat, squatting down. When Dad gives him the signal, he unties the line and tosses it onto the front of the boat. I look to make sure both lines are out of the water then give a thumbs-up signal to Dad, who's standing at the helm guiding the boat backward out of the slip.

"I'll be back around three-thirty," he says, waving to us. Todd and I watch for a few minutes before we walk back into the house to gather his iPad and summer-math workbooks to keep him busy while I work.

When we get to the seafood market, my dad's brother Henri is just opening up for the day. Todd makes himself comfortable in the back office, and I spend most of the day waiting on customers.

At the end of my shift, I announce, "Uncle Henri, it's time for me to take Todd home. I'll see you tomorrow morning," I take my apron off and find Todd in the office, and tell him to grab his things.

We drive back down the dirt road and park next to the house. Even though Dad has updated a lot on the inside, the outside of the house looks old and weathered. The wooden siding has never been painted, so it has a rustic look, but it's what you'd expect from a house that overlooks a swampy river.

"Can I put my swimsuit on and go swimming?" Todd asks as we walk inside. "Will you come with me, Landry?"

"Yes, you can swim until Dad gets back. I don't know what he has planned for you later."

Todd comes out of his room wearing a swimsuit, carrying a towel he probably picked up off the bathroom floor, and he's holding a swim ring. We walk to the dock. I slip my shoes off and spread out the towel along the edge of the wooden pier. Todd puts the swim ring around his middle and jumps in. I sit down to watch him, stretching out my legs and soaking in the warm sun. A few minutes later, we hear the honk of a boat horn as Dad maneuvers the shrimp boat around the bend, making his way to the dock. Todd climbs the ladder onto the dock and waves to Dad before he leaps off the dock into the water again. As the boat enters the slip, I stand and catch the ropes Dad tosses to me. Todd climbs the ladder, slips out of his swim ring and bounds over to me wanting me to let him tie the line to the cleat. I watch to make sure he does it right. Then he goes back and jumps off the dock, forgetting about the other side.

"I'll get the other side, Dad." I cross the dock and tie the line.

Dad steps off the boat and asks if we can sit. We move to the bench swing in the grassy area just to the right of the dock. We take a seat and watch Todd splash around.

"I know we're still working through some things. You know I'm grateful to have you back in my life." His eyes tear up a little.

"Yeah, Dad, I know."

"When I sold the house, the car, and the business back in Seattle and got the insurance check after Paula died, I put some of that money into a savings account for you. There's $35,000 dollars in it now. It's yours, and I did the same thing for Todd. He won't be able to get to it until he's twenty-one. But if you want to use some of your money now, you can. I'd like to help you look for a car. I think if we look hard enough, we'll be able to find a decent used one. And you'd still have enough money in your account to use for other things later."

"Dad, I don't know what to say. This is unbelievable. Thank you." I lean over and hug him. I haven't done that in years. Like, eight, or nine years, that's how long it's been since I hugged my dad's neck.

"We can go car shopping this afternoon if you want," he says, smiling back at me.

It took four days of shopping every used car lot and every dealership from Madisonville to Slidell, but Dad and I found the perfect car and I love it. It's a 2017 Volkswagen Beetle convertible. It's royal blue, and the convertible top is beige. It has Bluetooth speakers, and a back-up camera and Dad had them add CarPlay.

I've found peace in my relationship with my dad. I've gotten to know my little brother, and I know he's adjusting well to his new life on the bayou. I've got a savings account with $26,000 in it and a checking account with a little over $700. And now I even have my own Visa check card. I'm feeling more grown-up and ready for the world. I only have a few more days before I head back to Natchez. KK and I have talked almost every day since we left each other in the parking lot back in May. Cole and I have talked every day -----and sometimes for hours ------with the cat snuggled up next to me on my pillow, purring loud enough that Cole can hear her too. We joke that Rocky's really a lover, not a fighter.

Jordan came into the shop one day while I was working. He looked good and seemed to be happy. He got into SCAD in Savannah and he leaves in August to move into an apartment with a guy he met while working for an artist in New Orleans this summer. It was good to see him. I wished him the best. We'll always be friends, and I know he'll always have a small piece of my heart. First love never dies, at least that's what I've heard. Maybe it just fades away.

Back to college day arrives sooner than I felt it would, but I'm antsy to get back.

"I'm all packed, Mom," I say, hauling two duffel bags and two backpacks toward the front door. Setting them down, I move back into my room to get my large rolling suitcase. Mom walks into the living room carrying the large plastic container filled with clean sheets, towels, pillows, and my bedding for the dorm. Grandma follows behind her.

"I don't know how all of this is going to fit into your tiny car, Landry," Mom says, looking around at all the stuff sitting next to the front door.

"Let's move it all to the car and see what fits where," I say.

I stop and hug my grandma. Then I pick up the bags and start moving them out to the car. The large suitcase ends up in the trunk, and the large plastic container ends up in the back seat.

"You think you have everything?" Mom asks after we've stuffed the car.

"Yeah, I'm pretty sure I do."

"Okay. Call me as soon as you get there."

"I will." As soon as I say that, Dad pulls up behind my car. He and Todd jump out.

"Oh, good. We made it just in time. Todd wanted to bring you some donuts," Dad says.

Todd hands me a Dunkin Donuts bag, and I peek inside.

"One is chocolate with sprinkles, and one is strawberry with sprinkles," Todd says, smiling up at me.

"Thank you for these. And thank you both for coming to see me off."

Dad walks over, leans in, and hugs me. I reach down and pull Todd in for a hug too.

"I'll call you, Todd. And you can call me whenever you want. We can even FaceTime." He nods, pulling away from the hug.

"I love you, Landry," Dad says.

"I love you too," I say, fighting back tears.

Mom steps up and hugs me. "Be careful. Drive safely. Don't forget to call when you get there. I put some envelopes with stamps already on them in your backpack."

"Okay. Thanks, Mom. Bye." I step inside the car, hit the Natchez College button on my Waze app, and start the engine. Pulling away from the curb, I begin my drive. Mom, Grandma, Dad, and Todd stand waving as I drive off.

I roll the windows down and push the button to lower the top of the convertible. It's the middle of July and perfect weather for driving with the top down. The wind whips through my hair. The sun beats down on my face and my arms. I'm headed home to Nacogdoches, where I'll be reunited with my teammates, meet new teammates, and see my coaches and my boyfriend.

A lot has happened in a year. I've got my dad back in my life, gotten to know my little brother, and found the guy of my dreams. I know things don't always go as planned. My team may not always hit zero. Life can change in an instant. I've been able to let a lot of bad feelings go. I've learned to pray and to lean on God for help when I need it. I've learned to live in the moment., to ponder things in my heart, and hold the best things in life close. I don't know what the future holds, but I know who holds the future. It's like the faith of a flyer performing her routine unafraid, knowing there will be someone to catch her if she falls.

For I know the plans I have for you, declares the Lord.
Plans to prosper you, not to harm you,
Plans to give you hope and a future.
Jeremiah 29:11

Find Out More...

For Young Life on your campus and in your area, go to
www.younglife.org
For the soundtrack for Hit Zero on Spotify search under Hit Zero
by Perrie Tucker (not author pen)
For more books by the author: www.perriepatterson.com
Follow me on social media:
Instagram: always.n.style
Facebook: Perrie Patterson
Twitter: @PerrieT TikTok: @authorperriepatterson

Questions for Group Discussion

1. Describe how you think Landry feels the night before she leaves for Texas.
2. After Landry meets Cole Collins and he sends her a text, were you thinking she should go out with him? How do you feel about him being bi-racial?
3. Was Landry right to feel the way she did on Christmas Day when she found out her dad had come back into town?
4. Did Landry do the right thing by calling Jordan on Christmas Day? At that point, did you think she still had feelings for him?
5. At what point in the book did you think Landry was in love with Cole or that he was in love with her? Was it obvious? Describe the characteristics in Cole that appeal to you and why.
6. How did it make you feel to read about the events that took place on New Year's Eve? Have you ever felt that you could not forgive someone who's hurt you?
7. Did your feelings about forgiveness change after reading the New Year's Eve chapter?

8. Where you happy when Landry found the letter from her dad? How did reading the letter make you feel?
9. Did you think Landry handled everything well with her dad before and after the showcase? What might you have done differently?
10. In what ways has Landry changed from the time she gets to Natchez College to the time she arrives home for the summer? Do you like these changes?
11. Start a discussion about racial injustice with ideas on how we as individuals can improve our relationships with our black friends as well as ways to support them.
12. Did the story end as you expected? Did you like the ending? If not, describe the way you would have like to see the story end.

More Books by Perrie Patterson

Walking the Crimson Road

My Blood Runs Crimson

All the Crimson Roses

(The crimson trilogy is set on the University of Alabama campus)

Acknowledgments

I always have so many people to thank. Thank you to my beta readers, Sara Thomas, Becky Blackwelder, Wilma Turner, and Eileen Tucker. Thank you to my editor Sue Grimshaw. You're the best cheerleader a writer could have. And to my copy editors, Emily Lawrence and Mary Beth Bishop. Kudos to my proofreaders, Kaytie Mashburn Swofford and Barbara Delgiorno. Thank you to the Polo Women's Club book club ladies for always being supportive and gracious. Thank you to my friends who've bought and read my books and loved them! Thank you to my children, James and Laine, and my very patient husband, Jeff. And thank you to Netflix for creating the best documentary about cheerleading you possibly could, which gave me the idea for this story in the first place. And thank you to Coach Monica Aldama, and the team at Navarro. You guys are awesome, and I hope you enjoy this book.

Made in the USA
Coppell, TX
22 May 2024